Th

on the Beach

Fiona Gillan Kerr

Ringwood Publishing
Glasgow

First published in Great Britain in 2023
by
Ringwood Publishing

0/1 314 Meadowside Quay Walk, Glasgow G11 6AY

www.ringwoodpublishing.com

e-mail mail@ringwoodpublishing.com

ISBN 978-1-901514-91-9

British Library Cataloguing-in Publication Data
A catalogue record for this book is available from the
British Library

Typeset in Times New Roman 11

Printed and bound in the UK
by
Lonsdale Direct Solutions

Dedication

For all the Highlanders, past and present, whose stories have inspired me and whose experience has informed me.

There is a land of the living and a land of the dead, and the bridge is love, the only survival, the only meaning.

Thornton Wilder, *The Bridge of San Luis Rey*

Men, at some time, are master of their fates. The fault, dear Brutus, is not in the stars, but in ourselves.

William Shakespeare, *Julius Caesar*

There's nowhere you can be that isn't where you're meant to be ...

John Lennon

Chapter 1

Meghan – September, 2017

It was my second day in the village when I found it – the bone on the beach. I say I found it, but it was actually Cassie who noticed it, tangled in the seaweed which had swept in on the storm surge, stranded at the high tide mark.

We had arrived the evening before. It was late September, the sun hidden by the dark clouds gathering on the horizon, the wind whipping patterns across the tall grass on the grazing land at the cliffside. Already, the crofters and farmers had moved their animals – cows and sheep – down to the lower fields where they might find shelter behind the stone walls, the territorial property markers.

The GPS had faltered at the entrance to the village, fixed firmly on the first house as we crossed over the cattle grid. The road had divided, two routes to choose from, but only one would take us to *Ar Bàthach* – the cottage I had found on the internet only a month earlier.

A simple stone cottage in a picturesque highland village. Tastefully furnished and fitted with modern appliances, including washing machine, TV & internet. Sleeps 2/1 queen size bed. Shop & pub within walking distance. £250 per week. Rates negotiable for longer stays. Email for further information.

I had printed out a photo of the cottage. I pulled the car over to one side, handbrake on. The houses on the left fork of the road were closer together. Others were scattered up and down the opposite hillside where the second road meandered. Then I saw it, a small stone building beside a larger two-storey house, set high up on the hill. As I put the car in gear and started to take the right turn, I heard a screech of brakes behind me, gravel spinning off the paintwork of my car, a horn blaring. A small white delivery van swept up the left fork, scraping my wing mirror as it passed.

The two-storey house was obviously a farmhouse, an open-sided barn set back on one side, our cottage laying on the other. Cassie was alarmed by the chickens roaming the yard between the buildings, the unfamiliar smells of silage and manure emanating from the straw-covered floor of the barn; she refused to leave the safety of the back seat of the car. I carried her over the threshold of our new home. We would be here for the next twelve months. She would get used to it.

The cottage had two rooms with bare stone walls. A small bathroom was slipped in behind the bedroom. Kitchen, sitting and dining areas were squeezed into the second room which had an open fireplace. Matching blue and white chintz covered the bed and the windows. A miscellany of china and cookware rested on the shelves above the stove. A black electric kettle and toaster stood out on the pine countertop. And a note, propped up against a jug filled with sprigs of heather, on the table tucked into the nook overlooking the valley.

Welcome to Ar Bàthach, Meghan – which is Gaelic for 'Our Barn'. I left some milk, eggs and bread in the fridge, and tea in the caddy. You're our first visitor, so please come over if you need anything or have questions. We live just across the way in the farmhouse. No need to lock the door every time you leave, but I left a key for the front door in the drawer of your bedside table. Ellen

It had been a rough night, that first night. I had curled up

2

under the duvet, Cassie in her own bed on the floor. But outside the wind howled, whistling down the chimney in the other room, and hurling squalls of heavy rain against the window panes. Outside was complete blackness. At home in the city, there would be streetlights. You could look out, watch the passage of the storm, put the ravages of its violence into perspective. Here there was only noise, rattling doors and windows, unknown threats echoing round the walls. I rationalised that our stone cottage – the barn – had probably been designed to withstand a highland tempest. Cassie was not equipped to analyse these possibilities and left the familiarity of her bed on the floor and crept under the covers with me.

In the early hours of the morning, the storm passed and we slept.

We awoke to a glorious day, the sun bathing the valley in colour and light, the air freshly cleansed by the storm. This was why we had left the city. Here I could find peace, reset my mind, move on. For more than three years, I had fought for a relationship which was destined for failure and taken each day's hurt and pain as my due; until the final showdown and my collapse. Under professional advice, I had decided to take a sabbatical away from the daily stress of working in a fast-paced, big city law firm. I would read every day, take up painting, keep a journal, go for long walks. It would be a year set aside just for me. But, at the last minute, I feared loneliness and went down to the Animal Rescue Centre and found Cassie – a three-year-old Cairn terrier who had been left behind when her elderly caretaker had died. She was timid and alone. We would be a perfect fit for each other.

A sign at the crossroads had directed strangers *To the Beach*. But the path down the side of the cliffside was slippery with mud, and the beach was pebbly and wet with seaweed. We might have been able to make it down, but climbing back up – for both of us – was more of a challenge.

Instead, I drove out of the village to the sandy beach I had noticed about two miles back the day before.

Golden sand stretched across the cove. Towering sand dunes, covered in sea grass, protected the beach from the gusting wind behind. Huge waves continued to roll into the bay, thundering and crashing against the cliffs and rocky outcrops on either side. And we were alone, completely alone. It was still early.

I took off my shoes and socks, felt the fine, warm sand squidge between my toes. I found a small stick and threw it for Cassie to fetch. She looked up at me, uncertain if this was a game for both of us to play, and I laughed. Yes, I laughed. I really laughed.

'Fetch, Cassie. Fetch.'

Cassie barked and chased after the stick, dropping it at my feet, tail wagging. And I threw it again and again, and ran along the beach after her. Together, we ran back and forth, up and down the beach. Together, we chased the receding waves and ran squealing and barking in mock terror as they swept back in. Eventually, out of breath, I walked back up the beach and found a dry spot to rest.

I don't know how long he had been there – the man with the basket on his back. In the distance, I could see him criss-crossing the beach, up and down from the tide line to the edge of the water, occasionally stooping down to pick up something and putting it in his basket. I imagined he was collecting some kind of shellfish for his dinner, or perhaps he was simply a shell collector. The best ones always came onshore after a storm. As a child, at the seaside, my father and I had been avid collectors. I liked the brightly coloured ones. My father looked for perfection. Perhaps, this man here today might even be a beachcomber looking for treasure, ancient artefacts or lost wedding rings.

In the meantime, Cassie was pulling at a tangled heap of seaweed which was already beginning to steam in the

4

morning sun. After a minute or two, she fell backwards, a large bone clutched in her mouth. Bleached and smooth and unbroken, it was large and jutted out on either side of her jaws.

'I think that's rather too big for you to handle, don't you? Perhaps, we could find you something smaller to take home.' I leant forward to take it from her mouth and she growled.

'Okay, perhaps not! Let's just see if you can make it to the car.'

As we started back up the beach, Cassie stopping and starting as she negotiated the peaks and troughs of the sand, I noticed the man in the distance striding out now in our direction, waving. I waved back casually, picked up Cassie still clutching her prize, and hurried up the path to the car park. It wouldn't do to be unfriendly on our first day here; but I wasn't yet ready to get into conversation with strangers. And we were quite alone on the beach.

Chapter 2

Deirdre – September, 2002

The day of her mother's funeral was when it all started, when she discovered she had power. Not the kind of power you acquire with free will or determination, but an innate power over which you have no control, either for its presence or its untimely departure. It is the power which inspires poets and storytellers, which men are prepared to kill and die for; the power from which legends are born.

*

The funeral procession wound its way slowly up the hill to the cemetery, the coffin carried on the shoulders of six men, straining step by step together up the twisting incline. The minister strode out ahead, leading the mourners away from the musty darkness of the old stone chapel at the roadside. He had read a few verses of scripture, solemnly intoned Psalm 23 – *Yea, though I walk through the valley of the shadow of death, I will fear no evil* ... and now, surrounded by the men of the village, he was taking Máire McIntyre to her final resting place. The path was steep, and the gravel shifted and slipped under the leather soles of Sunday shoes. James McIntyre, already unsteady after a night of cradling a bottle of whisky in front of a cold hearth, stumbled from time to time, obliging the funeral cortege to slow down to match his pace.

In other parts of the country at this time of year, the sun

would still be warm and bright, but here in the north, it had already paled, moving further south across the horizon each day and setting earlier each evening behind the distant hills. Deirdre took in deep draughts of the cool air, and held her face up to catch the waning light and the warmth. Surrounded by the women of the village, she stood taller and straighter, her red hair streaming behind her in the gently gusting breeze blowing in from the sea.

'Mark me, there'll be trouble now with that one. She's not even dressed for it, wearing that plaid skirt and yellow blouse, as if she's off to a ceilidh, with her hair loose and her head held high.'

'Aye,' replied Janet's sister, 'she thinks she's too good for the likes of the rest of us.'

'Proud, aye. Always a wilful child. But handsome too, awfu' handsome. With her mother gone, living alone with her father in that old farmhouse, what'll become of her now?'

Deirdre turned around and smiled at the two spinsters.

'Miss Janet. Miss Maud,' she nodded at each in turn. 'My mother would've loved this beautiful day up here on the hill, don't you think?'

'I daresay she would,' Janet Munro frowned. 'But see there, out on the horizon, there's a storm brewing. It'll be here before the night is out.'

The procession stopped at the entrance to the graveyard, and the minister unlatched the iron gate.

'The men will take Máire on now to her lair. We will see all you ladies later at the wake.'

'I shall be coming with you,' Deirdre moved forward and rested her hand on the brass clasp on the side of the coffin.

'It is not how we do things, Deirdre McIntyre,' the minister said loudly.

'She is … she was my mother. And I'll not leave her internment to the men.'

'I told you so,' Janet whispered to her sister. 'Her mother

7

not yet cold in her grave, and already there's trouble.'

'Who'll come with me to lay my mother to rest?' Deirdre turned back to face the women.

An old woman stepped forward, 'I'll go with you, child. Máire was my dear niece and I'll not be leaving her alone with the menfolk on her last journey.'

Deirdre took her hand, and together they followed the men through the gate towards the open grave. The other women hesitated. Most turned back and started down the hill again. But a few fell in step behind Deirdre and Brigid.

The graveyard itself was balanced precariously on the hillside, the sand beneath the sod shifting each year as the wind and the rain wore away the headland. Here and there, graves had carved out a level space, but most seemed angled to the slope of the hill. At the highest point, landowners and wealthy merchant families had erected monuments, decorated with angels or replicas of a grieving Madonna, some carved with the coats of arms of their clans. Families were clustered together here, even in death. But all seemed to have lost traction, resigned to the march of time. Mosses now grew in the crevices where names had been engraved. The salt air had eaten into the headstones, many of which had now lost their footing on the hillside. Identities were eroding, self-importance slipping inexorably towards the incoming tide.

The sun had disappeared briefly behind a bank of clouds sweeping inland, a sign of the storm building on the horizon. Máire's freshly-dug grave gaped open at the lowest part of the graveyard. Deirdre shivered at the sight, imagining how it would feel to be a warm, sentient being consigned for eternity to the cold darkness below. Perhaps she should have left with the women, remembering her mother as she had been before the long, lingering sickness had taken away the colour from her cheeks and the smile from her eyes. She put out her hand to steady herself on a headstone as she made her way downhill and felt the warmth of it, accumulated by the late afternoon sun.

They had stopped now. The pallbearers set Máire onto the grass beside the grave and looked around for James McIntyre. Tradition dictated that the coffin was lowered into the ground by male family members, but James was alone now, and he was lost.

The minister continued unperturbed –

In the sweat of thy face shalt thou eat bread, till thou return unto the ground; for out of it wast thou taken: for dust thou art, and unto dust shalt thou return.

Deirdre stepped forward and took her father's arm.

'Come, Father, we'll do this together.'

The minister looked up sharply from his text.

'It is not …' he began.

'I know,' Deirdre interrupted, '… not how we do things. But today, it will be.'

Brigid smiled.

Deirdre led her father forward, and together, at the midpoint of the coffin, each of them bore the weight of it into the ground, with two pallbearers at the head and two at the foot. And together, they all picked up the shovels which lay nearby and began to cover the oak box, with its shiny brass name plate and buckles, in soft damp sand. At first, their erratic shovelfuls thudded against the lid, echoing in the cavern below. And then, as sand covered sand, they settled into a gentle rhythm, an accompaniment to the sound of the waves of the turning tide.

Finally, all the sand was tamped down, a strip of turf rolled over the top, and Máire McIntyre had been laid to rest.

The sun came out again but lower now, drawing nearer to the distant headland. The minister turned away, the mourners following his example as he led the way back up the sloping path to the iron gate. Only father and daughter remained.

'She's gone and we can't even see where she lies. How

9

will we find her?' he swept his hand across the graveyard.

'There'll be a headstone, Father, but we need to wait until the ground settles over her ...'

Deirdre hesitated. She did not want to remind her father of Máire's body lying now under six feet of sand, shifting and sinking around her coffin until she was imprisoned inside for eternity.

Deirdre put her hand on her father's shoulder.

'I'll bring *flùraichean* – heather blooms and bog orchids from the moors, all the ones she loved.'

'Aye, that'll be good.'

'And I'll plant some too, in the season. Then we'll always be able to find her,' she paused. 'But now, Father, we need to go back for the wake. They'll be waiting for us.'

Together, they walked away uphill. But as Deirdre turned to latch the iron gate behind her, a shadow passed overhead. She turned and looked up, her hand raised in greeting. An eagle – its dark and powerful wings beating as it swooped low over the graveyard – circled once, twice, and then soared up and over the hillside, calling with short, shrill cries.

Chapter 3

Deirdre

Deirdre longed to climb up the hillside, to follow her friend Iolaire, the eagle. To lie back among the tussocks of the moorland grasses and the small purple blooms of the flowering heather. To watch the sun set and listen to the sounds of life settling into the night – the ewes calling to their lambs, the curlews trilling in the sky above as they prepared for their winter trek to the northern isles, the triple bark of the dog fox calling to his mate as they set out on their nocturnal hunt.

Instead, with her father leaning heavily on her arm, they made their way past the darkened church and up the road, past the campground where tourists had pitched their tents and lit fires, the smells of roasting meat drifting on the air, past the village shop with its hand-painted sign advertising hot food and coffee and tea and snacks. Brigid's son owned the village pub – The Piper and the Swan – and it was where she had arranged to hold Máire's wake.

Many of the villagers had tried to attend the funeral, but now it seemed that everyone had assembled for the wake. Light and noise spilled out of the open door, shadows lengthening with the setting sun. Deirdre nodded to a group of older men who were outside smoking, and led her father inside.

Fergus stood behind the bar as usual, the jovial landlord. A sturdy man with sandy hair and blue eyes, he ran a tight house. Mindful of the alcoholic intake of some of the heaviest tipplers and a strict observer of closing time, he was respected in the community and had recently been elected mayor. It was largely a ceremonial title, but its bestowal indicated a level of popularity which his wife, Liane, believed included her and their two children. Tonight, standing behind the bar, beside her husband, she bobbed and smiled as each pint of beer and each dram of whisky was passed across into welcoming hands.

Brigid had taken responsibility for the food – the pork pies and the sausage rolls, the sandwiches and the shortbread. All of which she had prepared herself. A small-framed woman, with her grey hair wound in a knot on top of her head, she seemed slight beside her son and daughter-in-law. Busy with plates and serving dishes, she looked up as Deirdre and her father came in; and with tray in hand, took them to a corner table.

'I'll not sit, Brigid. I want to help.'

'Nay, lass, there's no need.'

'I need to,' Deirdre smiled, and took the tray.

For many months, since it became obvious that her mother was seriously ill and would not recover, Brigid had come to the house every day. She cleaned, prepared meals, and sat with Máire while Deirdre was at school and James was out working in the farm.

Deirdre had drawn close to Brigid, breathing in the fresh air of another life.

Brigid had lived in the city once. Apprenticed to a kiltmaker and working long hours each day, she had shared a small bedsit with another girl. On summer evenings, they had walked together along the riverside, and sat outside a pub drinking halves of cider. As the nights got darker, they had sheltered in cafés, sitting at plastic-covered tables with endless mugs of stale coffee, and talked about how it would be to leave this place, this country. They could sail halfway round the world to New Zealand, visit the temples and shrines of India and China, live on a tropical island in the Pacific, settle in the Wild West of America. Anything was possible, if they dared, wasn't it? And sometimes, on a Saturday night, they had been invited to a party where no-one was older than twenty-five and there were no rules. Brigid had met her husband, Iain, at one such party, and together they had returned to the village, to manage and eventually buy the pub.

Máire had never left the village. Brought up on a small croft, she had married young and had always given James McIntyre the kind of loyalty and obedience which she believed was her role in life. Deirdre had begun to imagine a different life for herself, to dream as once Brigid had dreamed.

But as Máire had drawn her last breath, Deirdre had made her a promise:

'When I'm gone,' her mother had said, 'your father will need you. Alone, he's not a strong man. You must promise me you'll take good care of him.'

'I will, Mother,' she had replied. 'I promise.'

Now, she wondered, what had been the depth of that promise. What limits and what conditions did it imply? Across the room, her father sat mumbling as he told the story of his courtship of Máire and their life together, barely able to articulate the words as his friends plied him with whisky and empty words of comfort.

At the bar, Deirdre refilled her tray with sandwiches and sausage rolls. Four young men lolled against the brass rail, pushing and shoving each other, ogling as she leant forward to retrieve some paper napkins.

'We're sorry about your ma, Deirdre,' one volunteered.

'Aye, so we are. You'll be wanting to leave your father's house soon enough.'

'And then,' another chimed in, 'you'll be looking for

a man of your own. Emily Gunn's already told me she's gaggin' fer it, and she's in your class at school. You might want to hurry before all the good ones have gone!' he laughed suggestively.

'The good ones, eh, Tom Mackay? You'd better take Emily up on her offer quickly then. Before she realises she's made a mistake,' Deirdre smiled as she turned to walk away, laughter in her wake.

Fergus banged the small gong behind the bar.

'Welcome everyone. I don't want to stop your drinking ... '

'No, Fergus, you'd best not be doing that,' a voice called out from the doorway.

'But tonight, we're all here to remember a sweet woman,' Fergus continued. 'Máire McIntyre, who will be sadly missed by all who knew her, especially her husband, James, and her child, Deirdre. So, raise your glasses, everyone. To Máire, may she rest in peace!'

'To Máire, may she rest in peace!'

There was a clinking of glasses and a brief moment of silence.

'And now, Deirdre, a song? Your sweet voice to send her soul to the other side with the angels,' Brigid had spoken.

Deirdre looked up. She had known she would have to sing. She had expected the invitation since the sun rose over the hills behind the farm that morning. At first, out on the hillside, climbing up to the cemetery, she had felt a sense of well-being. She was relieved that her mother had been spared any more suffering and the late afternoon sun had been a perfect complement to that feeling. But at the graveside, she had been overwhelmed with a sensation of claustrophobia and doubt. All she could see was the coffin hidden in the gloom and dankness of the open grave, in a place consecrated by the fond memories of family and friends in the daylight, but shunned by the living after dark. No birds nested there, no rabbits built their burrows, no field mice or voles harvested the grass which was cut each week before it had a chance to seed. Only Iolaire had crossed the boundary into the graveyard, fearless and proud, his spreading wings casting their own shadow, his call mocking the silence.

She was surprised at the phrasing of Brigid's invitation because she knew that Brigid did not believe in souls or angels. The word spirit was more a part of her belief system. Deirdre did not know what she believed about death and dying. But if Máire had a soul or a spirit, where was it now? Would it remain in the village, be at her side throughout her life, or would it soon depart? Nothing she had learned in the kirk or in the classroom had prepared her for this moment. So many words had been spoken, and yet so many questions were left unanswered.

'Sing, Deirdre,' Brigid coaxed. 'The new song which you sang for Máire – *Mo Rùn Geal Dìleas* – My Fair and Faithful Love,' she translated for the non-Gaelic speakers in the room.

So, Deirdre sang, first the chorus and then each verse. Her voice had a childish quality to it, slightly high-pitched, but which rolled softly around the Gaelic words. Some understood the words, listening carefully as Deirdre told a familiar story of love and loss, and death. Others simply registered the emotions as her voice rose and fell, pausing between each verse. Soon everyone had mastered the rhythm and the words of the chorus – a repetition of those in the title of the song – and joined in the singing and clapping, keeping time together.

She finished singing the last verse –

My fond farewell to you if you have left me,
The sea never ebbs, but follows the flow.

Then she began the final chorus. The familiar repetition of the words and notes and rhythms filled the room, everyone now drawn into the sadness and regret they evoked, some for Máire and some for a loss of their own. For a moment or two, the room settled into silence – and then James stood up, glass in hand.

'Máire! My Máire!'

As some raised their glasses, others turned towards the door. A man, a stranger, stood in the doorway, a large white dog at his side.

'Can I help you?'

Everyone turned to stare at the new arrival.

'I heard the singing. I thought you were having a party in here.' The accent was not local. It spoke of education and privilege.

'The pub is closed tonight to outsiders,' Fergus continued. 'If you're wanting a drink, the hotel up the hill will serve you.'

'I'm not …' the stranger paused.

'But you'll no' find any good music up there the night,' one of the young men joked.

The exchange had broken the moment. And now, it seemed to Deirdre, there were too many people in this small space, with its low-hanging beams and tightly-packed tables. The lights were too bright, the air too stifling.

'And this is not a ceilidh,' said Deirdre, as she pushed past the stranger who remained standing in the doorway. 'It's my mother's wake.'

Chapter 4

Meghan

Two days later we went to the pub, The Piper and the Swan. The sign over the entrance – a boy playing a panpipe to a large white swan – creaked as it caught the onshore breeze.

It was a Friday, and the pub special that night was fish and chips. There was a black slate board outside, which I'd noticed the day before on my way to buy a few groceries at the store. A fish supper would be a treat before the weekend, and it would be a low-key way to get to meet some of the locals. If Cassie and I were going to be here for the next twelve months, I didn't want to give the impression that we were standoffish city folks. We would get there early, find a corner table, and ...

I had not anticipated the noise, or the crowd. Cassie drew back, terrified by the whole scene, and I had to scoop her up under my arm to carry her inside. A crowd hovered around the bar, chatting to an older woman behind it, as she continued to pull pints and take food orders on post-it notes which she stuck on the overhead rack. A young man appeared from the back room, balancing a tray over his head, and made his way through the crowd to one of the tables. People moved back and forth, carrying glasses and calling out to others as they passed. A shout went up from the group at the dartboard.

'Losers buy the next round, Cathel!'

I recognised the name. Cathel and Ellen Sinclair were my landlords. I was staying on their property.

Cathel laughed, 'I canna lose the night, man. I'm on a winning streak.' And, as he turned, he saw Cassie under my arm, 'Ah, Ms. Bell,' he put out his hand.

'Meghan, please.'

'Meghan, then. Good to meet you and the wee dog. Perhaps this wasn't what you were expecting in a quiet village up here in the hills. It's not always like this.'

'Fish supper night?' I smiled.

'Aye, indeed. And you'll be in need of a place to sit. Dougal is propping up the end of the bar as usual, with an empty stool at his side. He loves a good blether, and it'd improve his reputation no end to be seen chatting with you,' he smiled. 'Just don't tell him anything you don't want anyone else to know – it'll be all round the village by morning.'

The sound of the local accent, the easy warmth of the place, Cathel's casual greeting. They all felt right. The bare stone cottage, the storm which had unleashed its fury on our first night, and the beach where you could be quite alone – it had all seemed part of a different world from the one I knew. But already, I could feel myself relaxing in a place where everyone would soon know my name. I had not expected, I had not wanted, to get too close to people, be involved in their lives, or for them to be involved in mine. Perhaps I had been mistaken. Perhaps I had chosen the perfect place, just for the wrong reasons.

Dougal smiled as I walked over. A small man, in his late sixties or early seventies, his hair was snowy white, and his eyebrows were sandy-coloured. His short-clipped beard was a mix of the two.

'There's a place right here, waiting for ye,' he patted the stool.

'Thank you. Cathel said you wouldn't mind my sitting here?'

'I wouldna refuse a pretty wee lassie like you a place at

my side.'

'I'm Meghan.'

'Aye, I know that well enough. You're staying up at the McIntyre place.'

'You mean at Cathel and Ellen's farm? I thought their name was Sinclair.'

'Aye, so it is. But it'll always be the McIntyre place to us.'

For a minute or two, Dougal stared at me, smiling.

'You're a wee bit like her, James' daughter. With your red hair and green-tinged eyes. Not so prominent, your colouring, though, nor so tall,' he paused. 'Perhaps not so *tappet thrawn* either, eh?'

'I've been called a lot of things in my time, but never that.'

'It means wild and headstrong.'

'Well, Dougal – may I call you that?' He nodded. 'I should warn you that I can also be *tappet thrawn* ...' He nodded again, 'under the right circumstances.'

Dougal turned towards the woman behind the bar and laughed then.

'Meghan here says she can be *tappet thrawn*, under the right circumstances! She even looks a wee bit like our Deirdre, don't you think, Liane?'

'I'll not have that name mentioned in my bar, Dougal. Ye ken that well enough,' she turned to me. 'Will it be fish and chips, and something to drink?'

Dougal was quiet for a few minutes, apparently silenced by Liane's warning. It was obviously a private matter, so I thought it was best left alone, even though it was intriguing. Perhaps this Deirdre had caused trouble in the village, with her wild and headstrong ways. I'd better be careful not to do the same.

When the food and drink arrived, Dougal raised his glass of beer, as I took the first sip of my shandy.

19

'You arrived on the night of the storm, the beginning of winter, on *Gore Vellye*.'

I laughed then.

'I can see I'm going to need an interpreter while I'm here.'

'Och, you'll soon begin to understand us, even though some lowlanders say we have strange and primitive ways. *Gore Vellye* is an island myth. The Vikings believed that the sea and the weather were controlled by a battle between the *Mither of the Sea* and *Teran*. In winter, *Teran* – the monster – breaks loose from his shackles and rises again from the bottom of the sea to confront the *Sea Mither* – who cares for the world. At the start of spring, she wins, bringing warm, calm weather. But, as winter arrives, he's the victor. He brings storms and dangerous seas.'

'That's a great story. Not just a weather forecast, with algorithms and graphs. A myth, and a glimpse into another dimension.'

'Here in the Highlands, Meghan, there's aye another dimension.'

*

It was after ten when I walked back to the cottage. The light had gone, and I had to use the torch on my phone to see the way. I had forgotten how quickly night settled in here and how the darkness was absolute. Cassie seemed to enjoy the walk, sniffing at fence posts and the tall grass along the verge. Perhaps she, too, was beginning to relax in our new environment.

I had not looked at my mobile phone at the pub. The reception was not good away from the internet at the cottage, the surrounding hills sheltering the village from the nearest cell tower. But, when I walked in and turned off the light on the phone, I could see the message on the screen and Richard's number –

20

You left without saying goodbye. I told you it was too soon. You can go, but you can't disappear. I will find you. One day you'll open your door and I'll be standing there. You need me, just as I need you. We are inseparable.

Chapter 5

Deirdre

The sea mist had begun to curl inland. An almost full moon hung low over the distant hills, encircled by a muted rainbow, pale light piercing the droplets swirling slowly in the air.

'A lunar halo,' Brigid said as she came outside and stood beside Deirdre. 'It's a sign.'

'A good sign?'

'Some might say so, child. It warns of danger, but promises the means of escape.'

'Janet Munro said there'd be a storm tonight.'

'Miss Munro says a lot of things, Deirdre. But she was only talking about the weather.'

'I don't want to go back in there, Brigid.'

'Then don't. Take a wee walk down to the cliffs and listen to the voices in the waves. Perhaps, they'll bring you some peace tonight. But take care on the path, and get home before the rain starts.'

'And Father?'

'I'll see he gets home safe. I don't think he'll be wanting to leave for a wee while.'

*

Deirdre turned away from the lights and the noise of the pub, and started down the path. She had intended to stop at the headland as Brigid had suggested. But, when she got there, she continued walking as far as the steps which led down the steep cliffside to the beach. The steps were roughly hewn, in some places filled in with uneven planks of driftwood, in others left to the natural mud and bare rock of the landscape. Someone had hung an old rope as a handrail along one side, but the hooks which originally held it in place were rusting in the salt air, and it had pulled loose and was a precarious handhold. Underfoot the steps were slippery, and Deirdre found herself crouching down to clutch at the grass and heather alongside to steady herself.

There was an ebb tide, and she could smell the exposed seaweed on the rocks and pebbles which led down to the water. The moon had disappeared behind a cloud, but Deirdre knew the beach well, and she followed the sounds of the receding waves which lapped against the side of the old, concrete jetty. Out at sea, she could see brief flashes of lightning followed by the murmur of muffled thunder. She made her way to the end of the jetty and sat down, her back leaning against one of the concrete bollards, her feet dangling over the edge. The wind was picking up now, driving against the outgoing tide; Deirdre lifted her face to feel the fine mist wafting inland on the air. As a child, she had once taken a ferry to the islands with her mother; and she had stood in the prow of the boat with some of the other children, squealing in mock terror as they slammed into the oncoming swell and the spray swept over them.

She closed her eyes and imagined herself drifting out to sea. It was not a frightening thought. She felt buoyed up by the waves, as if they were taking her away to a calmer place where she could rest for a while. Brigid had understood.

She did not know how long she had been sitting there before she became aware of another sound, a panting, approaching nearer and nearer. She remained completely still, alert now, in the present. Perhaps, whatever it was would not see her. Unless it could pick up her scent on the wind.

23

For a moment, the sound ceased; and then she was startled by a wet nose nudging her elbow. It was the white dog she had seen with the stranger at the pub. She jumped up quickly, aware now that the stranger was nearby. As the moon appeared briefly from behind the clouds, she saw him, standing, watching her from the end of the jetty. He raised his hand and started to walk towards her, the light from his torch barely penetrating the dense, dank air.

'I didn't mean to alarm you.'

'You followed me?'

'I saw you walk away from the pub. Then Magnus here took off after you. We reached the end of the path, and there was no sign of you. I thought you might've turned back on a side track, and then I worried you'd fallen. Magnus started down the steps so I followed. He's not usually so persistent.'

He was not a tall man and had short, fair hair which spiked in the wind. Although she could not see clearly in the mist, she felt his eyes on her.

'As you can see, I'm fine.'

'I know you, don't I?'

'I'm sure you don't. And I certainly don't know you.'

'Sebastian St. John Carlyle at your service,' he gave a mock bow.

'You're a Carlyle from the Big House?'

'The same. And you are …?'

'Deirdre, Deirdre McIntyre. And, as I told you, today we buried my mother, Máire.'

'I was sorry to hear that.'

Deirdre turned away.

'You won't remember who I am. I see that now. I was at uni, Oxford, around the time you were born. Since then, I've been away, in London and overseas. But they were right, what they said.'

'What who said?'

'There was a woman. Her husband owned the pub.'

'Brigid?'

'Brigid. They said she could see into the future.'

Deirdre nodded, 'She has the gift – *an dà-shealladh* – second sight.'

'She said you would become a dangerously beautiful woman. And I can see she was right.'

Deirdre laughed, 'You're a flatterer, Mr Carlyle.'

'Sebastian, please.'

'As I said, Mr Carlyle, you can go on your way.'

'How old are you, Deirdre?'

'Not that it's any of your business, but I'll be eighteen tomorrow. And how old are you, sir?'

'Old enough to recognise a beautiful woman when I see one.'

'Well, now you've seen me. I doubt we'll meet again. But thank you anyway for ensuring my safety on this wild highland night.' And she laughed again.

'I'm not going anywhere.'

'Excuse me?'

'What I meant was that I'm moving permanently into the Big House. My father died late last year. I'm taking back control of the estate, looking for new investment opportunities,' he paused. 'So, Deirdre McIntyre, I certainly hope we'll meet again.'

'You and I move in different circles, Mr Carlyle.'

'We're living in a new world, Deirdre. Times have changed.'

'I can see, Mr Carlyle, you've a lot to learn about our highland ways. And, as for opportunities at the Big House … Well, we'll see.'

And, once again that night, Deirdre slid past him, disappearing into the mist.

Sebastian St. John Carlyle called his dog to heel and slowly picked his way back across the beach, his torch swinging back and forth to light the way.

Chapter 6

Meghan

Why, I wondered, had I not deleted and blocked Richard's number? Had I really imagined we'd get back together? I had told him it was over. I'd asked him to return the key to my flat.

Richard and I had set a date for moving in together. I had already signed a year's lease for a flat with a newly-wed couple who both had jobs in the city. I'd bought new sheets, sets of dishes and pots, kitchen stuff. It was to be a new start. And then, the day before we were to spend our first night in our new home, he cancelled everything. He couldn't leave his daughter. She was only seven. It would break her heart. They'd have to wait until she was old enough to understand why her father was leaving home. It was the same mantra he had repeated since the beginning.

This time, I'd have to face up to the reality that I was the 'other woman'. That was apparently what I'd always been destined to be. Richard was a senior partner in the firm, assigned as my mentor. A good-looking man in his late fifties, but already on his second marriage, with a young daughter. Why had I not foreseen that getting into a relationship with him would be a disaster waiting to happen? Rejection was not an easy pill to swallow. But now the reins of power would switch hands. I'd take control of my own life.

*

When I awoke the following morning, the scene outside the window was dreary. A steady drizzle streamed across the landscape, whipped into little squalls by the wind which swept down the hillside behind the farm. I had to persuade Cassie to go outside after she'd eaten, sheltering us both in the lee of the cottage where, for a minute or two, we could avoid the worst of the weather.

I was clearing away the breakfast dishes, Cassie snuggled up in her basket, when I heard the knock at the door. Cassie looked up, ears pricked. I froze. There was a pause, and then another knock, louder this time. I opened the door slowly, blocking the entrance with my body, my foot ready to slam the door, afraid that Richard had found me. But it was a woman, sheltering under the hood of her anorak.

I stepped away so that she could come in out of the weather.

'Who were you expecting? The bogeyman?' she laughed. 'I'm Ellen. I just dropped by to ask if you'd like to come over for a coffee. It's Saturday, so the boys are home, but they're playing video games as usual; Cathel's gone out to feed the sheep. It'll just be the two of us,' she walked over to Cassie's basket. 'And you can come too if you like.'

She bent down to pat Cassie, who suddenly bared her teeth and growled.

'Oops. Doesn't like strangers?'

'She's usually really good with people. But she found a bone yesterday, and …'

'I understand. Our two sheepdogs are just the same.'

*

The farmhouse was warm and comfortable. A scrubbed pine table with four chairs sat in the middle of the kitchen area, the undercounter washing machine whirring spasmodically. A television, a chintz-covered sofa and two armchairs, and a dark wood coffee table lay at the other end of the open

27

room, in front of a stone fireplace, glowing now with a small pile of peat logs. Between the two rooms, a narrow staircase wound upstairs. In the distance, the sounds of gunfire.

Ellen smiled, 'Seven- and eight-year-old boys already wanting to conquer the world. It doesn't get better than this.'

We sat in front of the fire together, drinking coffee and eating Ellen's shortbread. She was an easy companion, and an attentive listener. Even without makeup she looked good – soft blond hair pulled back in a clasp, a fresh rosy complexion, expressive eyes. I had always felt the need to examine myself critically before I left the house. We were about the same age, but very different. She seemed content with her life. I, on the other hand, had lost my way somewhere along the road.

I asked about the farm, and she told me about the farmer who'd sold it to them. She told me the difference between crofters, who only rented their land from the landowner, and farmers. They'd been lucky, she said, to get the freehold here and also to have inherited her father-in-law's place up in the hills. Her grandfather had not been so lucky. She hadn't been brought up on a farm. She'd come from the islands, studied land management, and now had a permanent job on the nearby estate, having been taken on after a short internment there. She liked her job because she was given a free hand to manage everything. All she had to do was turn a reasonable profit each year.

And I told her about my job – a junior partner in a top-ranked law firm which specialised in criminal cases, a frenetic environment where there seemed no beginning or end to each work day, and emails and texts required your immediate attention. I also mentioned a failed relationship with a married man, but I didn't go into specifics.

'You came here to reset your life. And you couldn't have found a better place,' she paused. 'Although, don't delude yourself into believing this is a sleepy little backwater where nothing happens. We've had quite a bit of drama over the years. Every place has its secrets.'

'I met Dougal at the pub last night.'

'He's an old blether. You'd best not be telling him too much about yourself, or ...' she paused, '... just don't believe everything he tells you either.'

'Cathel warned me.'

'Good man, my Cathel. He helped James, who owned this farm for years. He liked the man, even though he could be an old grump. And he was a good friend to James' daughter too. There was a lot of talk when they lived here, some true, some not so. Either way, the past is often best forgotten.'

'Are you advising me not to ask too many questions?' I smiled.

'You're here to relax, recuperate from your past experiences, perhaps reorient your life. All I'm saying is that it's probably better to let others do the same.'

*

I had enjoyed my morning with Ellen, although her comments had piqued my curiosity.

When I got back to the cottage, I couldn't find Cassie at first. I called her name several times before I found her cowering under my bed, shivering. I wrapped her up in the blanket at the foot of my bed and carried her into the sitting room with me.

'What's the matter, girl? Were you frightened, left all alone in a strange place?' Gently I stroked her head, 'I promise, from now on, I'll never leave you alone here again. We're going to be the best pals ever, inseparable.'

There was that word again, the same one Richard had used in his text – inseparable. Some people were inseparable, weren't they? From the people they loved? From their pets? It was part of human nature to want to feel part of someone else's life, to feel relevant and included. Humans were gregarious by nature, and some animals had become part of their human families as they became domesticated. It was all about survival, safety in numbers.

So, that night, Cassie slept at the foot of my bed. But I, for some reason, still felt uneasy. Since I had left to visit Ellen this morning, something had changed in the cottage. Nothing had been disturbed, as far as I could see, and nothing taken. It was probably just Richard's text which had unnerved me, because now I felt as if I were being watched. I'd never taken him for a stalker. He'd never been the jealous kind. But then I'd always been available, every time he called, every time he wanted to get together. My life had revolved around him, his life; he'd always known that ... until now.

Cassie was sleeping soundly. I listened to her snoring, and realised I hadn't seen her bone all day, not since returning from the farmhouse. She'd always kept it beside her in her basket, but I couldn't remember seeing it all afternoon. She'd probably hidden it somewhere when I was out. She'd never actually gnawed at it, just kept it beside her. It was probably too big for her anyway. I'd have to buy her something smaller to match her jaw size.

When I did eventually fall asleep, I dreamed of bones accumulating in Cassie's basket, which she guarded more and more fiercely until no-one, not even I, could get near her.

Chapter 7

Deirdre

By the time Deirdre was on the path leading up to the farm, the storm had settled in overhead. Rain squalls were sweeping in over the headland, forcing her to lean into the wind to climb up the hill.

Wet and cold, she ran indoors in anticipation of warmth and shelter. But the house was dark and cold and silent. There was no fire in the hearth, no light in the upstairs window. The wind whistled and moaned down the chimney flue, into the house, crying like a wounded animal. The bravado of the day behind her, Deirdre collapsed on the threadbare hearth rug and wept. This, she realised, was how it would be from now on.

Upstairs, she tore off her damp clothes, throwing them into the hamper in the bathroom. As she turned to go, she saw her reflection in the mirror. The copper and amber highlights in her hair glinted in the overhead light, her wide green eyes stared back at her. Today, she had been called 'awfu' handsome' and 'dangerously beautiful'. At her age, there were very few girls who did not attract the attention of the hormone-driven young men in the village, but she was not impressed or really interested in the boys' crude overtures. She wanted to make her own way, plan her own life, have a few adventures. Time enough for marriage and motherhood. The idea that she might be considered beautiful had never crossed her mind. But this stranger, Sebastian Carlyle from the Big House, a man who was in his thirties and who had travelled the world, had called her so.

In her parents' room, she stood naked in front of the full-length mirror on the door of her mother's wardrobe. She was too tall, much taller than her classmates, taller than most of the young men in the village. Her high cheekbones were too prominent, above a sharply accentuated chin. Her complexion, although unblemished, was burned a pale gold from the hours she spent outside on the moors. Her breasts were small, her hips broad. But, even in the dim overhead light, her hair burned and glistened, tumbling over her shoulders and caressing her body. And her green eyes glowed fiercely, challenging, and perhaps even dangerous, as Sebastian Carlyle had said. She turned this way and that in front of the mirror; and then, smiling, closed the wardrobe door.

*

She had been in a deep sleep, dreaming, when she became aware that she was not alone.

In her dream, she was walking down a wide corridor illuminated by candlelight sconces. At the far end, she could see an open door and a brightly-lit panelled room. She could hear musicians tuning their instruments – a fiddle and the pipes, a drummer warming up. There were alcoves and window seats along the way, where groups of people – young and old – were talking quietly together, their words a faint background murmuring. All were dressed formally. Most of the men wore kilts with leather sporrans and dark velvet jackets, long white socks with garter flashes and *sgian dubhs* tucked inside. Deirdre recognised the clans – Mackay, Gunn, Sinclair, Mackenzie. Occasionally, she saw a bright blue tartan she had not seen before. The women wore long dresses of velvet and silk and moiré satin, most with clan sashes draped across a shoulder; all wore jewellery which

32

glinted seductively in the candlelight. Everyone nodded and smiled at her as she passed, but the faces were unfamiliar. And, although she continued walking, the room at the end of the corridor never seemed to get closer. The faces changed but the corridor seemed endless. She stopped and turned towards a tall window, set midway along, to get her bearings. Outside, in the moonlight, she could see a well-ordered garden, with row upon row of rose bushes planted in the beds. In the distance, the sea seemed motionless, the moon above, a perfect reflection below.

As she turned back from the window in her dream, she heard the creak of a floorboard. The warmth and the soft lighting fell away as she woke to the darkness and cold of her own bedroom. She waited. The floorboards of the farmhouse were old and warped. No-one could move across its floors without betraying themselves. And then she heard it again, another creak, nearer this time. She was not imagining spirits in the night, phantasms escaping from her dreams. Someone was definitely in her room.

Here, in the Highlands, nobody locked their doors. Everyone knew and trusted their neighbours. She could not imagine any of the young lads in the village daring to break this unspoken code, even after a night of heavy drinking in the pub. And the new arrival, Sebastian Carlyle? It hardly seemed his style. Should she call out, demand the intruder identify himself … or herself? Or turn over noisily and pretend to mutter loudly in her sleep? Whoever it was probably imagined she was still asleep. If she lay completely still, the intruder might simply leave like a burglar in the night.

As her mind was racing with thoughts of escape, she felt a rush of cold air as someone slowly pulled back the bedclothes. The mattress sank to one side as the intruder sat down. Whoever it was had been nearer than she thought. Once again that night, she felt eyes staring at her in the darkness. She froze, trying to make herself as small – as unavailable – as possible. Her only thought now was to wait until the threat had passed. If she did not react or pull away, perhaps he or she would change their mind and leave. And then she felt a warm hand grasp her bare breast. She could smell the musk of his sweat and the alcohol on his breath, as he fell, fully-clothed, on top of her. Her face now smothered by a rough wool jacket, and struggling for breath, she grabbed onto the cloth and pulled and pushed him until he fell to one side. Rolling over, she picked up her bedside lamp and brandished it over where she imagined his head to be.

'Get out,' she shouted into the darkness. 'Get out now before I smash your brains in.'

'Máire, don't say no, not tonight. Stay with me. I need you. You know I always need you. Please.'

Deirdre sighed. The words were familiar. She had heard them often through the walls, in her parents' bedroom. Even as her mother had been weakened by illness, James had continued to claim his conjugal rights. It had sickened Deirdre to hear her mother crying in the bathroom afterwards. James, satisfied and oblivious to the pain he had caused, immediately fell asleep, snoring loudly. Tonight, he had mistakenly stumbled into her bedroom, and imagined Máire waiting there.

She leaned over, shaking him by the shoulder, 'Father, it's me, Deirdre. Mother has gone. Remember, we buried her today.'

'No games tonight, Máire. You're always so warm and soft,' his hand stretched out, clutching at her arm.

Roughly this time, she pushed his hand aside, and got out of bed.

'Go to sleep, James,' she said, as she pulled on her dressing gown and closed the door quietly behind her.

Her parents had always loved each other; her mother had

34

never refused James anything. But it was not how Deirdre imagined love. She wanted to be able to refuse or accept a man's advances. In the closeness of her home, with her father clawing at her body, she had only felt revulsion. If this was love, what Tom Mackay had proposed in the pub just a few hours earlier, the kind she had heard in his laughter, she would do without.

Chapter 8

Deirdre

She awoke to the sound of Cathel's old car arriving in the yard, the telltale backfiring as the engine shut off. She had spent the night huddled on the sofa under a blanket, only falling asleep as the light came up around five. Now, she knew, it would be nearly eight o'clock. In a few minutes, he would be coming into the kitchen for a cup of tea, to talk to her father about the day's schedule. Cathel was nineteen, the son of a hillside crofter. She was naked under her dressing gown, and the school bus left in half an hour. The tea would have to wait. Upstairs, she heard the toilet flush.

*

'Where's the porridge, child?' James sat hunched over the kitchen table.

Deirdre stopped on the last step, grabbing her backpack from the banister as she passed.

'I made the tea,' Cathel interrupted. 'I said I'd make the porridge too, but ...'

'It's no' your job, man. It's hers now.'

'I'm late already.'

'That's because you didna sleep in your own bed last night.'

Was her father so drunk last night he really did not remember what had happened? Or was he in denial?

Cathel looked up at Deirdre, eyebrows raised.

'I waited up for you, Father. You were late coming in from the wake. I must've fallen asleep.'

'Aye, well. Brigid wilna be coming in each day, now your ma has gone. You'll need to get to it earlier, that's all.'

Outside the air was cool and fresh. The northerly had blown through, an early harbinger of the long, dark nights. This year, they had forecast a colder than usual winter, with snow storms and gale force winds coming down from the Arctic. Already, Cathel had started baling the hay, and strengthening the timber beams, and repairing the roof of the byre. The sheep and the cows would need extra food and shelter.

But today the sun was out, the sky was cloudless. And she had turned eighteen.

Her father had not remembered. It was just another day, the routines uninterrupted by a personal milestone. The almanac of the village revolved around the seasons for lambing and calving, planting and harvesting. A young girl's coming-of-age birthday, the day after her mother's funeral, was just another day for a crofter in the village.

In the distance, she could see the school bus making its last turn into the village over the cattle grid. And she could feel the warmth of the sun on her back. She looked back at the farmhouse. Cathel and her father had not appeared. Perhaps, even now, they were enjoying Cathel's porridge. She skirted the wall of the byre and started to climb the hill. At school, they would not be surprised if she was absent today. Her father would not know, or probably care, either way. This was her day, and she would celebrate it on the moor with a friend.

The climb up the hill to the top fence was steep. The heather, now in full bloom, stretched in purple swathes across the landscape, interspersed with dense patches of springy, bright green moss. A small rocky crevasse divided the property, where a small stream crossed the land and wound its way down the field below, over the cliffside and into the sea. Outside the perimeter of James McIntyre's farm, the ground became boggy, marked by deep cuts where the peat had been cut. Higher up, sheep were scattered in small groups of two or three, foraging amongst the rocks on small patches of grass and young heather plants, calling to each other as they moved. Flocks had intermingled. Some were McIntyre sheep, with large red circles painted on their fleeces. A blue stripe identified the Gunn flock, a green cross the Sinclair.

Deirdre climbed past them all and began the final ascent up the path to *Iolairean a'Neadachadh* – the Eagle's Nest. For as long as people could remember, eagles had nested on this mountaintop. And this was the home of her friend Iolaire.

She was only nine years old when she had climbed up the hillside and found the young fledgling fallen from his nest. Unafraid, she had taken him in her arms and cradled him against her chest, stroking his head and talking to him quietly. The down on his head was soft. His heartbeat fluttered beside her own. The nest was resting on a rock outcrop above her head, but there was no sign of the adult birds. She knew this youngster was still too young to fly. And his parents would not be able to return him to their eyrie because he was too big. If he was to survive, she would have to return him to the nest herself. Slowly and carefully, she had crawled over the rocks, with one hand clutching tightly onto his talons, until she was able to tip him carefully over the edge of the nest. He had flapped wildly for a moment or two. Then, settling down into the soft grasses and mosses which lined the huge twig nest, he had continued looking at her, this unfamiliar creature in his burgeoning world. She had barely noticed the blood and scrapes on her knees as she ran home to tell her mother. Máire had told Deirdre to honour the chick by calling him by his true name, his Gaelic name – Iolaire.

Every day for the next few weeks, she had gone up to the eyrie. After school, after she had done her Saturday chores, after kirk on Sunday. When she was certain he was alone, she would climb up to the side of the nest, with table scraps in her pockets. Expectantly, he would peep at her, his mouth wide open waiting to receive her offerings, as he would if she were his mother. All the while she talked to him, telling him stories of her life in the village. And, as he looked at her, his eyes locked with hers, her hand caressing his head, she believed he understood.

But one day, as she approached, she saw him take flight, launching himself effortlessly from the edge of the nest and soaring in wide circles over her head. Her friend had grown; he was ready to hunt and live alone. She had been left behind.

But Iolaire was not just any eagle; he did not forget. Now, nine years later, with another chick in his nest, he watched over Deirdre, calling to her as she went about her life below. And sometimes, she would want him closer, up at the nest, where they could sit together; a place where she could talk and he would listen.

*

For more than an hour, she sat with her friend, talking, telling him about the funeral, the stranger from the Big House and her father's fumbling in the dark. As usual they sat slightly apart, his head cocked to one side, as he followed the rise and fall of her voice. They spoke a different language. She knew that. But it was the telling that was important. In the silence which followed, one friend close beside another, there was complete understanding. Later, she raised her hand in farewell as he soared overhead, calling to his mate and his chick, before swooping over the hillside in search of prey.

The village below looked like a miniature version of itself. The houses – some bare grey stone, some covered in white harling – were clustered on both sides of the valley, walled-in gardens laid out with bushes and flowers in front, washing lines and garden sheds in the rear. Long rectangular fields stretched down the side of the gully, which carried the frothy peat-brown waters of the burn down to the ocean. The road wound around the houses, bridged in places as it crossed the burn. A yellow tractor criss-crossed a field in the distance, cutting the grass for hay baling later, seagulls wheeling and dipping in its wake. A man with a small pickup truck and his sheepdog were separating individual sheep from the main flock and herding them into a trailer. Fergus was taking a delivery from the brewery outside the pub. Greg, the postman, drove away from the village shop, his van loaded with the day's mail.

Deirdre turned her back on the village and took the path down the other side of the hillside to the Auld Village – the place where her ancestors had once lived. The landlords who had come from the south, Sebastian Carlyle's people, had invaded the country more than two centuries earlier, burning the houses and the crops, and driving the people out. It was a day to place three more stones on the cairn.

The *lochan* – a small body of dark water – lay along the route. Deirdre had taken this path with Brigid each year for as long as she could remember. Now Brigid was troubled with arthritis, and Deirdre was making the climb alone. Today, as on so many others, the water lay still. Tall green reeds clustered along the water's edge beside the path. The sun sparkled off its smooth, unrippled surface. On one occasion, they had surprised a lone stag who had come down from the hills to drink. On another, they had dared the journey just as the moon was rising and it had claimed its own reflection in the still water. Now Deirdre's own mirror image followed her as she hurried by.

Most houses in the deserted hamlet were just empty shells, cracking and crumbling more each year as the winds swept inland. Rain and sleet, snow and frost, had all taken their turn in the destruction. And no-one cared to return to live in a place where only bitter memories remained.

'This is sacred ground,' Brigid had told her on their first visit. 'Those who have departed this life leave remnants of themselves behind, on the stones of the walls, and in the air. Now they travel unseen through the empty spaces where doors were once latched and windows were hung with curtains. On dark winter nights, they still seek comfort beside the dank fireplaces which once offered heat and kinship.'

'Are they scary, like ghosts, Brigid?'

'You've no need to be frightened, child. You're one of their own. We both are. We're welcome here. We carry their blood in our veins. It's important to hold them in our hearts, always.'

Later, when Deirdre returned home and told her mother where they had been, Máire had told her, 'It's best not to dwell on the past. It surely won't put bread on the table or bring strong lambs into the world in the spring.' But, each year, Deirdre eagerly anticipated her excursion with Brigid. She welcomed the isolation, the uninterrupted silence of the place.

Brigid's family house stood facing the sea. Her great grandfather's family had been the last to live there. Only the chimney breast and a small section of the adjoining wall still remained. Beside the wall, Brigid's father had planted a rowan tree, which now hung low, festoons of bright red berries bending the branches. And, to one side of the tree, the cairn. Each year, she and Brigid had added to the accumulating pile of stones, carefully selecting them from the fallen piles around them. Today, Deirdre must choose three – one for herself, one for Brigid, and one in memory of her mother.

As she placed the last stone on the cairn, she heard what sounded like a wave surging onshore, and overhead she saw a shape-changing shadow swirling back and forth in the sky. Only once before had she seen such a display. A huge flock of starlings was searching for food and a roosting place for the night. Their calls like an orchestral chorus, their flight path a carefully choreographed ballet. Here, in the Auld Village, they had found the crumbling houses and the resplendent rowan tree. By the morning, the birds would be gone, and the tree would be stripped bare of its fruit.

And, in the late afternoon sunshine, alone in the abandoned village, Deirdre wept silently.

Chapter 9

Meghan

It rained steadily for the next three days. Relentless, unforgiving rain that blurred the window panes and rattled on the tin roof of the cottage. On my brief excursions outside with Cassie, the sky was a featureless grey. Indoors, I kept the table lamps on nearly all day. I had stocked up on the essentials, for me and for Cassie. And it was warm and cosy inside. The electric space heaters in both rooms pumped out more than enough heat. My only attempt at lighting the logs in the fireplace had not been a success. I'd need to get a lesson from Ellen the next time I saw her. But I had begun to feel trapped.

I wondered how the locals got used to the isolation, the days of dark skies, and longer nights. I had read how many of the younger people up here in the Highlands migrated to the cities as soon as they left school. They wanted more action, some night life other than the pub, and job opportunities that were not seasonal, not so dependent on the weather or the tourist industry.

I began to watch more television, even scrolled through YouTube videos on my mobile. I looked through the selection of books which Ellen had set out on the alcove shelf beside the fireplace. A local guidebook pointed out hill walks and picturesque beaches; bird-watching and wildlife locations; the location of ancient ruins – cairns and brochs and villages. For the more active tourist, there was mountaineering and pony trekking and whale watching. On the enclosed fold-out map, some of these seemed very close to the village. But I would not be going to see any of these sights as long as the rain persisted. There was a historical account of the Highland Clearances. I remembered what Ellen had told me about her work on an estate nearby, the absentee landlord. And there were a few paperbacks. I began to read one about a disillusioned detective. He had returned to his childhood home only to discover the skeleton of his school friend buried in the back garden of his parents' house. It was fast-paced, temporarily engrossing, and I finished reading it in less than two days.

And then I woke to a day where the sun wasn't shining, but at least the rain had stopped. By mid-afternoon, there were patches of blue sky and clouds that were more white than grey. Though the sky glowered over the hilltops, threatening more rain to come. And the sea was still whipped into a frenzy of whitecaps. I determined that Cassie and I would take advantage of the respite and go for a good walk through the village to the cliffs beyond.

As soon as we opened the door, the wind nearly knocked us off our feet. Below the cottage, the thistles had gone to seed, and Cassie started jumping up and down chasing the thistledown, which raced past her on the gusting breeze. She pulled on the lead, dragging me in her wake. I went with the wind, letting it buffet me this way and that, enjoying the sensation of relaxing into its force. Beneath the bridge, which crossed up to the other side of the village, the brown water of the burn churned and foamed in its rush downhill to the sea. It was full and fast, overflowing its banks as it turned and twisted between the rocks.

We took a turn to the left, and made our way across to the edge of the grassy slope, away from the steps which I had seen leading down to the small harbour and its concrete jetty. All along the coastline, huge cliffs dropped off to the sea below. Together, Cassie and I stood on the precipice of one such cliff. This was a fierce landscape, without the sandy beach and warm sand dunes we had visited a few days earlier. Huge rock monoliths rose from the sea, sculpted by the merciless pounding of the waves. For centuries, the sea had eaten into the cliff faces, carving holes and arches as it moved steadily inland. The sea rushed through these now, roiled by the gusting wind, sending spray high up into the air.

I stood there, watching the ever-changing rhythms of the sea, enjoying the sensation of the thundering waves pulsing through the soles of my feet. And, at that moment, everything else seemed irrelevant. I was simply a small part of a universe, which would exist with or without me. The continuity of life, even mine, did not depend on one failed relationship, one wrong decision. I could stay here for the year, as I'd planned. Or I could leave. Instead of moping about, terrified that Richard would arrive on my doorstep, pleading with me to return with him, I needed to make a plan, one that would propel me forward. I'd thought about writing a journal. This would be a good way to start, each day writing down the good things I liked about my life here, and what I'd enjoyed back in the city. I would create pro and con columns for each, weighing the balance, until ...

It was then that I saw it, the double rainbow. The sun had broken through the clouds and sat low on the horizon. I had not noticed the change in the light, but we had obviously left the cottage later than I thought. Now the rays of the setting sun were reflected through the sea spray which drifted up and over the cliff face. I remembered from my school science class that, with a single rainbow, the light is split into the traditional spectrum of colours. With the second rainbow, the spectrum is reversed. I had looked it up online. There had been several sites which mentioned the spiritual significance of a double rainbow. In many eastern cultures, and in mythology, it's considered to be a sign of transformation, indicating new beginnings for those who see them.

Regardless of the science, or the mythology, it was a magnificent sight. I had never seen one before. And today, I knew it would be the first thing I added to my list of things I loved about being here in the village.

Chapter 10

Deirdre

The flowers were on the kitchen table, arranged in her mother's tall china jug – a large bouquet of white roses with a single orange bud in the centre. Beside them, a small chocolate cake with candles.

Brigid, who was standing at the stove stirring a large steaming pot of what smelled like beef stew, turned and smiled as she heard Deirdre close the door behind her.

'Happy birthday, child.'

'I wasn't expecting … thank you. But flowers *and* a cake?'

'It's a big day, even if James probably didn't remember. The cake is mine. But the flowers are from another.'

'Who? Did you see who left them?'

'They were on the doorstep. There was a note,' Brigid pulled a small envelope out of the pocket of her apron. 'I thought it best to keep it safe for you, in case your da got in before you.'

'I went to see Iolaire and then up to the cairn.'

'I thought so.'

'But it wasn't the same without you. The Auld Village really felt lonely and abandoned today. I don't think I'd ever noticed it so much before. And, just as I was leaving, a flock of starlings flew in over the water. A huge black cloud of them moving together overhead.'

'A murmuration. A rare event, when those small birds

make music together.'

'The rowan tree had so many berries this year, but I'm sure they'll all be eaten up and gone by the morning.'

Brigid smiled, holding out the envelope, 'You need to read the note.'

Inside was a cream-coloured card, with a message written in large black script. Deirdre read it aloud –

Happy Birthday, beautiful lady,
S.

Deirdre hesitated. 'It can't be, can it?'

'Sebastian St. John Carlyle, the new laird up at the Big House? Aye, it would be him. He followed you. I watched him pass, and wondered if you'd talked.'

'We spoke, for a few minutes, yes. But why would he send me these? No-one has ever given me flowers before.'

'Because, child, he saw you. And he's no fool.'

Behind Deirdre, the door swung open, slamming against the coat hooks on the wall behind.

'Is my dinner ready?' James paused as he saw Brigid at the stove. 'And what are you doing here, woman? We've no need of you now that Máire has gone. The girl can take care of all our needs.'

'Nay, James, not tonight. It's your child's birthday – eighteen today.'

'This isn't the time for the likes of that,' his eyes scanned the table, the flowers and the cake. 'And I'll have none of this either. I'm surprised at you, Brigid, wasting good money on flowers, when Máire is barely cold in her grave,' he moved forward to grab the flowers. 'These are going in the midden.'

Brigid shook her head at Deirdre, and put her hand on the jug.

'I'll spend my money as I see fit, James McIntyre. You'll not be tossing those flowers out as long as I'm here. Go and wash up. I've made your favourite, beef stew.'

'Aye I can smell that well enough. But I'll not sit here

and play this foolish game. I'll away to the pub to get my dinner there.'

'Where you can wallow in self-pity, James? If Máire were here, she'd want you to be happy for Deirdre. There's just the two of you now.'

'I know that well enough. You've no need to be reminding me. And you,' he turned to Deirdre, 'better be sleeping in your own bed when I get home.'

As he slammed the door behind him, a draught of cold air rushed into the room. For a few moments, Deirdre felt it settle around her. Brigid crossed the room.

'Give me a hug, child. And ignore the man. He'll get over it.'

'But I'm afraid, Brigid.'

Brigid laughed. 'Of your father?' she held Deirdre at arm's length and looked at her. 'James has always drunk a little more than is good for him.'

'Last night, he came into my room. He touched my breast, tried to get in bed with me, to climb on top of me. He kept calling me Máire, thinking I was Ma.'

'Was that what he meant when he said …?'

'I got away from him, and I slept down here. But, in the morning, he noticed I wasn't in my own bed. He was very drunk last night, so I thought it was just that. But now, I'm not sure.'

'Would it make you feel safer if I stayed tonight?'

Deirdre smiled, 'I'm just being foolish, aren't I?'

'I can't believe he'd really mean you any harm.'

'No, of course not.'

'You can lock your bedroom door, can't you?'

'Yes.'

'Good. So do that from now on. But be sure to let me know, lass, if he makes you feel uncomfortable or afraid,' Brigid paused, smiling. 'And now perhaps, as it's a special day, you'd like to start with the cake? And I can tell you all about the meaning of the flowers your new admirer sent to your doorstep.'

But later, alone in the house as it settled into the darkness, huddling under the blankets behind the locked door of her bedroom, Deirdre lay awake listening for the sounds of James' return and the creak of his footfall on the stairs.

Chapter 11

Meghan

'Here in the Highlands, Meghan, there's aye another dimension' – Dougal's words to me as I'd left the pub that first night. Was that the start of it all, when I became more aware of that other dimension, that connection with people and events which had taken place here in the village several years earlier, before my arrival?

*

I'd happily settled into the routine of writing in my journal each day. I'd created one online with iCloud, so that I could add my photos and copy Wikipedia entries as background information. The double rainbow was a great beginning. I added Cassie into the village pro column. If I'd not decided to leave the city and come to the village, I'd never have gone to the rescue centre. Our only family dog had died when I was five, and my parents had decided they didn't want another.

Cassie was a great companion and, I'd begun to think, an excellent watchdog. But, when I'd returned from my coffee morning with Ellen, and I'd found her cowering under my bed, she'd alerted me to something that I'd slowly and surely begun to feel too.

We were not alone in the cottage. Something, or someone else, was here too. There were no strange noises. Nothing seemed to have been moved, or taken. It was simply a

51

sensation. We were being watched. As if I were at a party or in a crowded bar and I could feel someone's eyes on me, behind my back. And, if I turned, I'd see a stranger staring at me from the other side of the room, a stranger who seemed to want to attract my attention.

For a while, I mused that there might be a hidden camera somewhere, monitoring and recording our lives. But it seemed too weird to be true. Neither Cathel nor Ellen seemed to be the kind of people who would snoop on their lodger.

Yet, sometimes, I could definitely feel the presence of something or somebody else. A drift of cold air would creep into the room, the flames in the fireplace bending and swaying as it passed. And, each time, Cassie, shivering, moved a little closer to me on the sofa.

I'm not a spiritual or religious person. But neither would I dismiss the notion that old buildings retain something of those who have lived – and perhaps died – there before. Our knowledge of DNA assures us that this remains locked in places we've been and things we've touched. We never really disappear. But I've never seen a ghost. Although I know a few people who claimed to have seen one. Perhaps living alone in an old stone cottage, in an isolated village, where even a casual encounter in the local pub could elicit the memory of an ancient myth to explain a common weather phenomenon, was filling my imagination with foolishness.

Instead of worrying about something which might or might not mean us harm, I needed to develop some activities to keep me centred. I ordered some books online – where to look for and how to recognise local birds and wildlife, how to identify and use native plants, interesting facts about life along the seashore. I would collect samples and take some really good photos. I added a high-quality zoom lens for my camera to my order. I'd thought of taking up painting, hadn't I? Perhaps there was an art shop in town where I could get some advice. We hadn't ventured that far yet.

*

The road to town wound over the hills and along the coast. Sometimes the sea was hidden by the streets and houses of the small villages we passed through, or tall stands of trees with driveways leading away into the darkness. At others, it seemed to be just a short walk across the heathland to the edge of cliffs or the slopes of sandy beaches. It was a slow drive, but I was in no hurry. Cyclists, two or three abreast, made it difficult to overtake. Slow tractor-trailers eased out of one field and trundled along to another, trailing farm waste in their wake. And the locals sped past at breakneck speeds, oblivious to the obstacles ahead.

A small town, it had three banks, a handful of tourist shops and discount stores, an old-fashioned fish market, two small chemists, a camping gear emporium, three charity shops on the main street, a bakery, a fish and chip shop and an Indian takeaway, and an Italian ristorante. There was also a picture-framers which doubled as a gift shop and sold art materials. The owner was helpful, and delighted to send me out with a huge bag of art supplies, and a beginner's 'how to' book. I staggered back to the car park with my treasures.

It was midweek and, apparently, half day closing. But I needed a coffee. Cassie and I sat in a corner of the bakery café. Surreptitiously, I fed her scraps of my buttered scone under the table. The shelves were already being cleared. We seemed to be the last customers of the day.

I drove to the large Tesco supermarket on the outskirts of town, stocked up on groceries, and turned back onto the road home.

I was more familiar with the route now, and took my time to look around. Many of the houses resembled the stone cottages in the village, some bare and grey, others harled white. But the uptake in the tourist industry of the Highlands had encouraged some people to build with new designs, and larger premises.

We were about halfway home, when I noticed the large house in the distance on my right, set right at the edge of a long sandy beach. The signpost at the side of the road read *Annanside Bay.* For a moment, I considered driving down the gravelled road to see the house up close. But then I remembered all the food I'd bought sitting in the back of the car. The beach and the house could be an excursion for another day.

*

It took me some time to find places for all the groceries, and I was excited to lay out my art supplies on the table and take stock of what I'd bought. So, I'd probably been in the cottage nearly half an hour before I went into the bedroom and noticed the quilt. It was slightly rucked up at the corner, caught under the mattress. I knew I wouldn't have made the bed like that, and it was certainly not something Cassie could have done. And the guidebook was no longer in the centre of the bedside table where I'd left it, but was set further back. I'm rather particular about the way I live and have an exact place for everything. It used to drive Richard crazy. There was no doubt that someone had been in the cottage when we were out. I'd had all my money and credit cards with me. I checked the top drawer of the chest by the mirror, but my jewellery bag was intact. Nothing seemed to be missing. Yet someone had definitely been here.

It was time to talk to Ellen – about this, and our invisible visitor. I'd seen her car in the yard when we'd returned. The children were still at school, and I could see Cathel ploughing the field at the bottom of the hill. Now would be a perfect time.

Chapter 12

Deirdre

When she awoke in the morning, she could not remember
her father returning to the house, although she could hear
him and Cathel talking together in the kitchen. Tired after
all the exertions of the day, she had fallen into a deep sleep.
In her dreams, she had imagined her father rattling the door
handle and breaking into her room, wielding an axe.

It was Saturday and there was no school, but the work
of the farm continued. Today, Cathel and James would be
preparing the sheep for the autumn sale in town – washing,
trimming and combing their fleeces. In the past, she had
helped move the sheep down from the pasture into the
holding pen. Máire, as usual, had scrubbed floors, dusted
and polished furniture, and changed all the bed linens
in preparation for the Sabbath. Now this task would be
Deirdre's.

She had decided to finish by midday, and ride her bike
over to Carlyle House in the afternoon. Last night, Brigid
had told her about the significance of Sebastian Carlyle's
birthday bouquet. Eighteen white roses measured her years.
White was the colour of innocence and purity, often chosen
by a bride on her wedding day. The orange bud in the centre
of the bouquet represented passion. She had laughed at
the idea of Sebastian Carlyle thinking all this when he had
decided to send the flowers. But Brigid had warned her to
be careful.

'Mr Carlyle is a man with a purpose, and he has wasted

no time in laying the ground.'

'They're only flowers, Brigid. I'm eighteen and he's at least …?'

'Yes, Deirdre. And history is littered with tales of the shattered lives of young, innocent girls who have fallen for the seductive attentions of an older man, dreaming of love and a better life,' she paused. 'But enough of my doom and gloom. It's your birthday and, as your father is in no mood for cake, I think we both deserve another slice, don't you?'

Deirdre laughed.

'I feel a little bit like Marie Antoinette tonight, Brigid. The queen guillotined during the French Revolution? Who told the people to eat cake, if they couldn't afford to buy bread?'

'I remember that story.'

'Miss McDonald told us about it in history.'

'You like school, don't you? Have you thought what'll ye do after you've taken your exams?'

'I used to imagine I'd go to college, maybe even university. But now with Mother gone, and Father alone, I don't know.'

'Your mother and your father never understood as we do. You're eighteen. Your life is your own now, child. Mind that well.'

Deirdre hesitated. She remembered her dream – the one where she had walked down the long hallway and looked out through the tall casement window.

'Perhaps, Mr Carlyle picked the flowers from his own garden. Do you think they grow roses at Carlyle House?'

'I've never been inside the grounds, so I can't say. They look too perfect to have been out in all weathers though, at this time of the year.'

But outside the house Deirdre had seen in her dream, the one filled with strangers, she had noticed all the carefully-tended rose bushes in the moonlit garden. A high stone wall sheltered them from the onslaught of the salt air, which wafted inland twice a day on the tide.

Although Sebastian Carlyle had only just returned to the family estate, perhaps his father – and his father before him – had prepared the ground for just such an occasion.

Brigid had often spoken to her of the importance of dreams.

'Sometimes,' she had said, 'they allow you to see into the future. These you can believe in. They're the real thing. Others are reflections of your imagination, how you'd like your future to be, mingled with all your past memories. You want them to be real. So, you go out of your way to make them so.'

'But how will I know which dream is real and which just a fantasy?' Deirdre had asked.

'You won't.'

'So, either way, I can make dreams happen?'

Brigid had laughed then, 'Yes, child, sometimes you can.'

Now Brigid was gazing intently at Deirdre, 'Have you had a dream, child? Do you want to tell me about it?'

'No, no,' she said hurriedly. 'I was just wondering, that's all.'

A few days ago, Deirdre would have confided in Brigid. But now, she was eighteen, old enough to take care of herself, smart enough to make up her own mind about a self-important sassenach from the south, in whose grand house she may have imagined herself wandering in her dreams.

Her excursion to Carlyle House that Saturday afternoon would simply satisfy her curiosity. Would she find a garden with rose bushes? And, if she did, if indeed it was not a fantasy, would she find herself – one day – walking along a corridor in a grand house where strangers smiled and nodded at her as she passed?

*

57

Hints of winter were already in the air as she pushed her bike up the hill from the village and set out to cycle the five miles to Carlyle House. Low level clouds stretched overhead, swept along by a strong northerly, blowing inland. Like grasping hands, they seemed to pull the watery sun in and out of their shadows.

The road wound back and forth, skirting the heathered slopes of the hills and bare grey rockfaces on one side, and the fertile plain of the moors and the peat bogs, which stretched to the distant shoreline, on the other. Although Deirdre was wrapped well in her padded anorak, the hood tied tightly under her chin, she could feel the cold biting her nose and cheeks as she pedalled fiercely into the wind. But the traffic was light and she made the journey without having to pull over and let others pass.

Carlyle House lay in a sheltered bay, visible from the main road. A signpost indicating the route downhill simply read *Annanside Bay – No Campers*. The narrow gravel track took a couple of turns and then followed the curve of the bay. Rabbits and pheasants skittered into the undergrowth as Deirdre passed. At the bottom, it divided. To the right, where the main track veered up a slope, behind the house, a sign read *Private Property – No Beach Access*. The rest ended abruptly in a small clearing where a small, windowless van was parked, its driver sitting motionless behind the wheel. The sandy slope which led down to the beach was blocked by an aluminium turnstile supported by two weather-beaten gateposts. A rickety fence snaked from this, up the line of the slope and propped itself against the stone wall below the house. Deirdre dismounted and leaned her bicycle against one of the posts.

Carlyle House was a bleak three-storey building, its dingy-white harling displaying tinges of green mould growing along one side. The half-dozen narrow windows which fronted the shore, seemed to have been scattered haphazardly between the three chimney stacks. Only the slate roof, with its skylight windows, appeared to be in good repair. There seemed to be no curtains at the windows. If she had not spoken to Sebastian Carlyle two days earlier, she would have assumed the place had been abandoned.

She looked around as she heard the van engine start up behind her. It turned and pulled away. Now, she thought, she was alone. Perhaps she could slip through the turnstile and up the slope towards the house. A quick peek over the stone wall and she would know.

Close up, the wall was higher than she had expected and moss clung damply to the stacked stones. She found a foothold, and another, and then she lost traction, slipping and sliding halfway down the slope. She looked around, but she was still alone. She moved along the wall, testing the rocks where the grass and some heather had taken over. Once again, she pulled herself up the wall. Some of the smaller rocks shifted, a few tumbling below. But, this time, she found a larger rock which had been wedged halfway up the wall. It formed a perfect ledge for her to stand on. One more handhold and, at last, she could see over the wall.

There was no garden. It was a wasteland of sticky catchweed, patches of stinging nettles and dock leaves, and tall blooming thistles. No flowerbeds were laid out in neat rows, no swathes of carefully-manicured grass swept down from the house to the wall. Only a few straggly rose bushes sheltered in the lee of the house, their leaves yellowed and drooping. Sebastian Carlyle had not chosen his bouquet here at Carlyle House. This was not the garden she had seen in her dream. Nor, she imagined, would the interior of the house match her expectations.

The sun was lower now; the sandy beach, which seemed to stretch endlessly to the horizon, was bathed in its pale orange glow. There were at least two more hours before sunset, another hour before she needed to set out for home.

As she turned away from the turnstile, she noticed the warmth of the sun on her back. Towering sand dunes, held together by waist-high marram grass, smothered the force of the northerly. It was low tide; the beach sloped so gently that the distant waves were barely audible above the cry of the seagulls as they cruised overhead, searching for vulnerable lifeforms stranded by the receding water. She held her face up to the warmth of the sunlight and set her sights on the furthest part of the cove.

Half an hour later, she was lying back, her head resting against a tussock, her eyes closed, when she heard the growl. Alert now, her eyes snapped open. She remembered Sebastian's white dog, affectionate and curious. But this animal, only a few feet away, was growling menacingly.

'Don't move, Deirdre!' Sebastian's voice was urgent, commanding. 'Magnus, heel, now!'

The dog moved backwards slowly, his eyes maintaining contact with Deirdre's until Sebastian had his collar firmly attached to a short leather leash.

'I'm sorry. I didn't see anyone on the beach.'

'Is this the same Magnus I met the other night? He looks bigger, and definitely not so friendly.'

'This is home, and he's very territorial. A Dogo Argentino.'

'Which means?'

'Recognised as an aggressive breed. You can only own one if you have a special licence. Perfectly well-behaved when he knows who's the alpha dog.'

'And that's you, I suppose.'

Sebastian smiled, 'You got the flowers?'

'Yes, I did. They were lovely.'

'I told you we'd meet again, Deirdre,' he paused. 'That's why you're here, isn't it?'

'I was curious, that's all. Don't read too much into it.'

'What exactly piqued your curiosity? The flowers? The house? Me?'

'I was curious to know if you'd picked them from your own garden. Now I know that's not the case.'

'Because?'

'Because your garden's a mess. I've seen it.'

'Ah,' he smiled. 'But perhaps I have a greenhouse. Would you care to take a second look around?'

'A very generous offer, to be sure. But I need to be on my way. Good afternoon, Mr Carlyle. And thank you again for the flowers.'

'Sebastian, please. I thought friends used first names when they talked to each other.'

'Friends?'

'Can I give you a lift? It's a long ride home.'

'I'd prefer to enjoy the gloaming without the company of fierce dogs and …'

'We can leave Magnus at home.'

'And the company of a *fandan*.'

'A *fandan*? I'm flattered, Miss McIntyre.'

'Don't be. It means a pretentious …' she paused. 'Never mind. Next time I'll just call instead.'

'Until next time then.'

Chapter 13

Meghan

Ellen answered the door quickly when I knocked. I noticed a half-eaten sandwich and an empty coffee mug on the table as she stood back to let me in.

'I'm sorry. I interrupted your lunch. It's just that ...'

'What's the matter? You look...'

'Upset? Well, I am. Someone's been snooping around the cottage. And, before you ask, yes I did lock the door when I left to go into town this morning.'

'Has anything been taken?'

'No, not that I can see. But things have been moved. It wasn't you, was it? Or Cathel?'

'Of course, not. That's your private space, as long as you're renting. I'm sorry, if you think there's been an intruder. But I can't imagine who would want to break in, or even why.'

'Richard, my ex, sent me a text. Despite everything, he's still claiming we're inseparable and he knows where I am! But he's not the sort to just walk away. He'd stay, argue his case.'

'He sounds a bit like a typical stalker though, doesn't he? It might have been him, but do you think he'd go that far?'

There, in the warmth of the farmhouse kitchen, I should have been convinced by the rationality of Ellen's suggestions. She was right. Who would want to break into the cottage, and why?

And yet I had the feeling that something was not right, not normal. My mother had always told me, even as a small child, to follow my instincts –

In times of danger, or of stress, those first thoughts will be the signpost for you to follow. That's when your heart and your mind are in perfect union. It's how nature has made us, to help us survive – the fight or flight response.

She was a clinical psychologist. After my father died – a heart attack at forty-two – we had grown close. So close that my friends at school teased me about how I'd rather spend the weekend with her, than hang out with them in coffee shops or in the new shopping centre and wait for the boys to find us. Then, one day at university, I got a call. One of my mother's patients had broken into her office the previous evening, and stabbed her. He'd been high. She'd fought back, but there had been too much blood, and no time to find the signpost which would save her.

For too long, I'd lost sight of my signposts, ignoring my instincts about Richard and our future together. Since arriving in the village, I'd felt stronger, ready once again to follow my mother's advice. But, at times like this, I still missed her. It was an ache, a vacuum which I could not fill. She was the one person who would always listen, who would not judge, who really understood what it was like to be me.

'There's something else, Ellen. I feel as if there's a presence in the cottage, as if we're being watched,' I laughed then. 'You don't have any surveillance cameras in the cottage, do you?'

'That's not funny,' Ellen snapped. 'If you think we'd do something like that, then perhaps you need to find somewhere else to live.'

'I'm sorry. I really didn't think that. But there is something there. I feel it, and Cassie does too. I know it sounds crazy, but I wondered if, because it's an old building, someone might have died there. That it might be haunted.'

'Only Brigid would be able to answer that question,' she paused. 'Unfortunately, she died a few years ago. Your cottage used to be an old byre so it's probably only some livestock which breathed their last in there. Here, in the farmhouse – now that's a different matter.'

'You mean the man you bought the farm from? You said he and Cathel worked together. And something about his daughter, too.'

'James McIntyre is still very much alive. Living in a care home in town. He used to call Brigid, his wife's aunt, an auld witch.'

'He didn't like her.'

'It was much more than that. She had, what we call in these parts, *an dà-shealladh* – second sight. She could foresee things. And Deirdre was said to have it also.'

'Deirdre?'

'James' daughter. He didn't believe in it, and thought Brigid was filling Deirdre's mind with all sorts of rubbish – about him and everything else.'

'And what do you think about this second sight?'

'I say don't knock what you don't understand. There are lots of superstitions here in the Highlands, probably born out of our isolation. And everyone wants to believe in something, don't they?'

'Do you think any of this has anything to do with my cottage being haunted?'

'I'm not sure it is haunted. You're the first person to actually live there. A lot happened when the McIntyres lived here – as I told you, some good, some not so good. There were rumours, and insinuations. Even to this day, nobody knows what really happened,' she paused. 'But I've already said too much.'

'If it has anything to do with my intruders – real or imagined – I'd like to hear about it.'

Ellen sighed.

'Deirdre was an extraordinarily beautiful girl, who seemed to draw people to her. And it didn't always work out well for them. In many ways, she was an innocent, only eighteen. But she was also smart, and feisty with it. She knew no other way to be. That was just her. I liked her a lot, and so did Cathel. But we're not always aware of the effect we have on other people. We fall in and out of love. And, sometimes, we wreak havoc when we leave.'

'You said *was*. What happened?'

'As I said, nobody knows the whole truth. We probably never will,' she smiled. 'Deirdre wasn't a bad person. If it's her ghost haunting you in the cottage, she'll mean you no harm.'

'But, if it's her, then it might mean she's unhappy, restless or perhaps even unfulfilled. Maybe she needs help? Don't some people believe that a soul can be caught in limbo, marooned between this life and the next?'

'Yes, some do. Deirdre's mother, Máire, was a regular at the kirk. Deirdre would certainly have been baptised. But I'm not sure she was a believer. And having the sight? Well, who knows?' she smiled. 'You mightn't be surprised to hear that, not far from here, up in the hills, there's a place called the Hidden Glen – *Gleann am Falach*. Locals refuse to go there because they say it's where the devil goes looking for lost souls.'

'I think Dougal might believe that.'

'Of course he does!' she paused. 'If you're interested, I could take you …'

'To the Hidden Glen?'

'No, no. I've never been there. It's a rather desolate place – just a dirt track between two mountains, and a few ruined crofts. Even the shepherds prefer to keep their flocks away. No, I was going to suggest a tour of the Carlyle Estate, where I work. Deirdre lived there for a few months. In some ways, that's where it all began.'

And so, a week later, we drove down the track towards the large house which I had seen from afar, abandoned, standing alone on a long, sandy beach. It was the day when I started to write down names and places in my journal. They had nothing to do with my list of reasons for staying or leaving the cottage, nothing to do with centring my own life, and everything to do with an eighteen-year-old girl, whose beauty had apparently left a path of destruction in her wake. The girl named Deirdre, who lived on in everyone's memory, but whom very few wanted to talk about.

Chapter 14

Deirdre

Deirdre returned to school, her mother's funeral and her birthday behind her. She had, quite truthfully, told Brigid she liked school. But now she found herself looking forward to the autumn break, when she would not be shut up in a classroom with the likes of Emily Gunn, who spent her days talking endlessly, and in great detail, about her relationship with Tom Mackay.

Deirdre wanted more, so much more. For eighteen years, she had lived with her parents in a crofter's cottage in a small village. Her mother's death had not been sudden, but Deirdre had never visualised a time when she would be left to carry on alone. She had made a promise to take care of her father. But this promise now held threats her mother could not have imagined. She spent the daylight hours going to school and fulfilling the household chores, mindful of James' presence, just out of reach. Each night, she was haunted by a scenario when she might no longer be in control. Her world had closed in around her. Outside, she was still the girl who raised her hand in class a little too often; the girl who spoke her mind without heeding the consequences; the girl who tossed her hair at the boys as they catcalled her. But inside, for the first time in her life, she felt lost and a little afraid, as if all the landmarks in her life suddenly looked unfamiliar, and every way she turned led nowhere. She had imagined a life outside the village, getting a degree, having a career, even if the details had always been undefined. All this was still possible. But would she have to break the promise she had made to her mother on her deathbed?

Brigid understood. She had reminded her that everyone had their own destiny to fulfil. Even though **Máire** had gone, it was not Deirdre's responsibility to fill her mother's shoes in James' life. **Máire** knew no other life. But Deirdre was like Brigid, different from most of those around them, knowing and seeing things in another dimension. It was their fate to be misunderstood, but never to deny their right to be so.

*

In the meantime, the village was alive with gossip – in the pub, in the village shop, across the garden walls.

In the pub, with James–

'Yon new laird has been here today, talking about the vacant crofts. He'll be wanting to put the rents up next.'

'Nay, James, he was asking me if I wanted to buy my croft and the land. I'd be a farmer then, beholden to no-one.'

'And how will ye be able to afford that, you wee dafty?'

'He's offering a loan too.'

'I wouldna be falling for that, man. You're not …'

'I'm thinking aboot it.'

In the village shop, with Marge Ferguson –

'Mr Carlyle was in the day, asking about folks to work up at the Big House.'

'What kind of folks, Marge?'

'He's looking for a gardener …'

'Did you recommend Big Archie?'

'Aye. And he's wanting painters and all sorts. The house is in a terrible state, apparently.'

'There are plenty of folk who'll be pleased for that money at this time of year. He'll be paying good wages too, nae doot.'

Over the garden wall, with Brigid –

'Folks say that yon fellow up at the house is planning a Yuletide party, and him not long arrived. He's wanting some lassies to fix up the curtains and the chairs and such. I gave him your name, Brigid.'

'I'm no longer a lassie, Helen. And my eyes are not what they used to be.'

'No, but I'm sure he'd be glad of someone to take charge, organise a few of the good seamstresses.'

'Aye, well, we'll see. But has he no wife to see to that?'

'He never mentioned. And I never asked,' she laughed. 'He's a braw young fellow, all the same.'

Deirdre listened and smiled. Sebastian Carlyle was making his presence felt. He had promised change; and found a way to win the hearts and minds of some, at least, of the local population. And when, a week or two later, school closed for a fortnight, Deirdre decided that she, too, would make some changes.

Brigid had been asked to go up to Carlyle House on a regular basis, young seamstresses in tow. And, when she returned, she would tell Deirdre about their work and the house. The old laird's clothes had been sorted and taken to the charity shop. The curtains and the upholstery needed replacing, sofas and chairs dusty and threadbare. Swatches of new materials had been sent up from the city. Painters were systematically working their way through the house. Electricians and plumbers were everywhere. And Big Archie was weeding and digging and planting outside. There were to be roses in the walled garden – lots and lots of roses.

Deirdre cleared out her mother's wardrobe and dropped a bag in the charity box in the village. Cathel found some unused cans of white paint in his father's garage, and volunteered, one Sunday afternoon, to redo the walls of the downstairs rooms in the farmhouse. Deirdre dyed an old stained lace tablecloth with heather blooms and made new curtains for the kitchen; her mother's blue gingham skirt became curtains for her father's bedroom, and a patchwork of miscellaneous remnants for her own. Chair cushions were cleaned and turned; armrests reupholstered with swatches of unwanted fabric which Brigid brought back from the Big House. James muttered and grumbled each night as the renovations continued, but the sheep sale had gone well and Deirdre's efforts cost him nothing.

School had already started again by the time Deirdre turned her attention to the vegetable garden. The last of the neeps and tatties needed pulling, and the ground tilling, before the first frost.

*

There were only half a dozen students left on the school bus as it passed the layby. Deirdre was staring out of the window, barely noticing the landscape, when it caught her eye – the white shape beside the Land Rover.

'What's that?' Geordie leant forward on Deirdre's seat.

'A Dogo Argentino,' Deirdre said, without thinking.

'Whoa! That's some fierce beastie, barking at us like that.'

Deirdre smiled, remembering. But then, she wondered, why was the dog standing alone at the side of the road, unleashed, barking at the passing traffic? It did not seem like Sebastian Carlyle to leave Magnus unattended in a layby. This was not a friendly animal, especially if he felt threatened.

Cathel was pulling up the hill to the top of the village, as the bus made its last stop and Deirdre got off. She hesitated for a moment, and then she flagged him down.

'What's up?'

'Can you give me a lift to the layby, the one by the path which leads to the stacks?'

'It's a bit late in the day for bird watching. How'll you get back?'

70

'There's something wrong. Sebastian's dog is loose at the roadside. He can be quite aggressive and I'm afraid someone'll get hurt.'

'Sebastian?'

'Sebastian Carlyle.'

Cathel was a fast driver, and his old car rattled and shook as he accelerated round each bend in the road. The late October sun was sinking fast, the shadows lengthening over the moorland as he pulled over to the side of the road, a few yards into the layby.

'Wait here,' Deirdre said quietly as she opened the passenger door. 'Let me see if I can calm the dog down before you get out. I've met him twice before. He'll remember.'

'I'm not sure that's ...'

But Deirdre had already closed the door behind her. For a moment, Magnus stopped barking and stared. Then he ran forward, shaking his head and growling. Deirdre crouched down, the back of her hand outstretched, her heart racing.

'Hello, Magnus,' she said quietly. 'Where's your master, boy? Where's Sebastian?'

The dog bent down and pushed at her hand forcefully with its muzzle. Then turned and started down the path which led over the marshy ground to the stacks, where Deirdre came each summer to watch the nesting puffins.

'Come on,' she called out to Cathel. 'He's leading us somewhere. Hurry.'

The dog – silent now – was surefooted, keeping to the stony track which twisted its way across the soft ground. He leapt the narrow burn, its brown water gurgling and frothing as it flowed downhill towards the sea, and disappeared over the top of the hill. Ahead, almost to the edge of the cliff, lay more than a mile of meadowland, its spiky grasses and moss hiding the treacherous peat bog beneath – a man-eating bog. The sun had sunk below the horizon now, and the dips and shallows of the undulating landscape were being swallowed up by the darkness. But the white coat of the dog stood out, catching the fading oranges and reds of the sunset; his barking unmistakeable as he stopped and pointed into the distance.

Breathless, Deirdre stopped beside the dog, her hand resting on his back.

'I see him,' she called back to Cathel. 'Sebastian.'

'How bad is it?' Cathel, too, was breathing heavily as he drew alongside her.

'I can see his head, and one shoulder. He's not moving, though.'

'Good. I've got a tow rope in the car,' Cathel turned away. 'Make sure he stays exactly as he is.'

'We'll need a torch too. But, if he's weak ...'

'One thing at a time, lass. One thing at a time,' Cathel shouted over his shoulder as he took off back to the roadside.

The dog was pawing at the ground and growling. Deirdre moved her hand and began to stroke him behind the ears.

'We'll get him out, don't you worry, Magnus. But please just stay,' she said firmly.

For a few minutes, the dog relaxed, sitting back on its haunches. But, as soon as he saw the light of Cathel's torch returning along the path, he started to growl again. Cathel had the rope slung over his shoulder, a plank of fresh pinewood under his arm.

Cathel smiled, 'He had a pile of these in the back of the Land Rover. Thought it might be handy.'

Deirdre stepped forward.

'Nae, lass.'

'No, Cathel. This is mine. I'm lighter than you. And we're going to need your strength to pull us both out.'

'Your father'll kill me when he finds out.'

'Then we'd better do it right, and not tell him.'

Cathel sighed, but took the rope, wound one end of it around his waist, and tied it with a double knot. He passed the other end to Deirdre, who did the same. She pushed the plank out onto the surface of the bog and slid onto it, lying flat, as if she were a surfer.

'Let's hope the rope's long enough. Try seeing if you can rouse Carlyle, when you get there. It'll be a lot easier if he's working with ye.'

Deirdre started to edge her way over the waterlogged ground, her hands acting as paddles on either side of the board. Cathel shone the torch in the direction she was heading, but the beam was broken up by her shadow, and only the faintest of natural light was left to them. She could feel the cold, dank water seeping through her anorak, up her arms and creeping over her legs. Bog grass bent and was dragged under the board, as she pushed forward. Ahead lay the faint outline of Sebastian's head, tilting to one side, just above the waterline.

The rope jerked.

'Shit!'

'What's happened, Deirdre? Are you alright?'

'The rope's a bit short. I'm going to need ...'

'I'll untie it, wrap it round my wrists, and see if I can get another foothold nearer to the edge.'

For a few minutes, as Cathel worked at his end and Deirdre waited at hers, there was silence. When the rope slackened again, Deirdre paddled forward a few more feet.

'Sebastian, Sebastian, can you hear me? It's Deirdre,' she tapped him gently on the side of the head, but still he was motionless. She shouted louder, 'It's time to wake up, please. We can't do this without you.'

Both Cathel and the dog heard the faint groan as Sebastian Carlyle woke to the realisation that help had arrived. Magnus started to bark loudly. In the darkness, they heard Deirdre's warning.

'Don't move, Sebastian. For God's sake, don't try to move. Cathel's here with me, and we're both going to get

73

you out. But I need you to listen to me very carefully. I want you to lift each arm out of the water, very slowly. That one first. Don't jerk around or that'll be the end of you,' she paused. 'Good. Now the other one.' Another pause. 'Now I'm going to ask you to hook both of your arms under the rope, which is around my waist, then clasp them together in a fireman's hold. You know what that is, right?' Sebastian nodded. 'Do it very slowly. And, when we're both ready, Cathel's going to pull us back. But we're going to let him do all the work. I don't want you thrashing around thinking you're helping. That's only going to pull us both under … and I'll be going in headfirst!'

A few minutes later, Cathel started to pull. There was a jerk and a huge slurping noise as the suction of the bog released its hold on Sebastian. He fell forward, pushing into Deirdre, who felt herself slipping backwards on the board.

'Wait,' she called out. 'I'm slipping,' she clasped the side of the board, and felt the splinters from the untreated wood biting into her hands. 'Okay, I've got it now,' she shouted again. 'A little slower this time.'

Magnus was beside himself, barking, his tail wagging, as Cathel reached forward and grasped Sebastian's collar. Together, he and Deirdre pulled Sebastian onto his feet, but his legs immediately buckled and he began to shake, cold water streaming down his coat and legs.

Sebastian was not a big man, and Cathel had worked in manual labour for most of his life. It was not too difficult for him to hoist the laird over his shoulder and manhandle him back to the layby and into the passenger seat of the Land Rover.

Sebastian looked up at him. 'I should've known better. I won't forget this. You – both of you – saved my life.'

'Nay, man … Mr Carlyle, sir …'

'Sebastian will do.'

'Ah, well. You'll not be the first, nor the last that has

74

mistaken the bog for solid ground. And it was Deirdre who spotted the dog at the side of the road.'

'You're lucky Magnus raised the alarm so quickly,' Deirdre laughed. 'But perhaps you should take a human chaperone with you, next time you decide to take a hike across the moors.'

Already Deirdre could feel her splintered hands throbbing; in the torchlight, she noticed Cathel rubbing his swollen wrists, which had been bound tightly by the tow rope as they pulled Sebastian Carlyle to safety.

Chapter 15

Meghan

From a distance, Carlyle House looked splendid, with its tall pale-coloured walls reflecting the autumnal sunshine, overlooking a vast sandy beach. But, as we drew closer and made the final turn, I saw that its walls were streaked black and green, where mould clung to crumbling stucco.

'Is this where you work? It looks … depressing.'

Ellen pulled on the hand brake, the engine idling.

'My office is in the cottage. The one that's still standing.'

'Who exactly owns the estate? They obviously don't stay here.'

'Nobody lives in the Carlyle House now. I work through the estate solicitors. On paper, Sebastian Carlyle is the laird. But he disappeared.'

'Disappeared?'

'One day he was here, and the next, he wasn't. He didn't even wait around for Deirdre.'

Her name hung in the air between us, and I could not let it pass. Even Ellen, easy-going, contented Ellen, seemed reluctant to say more.

'You and Cathel liked Deirdre.'

'We did. She didn't make friends easily, but I'd like to think she trusted us, particularly Cathel, who knew her better than I did. Many of the folks round here would say she was wild and disrespectful. In fact, she was just a free spirit, who wanted to live by her own rules. Her father drank too much and could be a bully; her mother was a quiet wee soul who minded home and hearth. But it was only Brigid – Deirdre's great aunt – who really understood Deirdre.'

'And Deirdre and her family owned and lived in your farmhouse.'

'Yes.'

'So, how did Deirdre come to live here on the estate?'

'There was some trouble at home. Máire, Deirdre's mother, had died and James had not dealt well with the loss. He took it out on Deirdre.'

'But why did she move here?'

'Sebastian Carlyle, the laird, fell in love with her, and he wanted to marry her.'

'And how old was he?'

'Twice her age, about the same as you and I today.'

'And she moved in with him? You said she was only eighteen.'

'She didn't move in with Sebastian. She and Brigid lived for a while in one of the two cottages on the estate. Come,' she said smiling, 'I'll take you on the grand tour!'

We drove over a rough track up behind the house, and then across miles of open moorland. The heather carpeted the landscape, purples and blues and whites sweeping up to meet the craggy outcrops beyond. Birds rose in alarm as we thundered past, the wheels of Ellen's Land Rover churning rocks in our wake. Sheep meandered across the track, seemingly unconcerned by our approach until Ellen made several determined taps on the horn. They scuttled aside and stared at us as we passed. Cassie, seated on my lap, panted excitedly at the possibility of a chase.

Ellen smiled, 'As you can see, even the sheep are not used to visitors up here.' She pulled suddenly to one side of the track, 'Look, up there, the stag with his harem.'

Beyond the bracken, on an open grassy slope, about ten deer were grazing. The stag had paused, alert to our arrival, ready to protect his troupe of female followers. Ellen handed me a pair of binoculars. I focused the glasses on the stag, the eight-pointed rack of his antlers, the glistening browns and russets of his coat. I felt as if our eyes were locked together, as if I could put out my hand and touch him.

'Just one of several herds you can see here this year. It's rutting season. A great time to visit.'

I handed back the binoculars. 'And this is your job?' I laughed. 'I definitely chose the wrong profession.'

We drove on, rabbits and pheasants scuttling for cover in the undergrowth as we approached, until we came back to the turn up to the house. Ellen turned aside, though, and took a small track down towards the beach, pulling up outside a small stone cottage.

'This is my office. I need to pick up some paperwork, and make a couple of calls. Why don't you take a stroll along the beach? I'll join you when I'm done.'

Sheltered by towering sand dunes, I walked along the deserted beach. A gentle wind was blowing inland, small whitecaps on the waves. The winter sun felt warm on my back. It was peaceful, unspoilt by the detritus of holidaymakers on a day out at the seaside. In many ways, it reminded me of our first outing near the village. But this beach felt very different from the one where I had seen the beachcomber, where Cassie had found the bone. Here I felt like an intruder, aware of the tall house set four-square on the slope above me, its narrow slits of windows keeping watch. No-one lived there now, but Carlyle House still dominated the landscape.

At one end of the beach, I could see the cottage where we had left Ellen. But, at the other, there was another building with the roof gone. And, as we drew nearer, I could see that the stones were blackened with soot.

I clambered up the dune below the house. The wind was harsher here. I could feel the sting of the salt on my cheeks. Cassie sniffed the air, but seemed reluctant to step over the threshold. The building was now merely an empty reminder of the past. It had been gutted by fire. The interior walls had disintegrated. Only the outer stone walls had endured. Inside the open shell of the building, weeds had taken over the interior, and moss now clung to the charcoaled roof timbers, which lay as they must have fallen. This was the other cottage, the one where Deirdre had once lived with Brigid.

I heard a sound behind me. I turned, expecting to see Cassie. Instead, the silhouette of a girl was framed in the empty doorway, her russet hair crowned by the light of the sinking sun.

'I'm sorry. I didn't mean to intrude. I was just …'

'Are you in there, Meghan? Who are you talking to?' Suddenly, Ellen was standing in the doorway and the girl had vanished.

'I saw someone. I thought it might be … her. But it couldn't be, could it?'

'Who ... Deirdre? No, it's only me,' she smiled. 'There's been too much idle gossip for too long. Now it's starting to get to you too, and you never even knew her. Don't let it. And just to put your mind at rest, Deirdre and Brigid were not inside when Sebastian set fire to the cottage.'

Chapter 16

Deirdre

'How do you know the laird so well?'
Together, they had taken Sebastian home; Deirdre grinding through the gears of Cathel's old car, as he drove the Land Rover. Now, returning to the village, sitting side-by-side, there was safety in the darkness.

Deirdre smiled, her face barely visible in the faint glow from the lights on the dashboard.

'He was the one who sent you the flowers, wasn't he?'

'It was my birthday. What's wrong with that?'

'Nothing, not really, as long as …'

'As long as what?'

'You're a beautiful girl. The local lads look at you, imagine all sorts, but they'll never touch. And that's because they're also afeart of you. You, on the other hand, aren't afraid of anything … or anyone.'

'Oh, I'm afraid sometimes too. Especially of becoming like my mother.'

'Your mother was a lovely lady – kind, hard-working.'

'But I don't want to be remembered like that. I want to …' she paused. 'And I'm afraid of Father too.'

'Aye, your da gets a little crazy when the drink's in him,' he paused. 'But this man, Carlyle, he's different.'

'Like me?' Deirdre laughed.

'He's not one of us. Flowers on your birthday? Perhaps. Rescuing him from the bog? Fine. As long as you don't lead him on.'

'Lead him on?'

'You're eighteen. He's what? Mid-thirties. Twice your age. And he's been around.'

'So?'

'Perhaps he wants a fling.'

'Brigid warned me.'

'Aye, or perhaps he's more serious. Older men are attracted to good-looking young women with attitude. You've the means to drive him crazy.'

'Cathel Sinclair, I've never heard you say so much or speak so eloquently in all the years I've known you.'

Cathel laughed, 'I'm just saying, you're playing a dangerous game, flirting with a man like that.'

'I wasn't; I haven't been flirting.'

'Perhaps not, not as you see it.'

'He's a little too sure of himself, that's all. I enjoy taking him down a peg or two.'

'And that's how it begins, lass.'

*

Two days later, it was the end of the month, October. For many of the young folks in the village, it was Hallowe'en. The time to wear masks and scary costumes, demand treats from neighbours and friends. And then, at the beginning of November, a bonfire would be lit on the cliffside and fireworks launched over the bay to celebrate Guy Fawkes' Night.

But for Brigid, and many of her generation, it was *Samhain*. The light and brightness of the summer sun was passing. The darker months of shorter days and colder weather had arrived. They, too, lit a bonfire. For them, it was a way to capture the light and hold on to it for the return of spring. And, as the trees shed their leaves and animals sought winter shelter in the darkness, the celebrants remembered

81

those who had departed this life for the next. From light into darkness, and into the light again.

As the sun set below the horizon, the bonfire was lit, high up on the hill behind the Auld Village. A beacon in the landscape, it drew a crowd every year – some who were attracted to the old beliefs and some who were merely curious. For Brigid and Deirdre, it was an annual pilgrimage.

Tonight is the night to call out to those who came before.
Tonight I honour my ancestors.
Spirits of my fathers and mothers, I call to you,
and welcome you to join me for this night.
You watch over me always,
protecting and guiding me, and tonight I thank you.
Your blood runs in my veins,
your spirit is in my heart, your memories are in my soul.

Brigid spoke softly; but, in the still air, her words carried across the hillside, only interrupted occasionally by the crackle of the logs behind her as they caught the flames. Beside her a group of older men and women stood with heads bowed. The watching crowd stood in respectful silence. But, as soon as she had finished, instinctively, they moved in towards the warmth of the bonfire. Conversations started again, groups formed and reformed, children ran around excitedly.

Deirdre stood a little apart, remembering her mother and how they had been here on the hillside together only a year earlier. She could see Cathel to one side of the crowd, holding hands with a girl she did not recognise. She remembered his advice, the words he had spoken only a few days ago, and she smiled.

'Now,' she thought, 'I'll have something to tease him about.'

After a few minutes, Brigid clapped her hands.

'Let's make a circle, and join hands,' she called out.

'A circle, a circle,' the children echoed, as they ran

forward, several carrying small *bodhráns*.

People jostled and laughed together, pulling friends and neighbours with them into the circle. As Deirdre found a place and spread her arms out to hold hands with her companions on either side, there was a voice in the darkness behind her.

'May I?'

She took a step back to make space for the new arrival, and held out her hand. It was a voice she recognised.

Sebastian Carlyle had arrived. And his arrival did not go unnoticed. Across the circle, Emily Gunn whispered to Tom Mackay, who looked up quickly, grinning and passing the word on.

Slowly, the group began to move around the fire, chanting the familiar lines of the children's *Samhain* chant, the steady thrum of the children's hands against the skin of the *bodhráns* keeping the rhythm –

Samhain is here, cold is the earth,
as we celebrate the cycle of death and rebirth.
Tonight we speak to those through the veil,
the lines between worlds are thin and frail.

Ghosts and spirits in the night,
magical beings rising in flight,
owls hooting up in a moonlit tree,
I don't fear you and you don't fear me.

As the sun goes down, far to the west,
my ancestors watch over me as I rest.
They keep me safe and without fear,
on the night of Samhain, it is our New Year.

Deirdre felt the warmth of Sebastian's hand in hers, her heart beating a little faster, as she danced in the firelight. Tonight, in the darkness, he had sought her out. Cathel had warned her of something she already knew – it would not be difficult to ensnare this man. All she had to do was be herself. If she encouraged him, made him believe that she too was interested, the possibilities were endless. He was an attractive man, in a citified kind of way. He was not muscular, or as tall as Cathel. But he was amusing. Educated, well-travelled and quick-witted – she did not believe she would ever be bored with such a man. And, of course, he had money. She did not know what it felt like to be in love. But his hand felt comfortable in hers. Was that perhaps the beginning of love? What would she regret if she pulled away now?

As the chant finished, the dancers broke away from the circle. Some of the children continued to bang their *bodhráns* for several more minutes.

Deirdre turned to Sebastian, 'It's good to know you're fit enough to join in the *Samhain* festivities.'

'My rescue party was of the highest calibre. How could I not be? So, what happens now?'

'People go home – eat, drink and make merry.'

'And you?'

'I shan't be going home. My father's not much for this. He'll be at the pub. I'll wait for Brigid, make sure the fire is under control before we leave.'

'Excuse me, Mr Carlyle, sir,' Roddy Sinclair tapped Sebastian on the back.

Sebastian turned quickly.

'I'm Cathel's da. He told me to speak to you. I was going to come up to the house, but now that you're here …'

'Of course, Mr Sinclair. I wanted to talk to you about your croft.'

'There's nothing wrong is there?'

'No, no. I thought you might be interested in owning it yourself, and some of the vacant croft land nearby.'

'Well, I'll need to think on that. It'd depend …'

Deirdre moved away. Roddy Sinclair would be embarrassed to discuss his business with her there. She walked around the bonfire, pushing the outside logs closer to the heart of the fire. It would probably burn for another hour or so before they could contain it within a circle of rocks, which had been piled in readiness.

Ten minutes or so later, when she returned to her starting point, she looked around for Sebastian. But there was no sign of him, or Roddy Sinclair.

'Yer man's gone,' Emily Gunn shouted as she ran past, pulling Tom Mackay in her wake. 'It's back to the pub and yer da, I'll be thinking.'

The breeze had picked up, and some of the embers were blowing inland. They would need to get water from the well in the Auld Village tonight to extinguish the fire completely. It would be too dangerous to leave it on the open hillside unattended.

Chapter 17

Meghan

Hallowe'en had arrived. A time to remember the dead, those who had departed this life and gone … where, I wondered. The date at the bottom of my computer reminded me. Years ago, it had been a day for fun and silly pranks. Now it was an annual reminder, a time for regret, missed opportunities.

Fifteen years earlier, I had been partying with university friends as the sun went down. Dressed up in cheap masks and crazy costumes, we drank too much, raised our glasses to the invulnerability of youth; and joked about the dead rising from their graves and wandering the streets in the darkness. I'd never heard my mobile phone ringing, never looked at the screen to see the calls I had missed. But, as I sang and danced and laughed, my mother lay dying in a hospital bed three hours' drive away. And just a few minutes before midnight, she had gone from my life forever. Today was a day to be endured, to distract myself from the growing list of *if onlys* one acquires over the years.

I had been practising my drawing skills – arranging the jug, a book, some cups and plates on the table or on the windowsill, trying out shading techniques and perspective ideas. And I had become engrossed in my book on seashore life, amazed by the mathematically precise way in which the whorls and patterns of seashells were developed. I had planned a hike in the hills, but a damp mist had crept in overnight and I didn't want to stray too far from the cottage and get lost in unfamiliar territory. Instead, I decided to go down to the beach, where Cassie could run, and I could collect specimens for my next drawing lesson. There I would remember my father, too, in happier times.

*

The tide had gone a long way out, the waves rippling up and back with barely a sound, and I could not determine whether the tide was coming in or going out. At first, I thought we were alone. But in the distance, I saw someone sitting on a rocky outcrop, exposed by the receding tide. A slight figure, with long hair drifting in the breeze. A dark silhouette against the pale grey sky. I wondered how long they'd be there, if they knew when the tide was on the turn and how soon they'd need to abandon their post. Most of the tourists had already gone south to warmer weather. So, it was probably a local.

The sea had worn its own pathways on the beach, merging with a stream flowing down the beach from the hills behind. Between the rocks, pools remained where some small fish flitted just below the surface. Cassie stuck her nose under the water in an attempt to reach them, and then leapt back when she felt them wriggle past.

I set out across the beach, criss-crossing the sand as I'd seen the beachcomber do a few weeks earlier. I carefully laid each of my new-found treasures – shells and seaweed, multi-coloured and pure white crystalline pebbles – in my canvas shopping bag. I found two coins and a red and blue plastic toy boat, and added them to my collection. Cassie was pulling on a piece of shredded rope, still attached to a small rusty anchor. Together, we hauled it up the beach and found a sheltered place to sit amongst the dune grasses. I smiled when I saw Cassie lay her paws protectively over her new possession. She'd become a perfect companion who liked to do all the same things I did.

I turned my face into the wind, taking deep breaths. Winter was coming and I wanted to enjoy every minute of it. At home, I would have dreaded the onset of the rain and the cold, the trudged commutes to and from work in the dark. But here, I realised I'd begun to enjoy each change in the weather. Each one gave a different complexion to the landscape. Mist cloaking the hills in mystery was a perfect complement to the swathes of colourful heather. The rain battering against the windows of the cottage meant a wild sea dashing its anger against the cliffs, offering a cathartic release of energy to those onshore. The sunsets promised hope and a fresh start. All this I'd felt since arriving here. If Cassie had become my perfect companion, this place had become my idyllic retreat from the past, and a place to restore my soul.

I don't know how long I'd been sitting there, when I realised that the late October light was fading quickly. Once again, I'd lost track of time. There would be no glowing sunset over the water tonight. Now I could see the tide was definitely on the turn, coming quickly up the gently sloping beach. I looked back along the shoreline. The figure I'd seen an hour or so earlier was still there, looking out to sea, motionless, unmoved by the changing tide. I should go to warn them. Perhaps they too had lost track of time. And then I saw another figure, an older woman, bent a little, walking out of the dunes towards the water. I could stop worrying and go home. But when I turned back to look out to sea, the figure had disappeared and I saw the older woman walking along the shoreline alone.

We were clambering up the path beside the stream, on our way back to the car, when we met the beachcomber on the way down, his telltale basket on his back. He stopped, blocking the way forward. A once tall man, he was now stooped over. His bright blue eyes stared out at us, beneath a crop of pale white, shaggy hair.

'You're the one staying at the McIntyre place, aren't you?'

'Cathel and Ellen's place, yes. I'm Meghan.'

'What've you got in that bag of yours?'

'Shells, seaweed, bits and pieces. Why are you asking? Is there a law against beachcombing? If so, I'm sorry. I didn't mean ...'

'It just depends.'

'Depends on what?'

'You can't take parts of the beach wi' ye, rocks and such. Nor can you take living creatures,' he paused. 'And you canna take stuff that belongs to other folks.'

I thought of my small collection of pebbles, but decided against mentioning those. I could always return them later.

'Well, I believe I meet all of those criteria. If you don't mind my asking, what is it that you collect on the beach?'

'I do mind.'

I hesitated.

'Actually, I was worried. There was someone – a girl I think – sitting far out on that rock,' I pointed. 'She was there for ages, and didn't seem to notice the incoming tide. I was going to warn her. Then an older woman walked out from the dunes. And when I looked back out to sea, the girl had disappeared. You didn't see her, did you?'

'You saw someone sitting out there?'

'Yes.'

'And an old woman?'

'Yes. Do you know them?'

He turned to stare out at the waves as they rolled gently up the sand, creeping up the foreshore as they did each day. Slowly, our footprints were being erased. But, beneath the damp sand, life was returning for those creatures who had burrowed their way down into the darkness as the sea retreated.

When he looked back at me, his expression had changed.

He was no longer an aggressive, surly old man. He looked sad, shrunken somehow.

'It would've been my mother and the lass,' he said quietly.

*

On my way home, I stopped off at the village shop and bought some sweets for Ellen's boys. As Ellen opened the door, she nodded behind her.

'It's already begun – the silliness, trick-or-treating. In Brigid's time, Hallowe'en meant something. It was a time to celebrate the spirits of our ancestors – the Druid festival of *Samhain*. My first year here, Cathel took me up to the Auld Village. There was chanting, music, a bonfire. It was magical. Now it's just commercial glitz and giving kids all those things we've been saying were bad for them the rest of the year,' she laughed. 'But thanks for the sweets anyway.'

Chapter 18

Deirdre

The first snow arrived. Usually, the early fall would be mixed with rain and melt before it could lie. But this year, the temperatures dropped steadily, and the flurries settled, layer upon layer. Snow ploughs worked throughout each night, clearing the main road, but refused to make it down the dangerous twists and turns into the village. Fergus drove his four-wheeler up to the main road, a small trailer behind, and collected deliveries for the inn as well as those for Marge at the village shop. Greg's postal run was restricted to twice-a-week delivery.

Cathel now worked with his father in the mornings, checking on their animals, moving them into shelter and making sure they had feed. But, each afternoon, he made it down into the village on his father's ATV to help James. James' animals were nearer at hand, and he could often manage them alone, but his tractor was in bad shape and needed a complete overhaul.

Although school was still in session, children who lived in outlying areas – where school transport was no longer able to reach – were given permission to work on projects from home. But Deirdre left early each morning, trudging slowly through the snowdrifts to catch the bus at the main road. She breathed in the fresh, cold air which took her away from the claustrophobia of the cottage, where James now spent much of each morning hunched over the kitchen table, waiting for Cathel and listening to the radio.

For ten days, the snow lay deep and crisp, until the villagers woke one morning to a clear sky and bright sunshine. Grit and salt were scattered, and the road turned first to a slippery slush and then became awash with streams of water which rushed down the hillsides and across the road, tumbling into the burn and out to sea.

Life returned to normal. The crofting committee met and organised a group to repair the sheep fence which encircled the village. The pub was full to bursting on Friday, as usual, for fish and chip suppers. James wove his way home from the pub each night, his feet creaking their way up the stairs, alerting Deirdre to his arrival as she lay still and quiet behind her locked bedroom door.

Brigid returned to the work at Carlyle House; coming back from the village, late one afternoon, with two envelopes in her pocket – one addressed to Cathel, and the other to Deirdre, each with the Carlyle crest embossed above their names. James had driven into town to collect some new parts for the tractor. So, Deirdre and Cathel sat together, mugs of tea in front of them at the kitchen table, Brigid hovering nearby.

'You first, Deirdre,' Cathel smiled.

'And read it aloud,' Brigid instructed. 'I want to know too.'

Friday, November 22ⁿᵈ – 7pm, Deirdre read,
You are invited to a casual supper at Carlyle House.
I hope you are free that evening.
Sebastian.
P.S. Let me know if you need a lift.

RSVP – 01641 666333.

'Rather formal,' Brigid commented.

'Now your turn, Cathel,' Deirdre nudged Cathel.

Friday, November 22ⁿᵈ – 7pm.
You and Ellen are invited to a casual supper at Carlyle House.
I hope you are both free that evening.
Sebastian.

RSVP – 01641 666333.

'So that's her name!' Deirdre leaned back, smiling. 'And who is she, this Ellen of yours?'

'Ellen's from the islands, staying at her granda's place. You know, Gavin Sutherland, who lives in the croft next door. She's studying estate management, and Mr Carlyle has offered her a three-month internship, part of the course requirement,' he hesitated. 'And she's not my Ellen. We've gone out a few times, that's all.'

'Ooh, Cathel, I do hope you're not leading her on!' Deirdre laughed.

'So, you're both going, right?' Brigid topped up their mugs of tea.

'Do you think there'll be lots of people there? What shall I wear? And what if Da finds out?'

'You make the call, lass. I'll deal with James.'

'And we can all go in my old car. All three of us,' Cathel said, smiling.

'Safety in numbers,' Brigid added.

*

The headlights of the car dipped and shivered as Cathel took the turns of the track leading down to Annanside Bay, bumping over the potholes left by the melted snow. Tonight, Carlyle House looked more isolated than Deirdre remembered, its pale walls standing stark and tall in the moonlight, its narrow-slit windows glowing like ghostly eyes in the wilderness, the only lights in the valley. But as they approached the leeward side of the house, up the private track leading away from the beach, the front of Carlyle House seemed more welcoming, more alive. The windows on both floors were ablaze with lights, each one draped with their new curtains. And Sebastian was waiting for them, under the porchlight, as Cathel pulled up into the drive.

Inside, the house seemed smaller, less grand than Deirdre had expected. There was no vast domed ceiling with a splendid sweeping staircase leading to the upper floor. No suits of armour playing sentry in the entrance. Just a few low oak beams, with a small chandelier suspended in the centre, its lights glinting off the polished wood floor and the wall panelling of the hallway. No music and laughter emanated from the doorway to the right, where she could see floor-to-ceiling bookshelves and a log fire burning. There was only the whoosh of the front door closing behind them and the ticking of a grandfather clock half-hidden in the shadows.

'Are we alone?' Deirdre asked. 'I was expecting ...'

'Quite alone. Are you disappointed?' Sebastian laughed. 'Because I'm also the head cook and bottle washer tonight,' he paused. 'I wanted to thank you both, properly.'

'There's no need, Mr Carlyle.'

'Yes, Cathel, there is. And it's Sebastian, remember?'

In the study, standing in front of the fire, Deirdre accepted a glass of sherry, even though she had never tried one before.

Glass in hand, Ellen scanned the bookshelves.

'May I? This looks interesting – *From the Good Earth: Traditional Farming Methods in a New Age*,' she said as she leaned forward to pull a volume down.

'Of course,' Sebastian smiled. 'For the next three months, the whole library is at your disposal.'

'Does that apply to all of us?' Deirdre laughed.

'You're welcome to come and browse at any time.'

'And Cathel too?'

'Oh, I'm not much of a reader.'

'But look,' Ellen showed him a double-page spread.

94

'You'd love this. We could look at it together, one evening at Granda's.'

Deirdre winked at Cathel, who scowled back.

Later, as they ate dinner – a spicy chicken dish served with rice – Deirdre accepted a glass of bubbly wine which Sebastian called prosecco; and another with the rich plum dessert. She found herself drifting in and out of the conversation, nodding and laughing, occasionally asking Ellen questions.

Ellen was petite with long blonde hair, which she had tied back in a bow, low on the nape of her neck. Her brown eyes darted from one speaker to another, as she leant forward, listening intently. She was knowledgeable and pretty, and was not afraid to contradict Sebastian. But she always did so with a completely disarming smile.

Cathel seemed enamoured.

'Tell Sebastian, Ellen, about the time ...' Cathel said several times, patting her hand.

Was this how it began, Deirdre wondered? The subtle shift from admiration to love, the small bud holding the promise of the full bloom, with its intoxicating mix of scent and colour and form. Had her mother felt this when she met her father? Had he? She would like to imagine that her father, before the drink took him, might have been much like Cathel, a gentler man. Yet the word love also implied something much more animal and basic, like the hormonal frenzy bandied about casually in the schoolyard. Its passion represented, Brigid had said, by the orange bud in her birthday bouquet of white roses. The physical implications of the flesh-on-flesh intimacy of the sexual act was not appealing. She could not, did not want to imagine losing herself so completely. In all the books she had read, and the films she had watched, there was always a dominant personality, the one who wielded power over another. Cathel had told her that she had such power, over Sebastian. But did she really want it? And would it last? Cathel was not educated in the same way as Ellen. Flowers faded, their seeds swallowed up by the dark earth below or scattered by the wind. Winter arrived. So often, even in fiction, love evolved into boredom or bitterness, only the dried husks of its seeds remaining, rotting in the ground.

*

Later, as Cathel and Ellen made their way outside to the car, Deirdre turned to Sebastian.

'Why did you really ask us here tonight?'

'I told you – to thank you both for rescuing me. And to ask for suggestions about the Yuletide party, what I should and shouldn't do,' he paused. 'What other reason might there be?'

'I thought perhaps …'

'You thought perhaps that I wanted to see you again, is that it?' he smiled. 'And, if I did?'

'Nothing, I didn't mean that,' she hesitated. 'The dinner was great. The food delicious. Thank you.'

'I do want to see you again. You know that, I know you do, Deirdre. But we're crossing into dangerous territory here.'

'Are we? Why?'

'Our ages, positions, background.'

'And you were the one who said, when I warned you about this place, that we're living in a new world and times have changed. Are you afeart, Mr Carlyle?'

'You're a tease, Deirdre. Did anyone ever tell you that?'

'No, sir. Just that I'm opinionated and proud.'

'That too.'

'But that's why you want to see me again, isn't it?'

He smiled, 'So, we have a date?'

She paused, 'Sunday morning, 11.15, when nearly everyone is at the kirk. Meet me at the top of the village on the main road. I'll bring my bike. We can put it in the back of the Land Rover.'

'And go where exactly?'

'You'll think of something.'

A few minutes later, Cathel, making a precautionary stop at the top of the hill, at the junction with the main road, turned to Ellen.

'It must be awfu' lonely being stuck away in that big old house?'

Ellen laughed, 'He's probably running away from a nagging wife and a brood of screaming kids. Or he's gay. He's good-looking anyway. And was very pleasant tonight.'

Deirdre closed her eyes and pretended to be asleep.

Chapter 19

Deirdre

Through the kitchen window, Deirdre saw the glow of the peat burning low in the fireplace, the shadows of the flames flickering on the newly-painted white walls. As she opened the door, along with the rush of heat expelled into the cold night air, she smelled the alcohol. And she recognised the silhouette of her father slumped in his chair by the fireside, glass in hand, a nearly empty bottle of whisky at his feet, and several beer bottles catching the firelight on the tile floor. Quietly, slowly, she turned to close the door; but the click of the door latch roused her father, and he stood up suddenly, alarmed by the presence of an intruder.

'I canna see you in the darkness, but I ken you're there.'

'It's only me, Father.'

'It's you, is it? And where do you think you've been? That woman …'

'Brigid?'

'Aye, Brigid. She said you'd be having my supper ready.'

'No, Father. She told you I was going out for supper – with friends.'

'Supping with friends now, is it? And your da sitting here alone waiting for his tea.'

'Can I get you something to eat now?'

'Nae, I'm well past that. If your ma were here now … She was my special girl.'

'I know. I miss her too.'

'You're my special girl now, you know that, child, don't you? I need you. You'll be here for me, won't you?'

'Of course. In the morning, I'll fry up some bacon and eggs and tattie scones for breakfast – all your favourites.'

She turned towards the stairs, her hand on the banister, her foot on the first step.

'But I need you now, tonight. Come and give your da a cuddle. I want to remember my Máire tonight, the smell of her hair, her soft skin. When we married, she was so young, so bonny, just like you are today.'

Deirdre remembered too – the night of her mother's funeral. The sourness of her father's sweat and the reek of stale alcohol on his breath, as he had lain on top of her. The suffocating roughness of his coarse wool jacket as his hand clutched at her bare breast. Since that night, she had convinced herself he had simply lost his way, had a moment of temporary insanity. Nevertheless, she had taken precautions to avoid another confrontation, locking her door carefully each night before he returned from the inn, feigning sleep in the darkness. But, tonight, she had broken her routine. She had relished a new kind of freedom, a chance to step away from her childhood, from the past, be an adult. She had even idly considered the prospect of love.

'Come, girl. Sit with me. I can hold you on my lap as I did when you were a wee bairn.'

'I'm not a bairn any more, Da. I'm tired. You're tired.'

'Too tired to give your da some love?'

'It's late, Father. And you're pished.'

'Aye, that's as maybe. But I'll no' have you talking to me like that!'

He launched himself away from the chair towards her. The glass fell from his hands, shattering on the hearthstone.

'As long as you're in my house, you'll do as I say.'

'No, not this. Not now, not ever.'

She turned quickly. Her foot slipped as she turned the

corner of the stairs, her heel catching on the uneven riser. As she lost her balance, she felt the tug of her father's hand on the hem of her skirt. Tonight, she had worn her tartan skirt and the same yellow blouse she had worn on the day of her mother's funeral, the same day she had first met Sebastian St. John Carlyle on the beach. It was her best outfit. The tartan was made of tightly woven wool, both strong and durable; James pulled hard on it, grabbing onto the handrail with his other hand. Despite his drunkenness, he was still a strong man. Deirdre felt herself being dragged backwards. Her blouse worked its way loose from the waistband of her skirt. She heard the thin cotton tearing as James caught hold of it. He stumbled. Deirdre kicked backwards as hard as she could. She felt the sudden jolt as her heel made contact with her father's nose, toppling him backwards. She heard the dull thud as his head fell hard onto the tiled floor below. For a moment, she hesitated; then she ran, into the safety of her bedroom, her hands shaking as she turned the key in the lock behind her.

In the darkness, she buried her head in her pillow and sobbed. Tonight had held so much promise – dinner in the Big House, wine and adult conversation, a little flirting. Despite her promise to her mother, she knew now she had no choice but to leave the farm. In the morning, she would call Brigid. Together, they would find a way to explain her moving out, reasons which would not harm her father and save her own reputation from the gossips in the village.

Chapter 20

Meghan

The days slipped by easily. I was enjoying my self-taught drawing lessons. Now I'd added washes of colour to my sketches, experimenting with the mixes. The blues and yellows and greys made my seashore collections more interesting, more memorable. I'd gathered sprigs of heather, some faded brown bracken and an empty bird's nest for my collection. The deep recess of the cottage windowsill was an ideal display area. I was reading more. There seemed to be an endless supply of ebooks about mysterious happenings in the Highlands. Downloading was all too easy.

And I started buying the local weekly at the village shop. The daily concerns of Highlanders were not so different from those who lived in cities or towns in the south, but sometimes they seemed to affect their lives more directly. A new farming regulation meant another hurdle for a farmer or a crofter to negotiate, and could spell ruin for their livelihood. A small business closing could mean loss of local access to the food chain or other essentials, and a takeover by the behemoths of the e-tail business. The influx of tourists meant the expansion of hospitality outlets, and the intrusion of visitors onto unspoilt landscapes and dangerous overcrowding on the narrow roads.

Yet the village still held its own. Set back from the main road, hidden from the casual passerby, only the adventurous ventured down the winding road into the valley.

I took photos of the houses, how they hunkered together in clusters. On the far side, most faced away from the sea. But on our side, more had chosen to take in the view, where they could look out over the ocean and watch the setting sun. I started to recognise where people lived, their names and their occupations. I made lists and links between the households. And I reserved a special page for Deirdre – those who had mentioned her name, or who had been mentioned as part of her story –

Deirdre – 18. How did she die? When? Why? And why did I keep seeing her?
Sebastian Carlyle – laird, Carlyle House – twice Deirdre's age, wanted to marry her. Where is he now? When did he disappear? Why? And why didn't he wait for Deirdre?
Brigid – Deirdre's great aunt, her mentor. When did she die?
Máire McIntyre – Deirdre's mother, also dead
James McIntyre – Deirdre's father, now in a care home
Dougal – in the pub
Liane – owner of The Piper and the Swan
Cathel and Ellen – landlords – friends of Deirdre. Ellen met Deirdre 15 years ago, when she arrived/met Cathel
Who is the beachcomber?
Who is his mother – the old woman on the beach? And who was the lass out on the rocks?

Just as the village was hidden from the eyes of casual tourists who were 'doing' the Highlands, it seemed that the villagers had decided to keep the story of Deirdre to themselves. Something had happened here that they were frightened, or ashamed, to admit. I was no longer making a list of why I should stay or leave the village. Tacitly, I'd decided to stay. I liked the place, and the people. The wildness of the landscape and the changing moods of the ocean stirred and soothed my spirit at the same time. The knowledge that I was known, perhaps had even been accepted in the village, reassured me that I was not alone. And yet, Deirdre had been lost to them, the very people who'd now welcomed me in. The mystery of what had happened to this young girl, living among her own kinfolk, seemed so wrong, when I had begun to feel so relaxed here. Everyone I'd talked to seemed to know something. But did anyone know the whole story? Perhaps, that was the problem. They had, for one reason or another, each in their own way, omitted to take care of one of their own and wanted to keep their guilt to themselves.

*

I received a text from a friend at work. Richard had been to the office, taken her out for a drink after work and asked about me. I'd not been answering his texts or emails. Did they have a forwarding address for me? Or a number? He needed to contact me urgently. She'd told him she didn't know where I was, but would pass on the message. And she wanted to know if I was okay –

Thanks, Liz – I'd replied – *I'm fine, enjoying my sabbatical away from it all. Richard & I have split up for good! He was never going to leave his wife. I've blocked him now on all my devices & social media. Tell him you haven't been able to contact me either. I hope you and the others are managing without me, Meghan xxx*
    P.S. I've got a dog called Cassie!

*

It was early December when I talked to Dougal again in the pub.
    The sky had been threatening another storm all day. The air was still, the sea calm, but the clouds were gathering, a dark blanket glowering overhead. With the prospect of being housebound the following day, I decided to go down to the pub for supper. I'd been there several times since my arrival, but there had usually been groups of drinkers – mostly men

– talking and laughing loudly together. On each occasion, Dougal had been at the centre of the noise. He'd waved at me, even beckoned me over to join them once or twice, but I'd always just collected my cottage pie, or fish and chips, or steak and kidney pudding, and taken it home.

Tonight, it was quieter, curry was on the menu, and Dougal was sitting in his corner at the bar. With my order in play, I went to join him.

'Folks are staying away tonight, lass. There's going to be snow, lots of it; everyone's taking their beasts into shelter.'

'I wondered about that. The sky looks different tonight.'

'Aye, indeed. Just another season turning. And you've been settling in, I hear. Walking on the cliffs, taking pictures. Cathel said you'd even been over to the Carlyle House with Ellen.'

'Everyone knows everyone's business around here, don't they?'

'Well, we like to think it's a neighbourly thing to do. Some might say, though, that we're just nosy folk,' he laughed.

'Perhaps, you could tell me then … Who's the old man I've seen on the beach, the beachcomber with the basket on his back?'

'You mean yon fella?' he pointed behind me to the other end of the bar, beyond where Liane, the owner of The Piper and the Swan, was standing.

I turned. A man hovered in the doorway to the kitchen.

'Yes, that's him.'

'Why that's Fergus, of course. Used to run this place,' he paused. 'Handed it over to Liane after the trouble, never quite got over it.'

'Never quite got over what?'

'It's all a long time ago, lass. I think it's best not to dwell on the past, don't you? You'll always be wondering what you could've done differently. Brigid, his mother, blamed him for it all though. That wasn't right, no' right at all.'

'Brigid was his mother? But she died, didn't she?'

'Aye, maybe twelve year' ago now.'

'But I met him the other day and he said …'

A young man came out of the back, carrying a tray with my curry. Liane moved along the counter and pulled me a pint of draft cider. At the other end of the bar, Fergus continued to stare at Dougal.

'It's not my place, ye ken, to talk about it,' Dougal smiled. 'And it's time I was away. I've got quite a wee walk up the hill to my house, and I'd like to be in before the snow arrives. It doesn't do for a man of my age to go slipping and sliding. Not good for my reputation!' he patted me on the arm. 'You take care too, lass.'

The curry was excellent, but I ate it hurriedly, uncomfortable now that I was sitting alone. I imagined Fergus staring at me, his eyes following my every move. But, when I looked back, he had gone.

Outside, the snow had already begun to fall. The road was slick with a thin white coating, ice crystals glistening in the beam of my torchlight. I shivered as the small swirling flakes crept inside my collar and melted. But Cassie was delighted, leaping up as the snow landed on her nose, as if the dark night sky was scattering confetti in our path, leading us home.

I'd been unsettled by Dougal's evasive answers to my questions. They made me want to know more, so much more. And there was something about Fergus, watching and waiting in the background, which had felt like an unspoken threat to both of us.

Richard had promised to find me, turn up at my door one day. I remembered the words of the text message he'd sent, not long after I'd arrived in the village –

You can go, but you can't disappear. I will find you. One day you'll open your door and I'll be standing there.

With all the internet research tools at his disposal, it would not be impossible. I'd spent a lot of time at work researching the online footprints of clients for the cases we'd worked on – social media, CCTV, telephone records, bank and credit card statements, the police national database providing access to criminal records. People could run, but eventually they would nearly always be found. It only took one moment, a casual mistake, and their lives became an open book.

What was stopping me from doing some research of my own, finding out more about Deirdre and why no-one would talk openly about her? Tonight, I'd discovered several links, relationships between some of the people on my list. Some others had died. But Sebastian Carlyle had, apparently, disappeared. 'He didn't even wait around for Deirdre,' Ellen had said. So, where had he gone? A man with property and money had connections. I might not have legal access to all the resources I'd used at work, but there was still the press and social media. He must have left a trail behind him somewhere.

Chapter 21

Deirdre

Deirdre woke suddenly from the dream. She was running, running down a long corridor away from a man who kept calling her name. The voice was familiar, but she could not see his face, nor remember his name. She only knew that she had to keep running. Now, awake, she could feel pressure on her temples, her head throbbing. Was it the dream, or a hangover? Her cool hand on her forehead felt good.

She swung her legs over the side of the bed and crossed to the window. Already the sun was rising over the hills, their shape-shifting shadows creeping across the valley. But the house was silent. A thick frost lay across the fields below, and glistened on the roof of the barn in the yard. Last night, she had made a plan, but in the morning light, she was frightened. Leaving home, staying with Brigid, it had all seemed so simple. But what about the rest of her life? What were her plans for that? And what would become of her father? Her father, her father … He had fallen, hit his head. Perhaps, even now, he lay dead on the kitchen floor. If she had killed him, she might go to prison.

Slowly, she turned the key and pushed open her bedroom door. There was no movement, no sound. She put one bare foot forward and peered round at her parents' bedroom door. It stood open, the bed unslept in. Testing the floorboards as she went, she crept across the hallway to the top of the stairs and peered down. Her father lay where he had fallen. His eyes were closed and he was breathing heavily. He was still

107

alive. But, when she reached him, she saw that his nose was twisted at an odd angle, blood had dried on his upper lip, and more had seeped from under his head.

She picked up the phone and dialled. It rang several times, and then the answering machine clicked in.

'Sebastian, I need your help. Now! It's Father. I don't know what …'

'Hello! Hello! Is that you, Deirdre? What's the matter?'

'Oh, please, please, come now,' she broke down crying.

'Are you at home?'

'Yes, yes. Will you come?'

'Of course, stay there. I'm on my way.'

And the phone went dead.

*

An hour later, it was all over.

Sebastian had arrived and taken care of everything. Constable Mackenzie had been called at the same time as the ambulance. He had taken Deirdre's statement and gone with James, in the ambulance, to the hospital.

'We all know James McIntyre, Mr Carlyle, sir,' he had reassured Sebastian. 'You'll be hearing no more from us on the matter. But our Deirdre … she looks a little peaky, if I may say so, sir.'

'Thank you, Constable. You've been very helpful. I'll look after Deirdre's welfare from now on.'

As the door closed behind the constable, Sebastian smiled.

'Good thing you're still wearing your clothes from last night. The constable couldn't dispute the evidence. But you do look a little peaky, my dear. A hot bath, some clean clothes and a good breakfast and you'll soon be right as rain. Then we need to sort out where you're going to stay from now on, before your father gets released from hospital.'

'With Brigid.'

'Of course, with Brigid.'

As she lay in the bath, the steam rising up around her and fogging up the window, she asked herself why she had called Sebastian. In the past, she would have called Brigid. Last night that had been her only thought. But this morning, seeing her father lying in a pool of blood, she had been afraid. Instinctively, she had realised she needed someone who had the kind of authority which would solve all her problems. Only Sebastian was capable of that. Brigid was her confidante, and Sebastian would be her good Samaritan. Of course, she argued, she had once been his, as he lay trapped in the peat bog. It was only right that he returned the favour. Yet part of her, she knew, had wanted him there. More alone now than ever, she needed someone. And, in the context of her life in the village, he was the only one capable of finding a way for her to escape. Besides, he was not an unattractive man. A little old perhaps, but not unattractive. Already, he was falling over himself to help, be with her, and …?

The *and* would have to wait. Her father gone, her safety assured, she sank under the water, her hair floating around her, long russet curls shrouding her from the daylight above.

Chapter 22

Deirdre

Sunday morning dawned, and Deirdre was waiting outside Brigid's house. Yesterday, Brigid had taken her in; and it was not long before the questions started.

Janet Munro was the first to call.

'Remember,' Brigid had said just before she picked up the receiver, 'we need to get our stories straight,' she paused, listening. 'Of course, Janet. It's so kind of you to ask after Deirdre. Yes, she's fine. The ambulance you saw at the farm this morning? Oh, it was for James – he had a turn in the night and fell down the stairs,' Brigid winked at Deirdre. 'No, no, nothing serious. He'll be back on his feet in no time. And yes, Deirdre will be staying with me for a while.'

In the afternoon, they had seen Marge in the village shop.

'Miss Munro was quite concerned about Deirdre, but she said she was to be with you ... after James' wee accident!' she smiled. 'A lot of people saw the ambulance this morning. It'll be company for the both of you, staying together. No need for Deirdre to be up in that old farmhouse all alone.'

Later, Fergus had dropped by Brigid's house and offered Deirdre some evening shifts at the pub.

'An extra pair of hands is always welcome at The Piper,' he had said. 'And young lasses like a little extra money to spend on themselves ... without having to ask their miserly old das.'

Since the night of her mother's funeral, Deirdre had

spent so much time running, hiding, evading her father. But today, in the crisp clear air of a November morning in the Highlands, she felt calm. Sebastian was coming to take her out for the day, and she did not care who saw her waiting for him or who noted the arrival of his Land Rover. He was her protector now. Beware, beware! She had the laird from the Big House on her side. She did not know what plans he had made for their outing, but she hoped he would drive her out into the hills or down to the sea, where she could breathe freely again. They might follow the deer track up into the forest, watch the red grouse foraging in the heather, sit by the river and see the pike jump in the midday sunshine, or walk along the beach and listen to the sounds of the ocean, the seagulls calling to each other.

Then, as she sat on the stone wall of Brigid's front garden, waiting for Sebastian, she saw him – her Iolaire. At first, he was only a speck on the other side of the valley, drifting down the hillside behind the farmhouse. He might have been looking for prey. But Deirdre knew, as he circled over the farmyard, that he was not interested in catching a stray chicken which had not noticed his shadow overhead. He was looking for her. She jumped off the wall and waved, her arms making large circles in the air, movements which she knew would catch his attention. And she called his name. For a moment, as he soared upward again, she wondered if he had not seen her. But he flew sure and straight over the burn, made two circles in the air above her head, and landed on Brigid's chimney pot.

'I'm here now,' she called out. 'I'm safe. I'm free. And I promise to visit you very soon.'

*

Sebastian turned off the main road, following the signs down to Annanside Bay, and Carlyle House.

'I thought we were going out today.'

'We are, Deirdre.'

He smiled, and then swerved away from the house and along a rough track, which led to a small jetty. At the far end, a small motor boat bobbed up and down on its moorings.

'I know you like the beach, Deirdre. I was hoping you'd like being on the water too.'

'Some people, Mr Carlyle, are afeart of the water. But I'm not one of them!'

'I'm delighted to see my Deirdre back to her old self,' he laughed.

'I'm not yours … or anyone's.'

'No, no, of course not.'

She helped to cast off from the jetty, and then sat in the small wheelhouse, watching Sebastian as he steered the boat out of the calm waters of the sheltered bay and into the open sea. The tide was on the turn, the breaking waves crashing on the rocky outcrops of the headland, and turning back on themselves, roiling and foaming as they fought their way to shore. For several minutes, the boat was tossed from side to side at the mercy of the cross-currents, leaping and plummeting as the rollers rose and fell. And then the swell settled, the boat gently rocking as Sebastian turned to skirt the coastline.

In calmer waters now, Deirdre moved outside and sat on one of the benches in the stern. In the distance, she could see the snow-covered tops of the mountains, stark silhouettes against a brilliant blue sky. Winter had already made its appearance, but today, the sun was out, and Deirdre held her face up to its warmth. She closed her eyes, and let her mind drift with the steady hum of the engine.

She remembered – it was the day after her thirteenth birthday – when Fergus had taken her out with him in his dinghy to harvest the small lobsters from the creels he had set out in the bay. Today, she and Sebastian both wore life jackets, but she and Fergus had not. Instead, he stood in the prow of the boat, while she held the tiller steady, as they moved from one orange marker buoy to another. Leaning over the side, he had hauled on the ropes and pulled the baskets onto the deck, before tipping the dazed lobsters into a bucket of seawater and tossing the pots back into the sea. Her mother had been terrified for her, as her two brothers and an uncle had drowned at sea. Although they were fishermen, none of them had ever learned to swim. Even though Deirdre could swim, she had not been allowed to go out again.

She had forgotten how good it felt to be out on the open sea in a small boat, almost weightless, rocked by the steady motion of the water.

Sebastian cut the engine and came to sit beside her.

'Was this a good idea?'

'It's perfect.'

'I have bread and cheese, and wine, if you're hungry.'

'Are you trying to seduce me, Mr Carlyle?'

'Do you want me to?'

'First, we need to get a few things straight.'

'Yes?'

'Are you married? Or have you been?'

'No, to both questions. I never felt the need.'

'I see. Because you got what you needed without the formalities?'

'If you mean, am I a virgin? Then the answer would also be no.'

'So, you might have children?'

'Not that I'm aware of. And,' he added, 'I never felt the need because I never met anyone I wanted to keep by my side for eternity.'

'Eternity is a long time.'

'I'm beginning to think it may not be long enough,' he paused. 'You're so, so beautiful. Every time I see you, you take my breath away. Yesterday, I was overwhelmed when you called, when you said you needed me.'

113

'I did. And I do. Still.'

'I know I'm not your idea of a Prince Charming …'

'I don't believe in such foolish stories,' she paused. 'Besides, you're quite good-looking, really.'

She gave him a quick peck on the cheek. He took her hand and put it to his lips, all the time gazing into her eyes. But Deirdre turned her head and looked at the horizon. If the eyes were the keys to your soul, she was not ready for him to assume that level of intimacy. She realised how vulnerable that could make her, especially now.

Since the day she had buried her mother, she had cast off the taboos of childhood. The funeral had been her rite of passage. In his twisted way, her father had sensed that. And Sebastian – at their first meeting – had seen the woman in her. That was all he had ever seen. He might be older, more worldly-wise. But even as he might want to show her a new way to live, with wealth and privilege, she was determined to hold onto the power she now felt was hers in their relationship.

As the boat drifted with the current, further away from the coastline and out to sea, she took long, deep breaths of the richly oxygenated air.

*

On their return journey, Sebastian had encouraged her to steer the boat.

He stood behind her, his arms guiding hers as they navigated the fury of the ocean at the entrance to the bay. The wind had picked up, and the outgoing waves were being whipped into a maelstrom of confusion. She leant into the warmth of his body, tensing and relaxing as the keel crashed from peak to trough, until they turned past the headland and into the haven of the bay below Carlyle House.

Chapter 23

Meghan

Ever since my arrival in the village, my imagination had begun to get the better of me. I'd started to feel, and apparently see, things which I didn't believe were possible. Yet, even down-to-earth Ellen had suggested that second sight – Deirdre's and Brigid's ability to see into the future – should not simply be dismissed as fanciful, or impossible. My mother had told me to follow my instincts, and I was still a realist. But I'd never felt this way before, never doubted the evidence of my own eyes. Perhaps living alone, away from familiar surroundings, was getting to me. Isolation can do that, apparently. I hadn't started meditating yet, or going off into trances; but maybe it was only a matter of time. If Fergus – my beachcomber – believed I'd seen his mother, perhaps he also believed the lass was Deirdre. Whatever had happened – 'the trouble,' Dougal had called it – had turned Fergus into a confused and unhappy human being.

Regardless of my scepticism about things which go bump in the night, I'd become obsessed with Deirdre's story. It was like a huge jigsaw puzzle, with a scattering of people, each holding one or two key pieces. If I listened carefully, I could assemble the outside pieces, the framework. If I asked questions, as the occasion arose, quietly and obliquely, perhaps the details of the whole might come together. And, if I tried to trace where Sebastian had gone, I might understand more about his relationship with Deirdre – when it had started, and how it had ended so badly. There was no hurry. I could wait. I had plenty of time.

*

The week before Christmas, a special event took place in the village. The primary schoolchildren were to stage a pageant in the church hall. It was an annual tradition and Ellen asked me to join her and Cathel.

Tables were laid out in the small entrance hall with tea and coffee urns, paper cups and plates of homemade biscuits. The children were ushered into a side room to change, while parents and family and friends milled around the tables, chattering and laughing. There was an exaggerated exuberance to greetings and conversations. I remembered occasions like this as a child. We'd been overexcited, giggly and nervous, anxious to please and mindful that the Christmas holidays were only a day or two away. Parents came with cameras at the ready, prepared for the worst, but hoping for the best. But, tonight, I sensed something more. A few people stood apart from their neighbours. Some hugged and spoke quietly to each other, as if this was not – for them – an occasion for celebration, but for sadness.

The minister, a tall, dour man with white hair, called the groups to order and began to usher everyone into the main hall. Chairs had been set up in a semi-circle around an almost empty space along the side wall. A large ship's anchor was propped up against the back of this makeshift stage. A wooden stool and a music stand were set off to one side. We found seats in the back row and, within minutes, there was standing room only. The audience was hushed now, speaking only occasionally in whispers. Above the anchor, tall bare windows revealed the darkness of the wintry night outside. But inside, the radiators were pumping heat into the room. And, with so many people packed into such a small area, I began to feel a little claustrophobic.

116

A kilted fiddler appeared from the back of the audience, playing a slow, muted melody, leading the children towards the stage. Everyone stood up. Little hands waved surreptitiously as they passed familiar faces. The minister brought up the rear of the procession. Now he was wearing a brightly coloured surplice over his black cassock. The front of the surplice was embroidered with a bright blue and yellow anchor; the back with a small blue and white saltire, and the words – *Saint Andrew, Patron Saint of Fishermen.*

'Tonight, we have again come together, to remember those who have left us,' he began as soon as the children had lined up behind him on the stage, his eyes scanning the assembly. 'Fathers and husbands, sons and brothers, who went to sea, and never returned to live among us again. Simple fisherfolk whom God, in his wisdom, took from us too soon. Some were returned to us, and buried in sanctified ground. Others lie still on the ocean floor, swallowed up by the fury of the waves. But all their names are inscribed in our hearts, remembered by the generations who have preceded us, and will continue to be by those who follow us. They will never be forgotten. And, amongst their number, there are strangers, whose names and faces we may not have known or cannot recall. Tonight, we honour them too – for their lives well lived, and for their sacrifice,' he lowered his head. 'May they rest in peace. Amen.'

'Amen,' everyone chorused.

He waved his hand across the room, and everyone sat down.

As he stepped back, a small girl came forward.

'You'll hear the Gaelic sung tonight, Meghan,' Ellen leaned over. 'I'll translate later.'

The girl was perhaps eight or nine years old, dressed in a pale, flowered dress with a white apron, her dark plaits hanging down below her headscarf. The fiddler started to play. The girl waited, looking over the heads of the audience.

As the intro ended, she began to sing. The words were unfamiliar, but their meaning was unmistakeable – a lament for lost souls, for unfulfilled lives, and for abandoned hope. Her voice was soft, but the notes she sang were crisp and clear, pure sounds which seemed to wrap around the hall and soar up into the rafters overhead. The fiddler was merely an echo to her song, keeping time, the bow on the strings a plaint answering her words.

When she finished singing, the hall was quiet. Some brushed away tears, others hugged their neighbours. I'd expected applause. Instead, in the silence, I heard the door open behind us, and turned. I saw Fergus, and he was leaving.

The girl returned to her place with the other children, and the minister moved to a seat in the audience to watch the pageant. It was the Christmas story, set in a fishing village. The boys fought storms at sea, hauled nets and sang a sea shanty about the days of ships under sail. The girls worked looms, tended the land and sang the nursery rhyme *Bobby Shafto's Gone to Sea*. There was no scenery, but the children held up pictures they had drawn on banners to depict the setting. Then, the nativity began – Mary and Joseph looking for shelter. Three children, dressed as shepherds, led in a sheep, a calf and a donkey, singing *While Shepherds Watched* as they walked. Finally, the boy playing Joseph sang. The carol was unmistakeably *Silent Night*, but the words again were in Gaelic.

Ellen nudged me, smiling, 'That's our Brennan.'

She hooked her arm in Cathel's; and I saw he had tears in his eyes.

*

Back at the farmhouse, Ellen made hot chocolate for the boys who were tired, but still hyped up by the evening's activities, and then hustled them up to bed. Cathel made hot toddies for us, and we settled by the fireside. In the corner, a

118

small green fir tree had been set up, waiting to be decorated.

'So, the song … I promised to translate,' Ellen began.

'It sounded so sad. The little girl …'

'Wee Aileen is quite something, isn't she? It's a true story, the words composed by Annie Campbell, who was to marry a sea captain named Allen Morrison – "Brown-haired Allen" or *Ailein Duinn*. There was a storm at sea, and he and his crew were all drowned. In the song, Annie repeats the words "I would go with thee" – *Ò hì shiùbhlainn leat*. I would make my bed on the sand and the seaweed, fish would be our candles, seals our watchmen – if I could be with you.'

'And his body was never recovered?'

'He washed ashore on a flood tide,' Cathel answered. 'It's said that Annie died of grief, her body discovered on the same beach where he was found,' he paused. 'Just like …'

'It was a sad story,' Ellen interrupted quickly. 'Romanticised, of course, but true.'

'Aye, and a sad reminder of a hard way of life for many. But now, ladies, I'm off to my bed. You can stay up all night, if you've a mind, but I've got animals to see to in the morning.'

'And I need to go too and let Cassie out.'

Ellen put her hand out and touched my arm.

'You'll spend Christmas with us, won't you?'

For the last three years, I had spent Christmas alone. Richard had promised to take me out for dinner on Christmas Eve, come and visit on Christmas night or on Boxing Day. But each year, it had been the same. He couldn't get away. There were too many obligations, family and friends arriving, his wife needing him to play host, his daughter needing him to be there to assemble the doll's house or the swing set. I refused invitations to spend Christmas with friends, always hoping he'd make it and I'd hear his key turn in the lock. Each year, he apologised and made promises which, in my heart, I knew he'd never keep. I expected to sit alone all day, eating my portion of roast chicken, heating up the store-bought mince pies, watching old movies and drinking too much, until only the twinkling lights on my small artificial Christmas tree shone in the darkness. And still I'd waited.

Looking back now, I recognised this had been the symbol of our relationship. Richard was in control, his life and his needs always took precedence over mine. He would make plans and, desperate to spend time with him, I would break my plans to be with him. He might cancel at the last minute, and I would make excuses for him. From my first day at work, I'd been assigned to shadow him, research clients' backgrounds, and back up in-court proceedings with a list of legal citations to be included at trial. Our affair segued naturally from this. He was the leader. I merely a follower in his wake. Neither of us ever talked about it. It was simply an established pattern. Only when he finally backed out from our agreement to move in together, did I realise the damage it had done. It seemed there was no way forward, no avenue to establish a new pattern, and I couldn't change the past. I had to be the one to break the chain.

This year, I'd expected to spend Christmas alone with Cassie, though I wasn't really alone anymore. I knew she wouldn't disappoint me.

I smiled at Ellen, surprised, but delighted, by her invitation.

'That would be wonderful … if you're sure I won't be in the way.'

'You'll be doing me a favour. Because there's one thing I should warn you about,' she paused. 'We always have James – James McIntyre – for Christmas. He used to live here, as I told you, before he sold this place to Cathel. He's losing it and can be quite a grouch, when the drink's in him. But we feel we owe it to him. It's not much fun spending Christmas with a lot of old folks, in a care home, who're nodding off over the gravy,' she laughed. 'He might even put on his best face, just for you.'

Chapter 24

Deirdre

Brigid was knitting, listening as Deirdre related the details of her outing with Sebastian. The intricate twists and turns of her needles, and the balls of deep purple and green wool bouncing up and down in her knitting basket as she moved from row to row, were the focal point in the room. Brigid maintained her concentration on her handiwork, without interrupting or commenting. And Deirdre talked, filling the room with her laughter and re-enacting the day's events, without having to look directly into the old woman's eyes, the need to explain and confide uppermost in her mind. Only when Deirdre seemed to have reached the end of her story, did Brigid look up.

'Will you put some more wood on the fire, child? The peat is low and we'll need the heat for a wee bit longer before we go to our beds.'

'And I'll make us another pot of tea, shall I, Brigid?'

'Aye, that'll be good.'

A fresh mug of tea cradled in her hands, her knitting resigned temporarily to the basket at her feet, Brigid returned to the subject of Deirdre's day.

'So, you enjoyed yourself, child? You liked being in the man's company? He was good to ye?'

'Yes, all that.'

'And have you thought about the future, where this will all lead?'

'Can't I just enjoy it for now?'

'You can. But what of your dreams, child? What have they told you?'

'My dreams?'

'We both know you see as I do. You used to tell me, when you were a wee 'un and our Máire did not want to listen, when she told you it was ungodly.'

'But it isn't, is it? You said so.'

'Nae, it's a gift. A gift from nature. And, although you haven't spoken of them, I know they're always with you.'

'I did dream, that first night after the wake. When I met Sebastian on the beach. I dreamt of a party in a grand house, and a garden filled with rose bushes.'

'You saw Carlyle House then. There once was a rose garden, and Sebastian Carlyle has planted one again.'

'After I went there looking for one!' Deirdre laughed.

'You didn't say.'

'No, it was foolish. But, after the dream, when he sent me those roses for my birthday, I wanted to know if he'd picked them from his own garden. I climbed up the wall beneath the house, and he saw me. The garden was a mess, and I told him so.'

'Indeed! Perhaps you wanted the dream to be real.'

'Why, why would I want that?'

Brigid smiled, 'And since then?'

'Later, it was Father trying to break down my bedroom door with an axe. But that was just me being afraid because … Wasn't it?'

'Perhaps. But you're safe with me now.'

'But then, the other night, I was running away from a man I thought I knew. He kept calling my name; but I didn't recognise the voice and I never saw his face. I'm afraid, Brigid. I don't like dreaming like that. Sometimes I'd just like the dreams to stop,' her eyes filled with tears. 'I feel so sad, Brigid. So alone without Ma, even without the Da I thought I knew.'

Brigid rested her hand on Deirdre's arm.

'You've been so good to me, Brigid, for as long as I can remember. But you're right. What about the future? What will happen to me now?' she hesitated. 'Sebastian is a good man. I know if I wanted anything, he would give it to me.'

'I know, child. Sebastian Carlyle seems like a good man. From everything I've seen, and what you've told me, I'm sure that's so. But you don't really know him, do you, not really?'

'What about the dreams?'

'Of course, you need to remember them, heed their warnings. But, more importantly, you need to listen to your heart. I know because that's how I found my Iain.'

'Your dreams told you he was your man?'

'I was so in love I don't even remember, child!' she laughed. 'But I never regretted one single day of my life with him.'

'I don't know what to feel about Sebastian. I just know ...'

'That, when you call him, he runs to your side?'

'Yes, that's it.'

'Love and need are different. And sometimes they make a good marriage. Many people settle for that and are content. But you can't pretend to have feelings for a man and then cast him aside when someone better comes along. If a man – like the laird – sees the prize he wants, believes it's within his grasp, he'll do everything to get it. But if he sees it slipping away, he'll do anything – and I do mean anything – to keep it. Sebastian Carlyle may be a good man, child, but he's a man ne'ertheless. Never go forgetting that.'

Chapter 25

Deirdre

Five days of school and then Saturday – four days before Christmas – the day of the Yuletide party at Carlyle House. Deirdre had thrown out her tartan skirt, along with the torn yellow blouse, the memory of both tarnished by her father's drunken assault. She had decided to wear jeans, a blouse and her ankle boots.

'Nay, child, you'll not be going to the Big House looking like some casual teenager, not if you're thinking seriously about Sebastian Carlyle,' Brigid insisted.

And so, Brigid found a remnant of red velvet in her fabric pile, left over from an old curtain project. By the time Deirdre had returned from school on Monday evening, she had cut out and tacked up a pattern for a calf-length skirt and a short waistcoat. She had also found a long-sleeved white t-shirt amongst Deirdre's clothes and lain everything out on the bed in Deirdre's room. On top, she had placed a small red garnet pendant with two small matching earrings.

'My Iain gave me these on our wedding day. I want you to have them.'

Once again, Deirdre's eyes filled with tears as Brigid hugged her.

'But you told me I shouldn't get serious.'

'No, child. I told you not to pretend,' she paused. 'So, will it be jeans or the red velvet?'

Deirdre laughed, 'The red velvet, Brigid. If I don't try, I'll never know, will I?'

Brigid drove fast, brakes squealing as she straightened out the bends of the small unpaved road leading down to Carlyle House.

'How do you like my new ride, Deirdre?'

'Aren't you perhaps driving a little fast, Brigid? Are you sure you can see in the gloaming?'

'My eyes are as good as they've ever been, except for a wee bit of a cataract in my right one. But I still see just fine. The car's automatic, so it'll slow down as it needs, as soon as I put my foot on the brake.'

As they turned the final bend, two sheep wandered lazily out into the middle of the road. For a moment, Brigid seemed confused by the white shapes caught in the glare of her high beams, belatedly slamming on the brakes and swerving sideways towards them, before screeching to a halt.

Brigid laughed nervously, 'Silly beasts, sheep. Wandering around in the dark when they should be bedded down.'

'Yes, Brigid. But they're probably not expecting a speed demon on the road at this time of night.'

'Och, well. It'll teach them to be more careful next time.'

*

The last rays of the evening light had disappeared over the horizon as they parked at the end of a long line of cars, which stretched up the track to the house. Cars and vans, and small trucks were also crammed into the beach car park, latecomers blocking the exit. Flares lit up the track leading to the house.

'Everyone's here!'

'Maybe so. It's a long time since a laird invited the villagers to his house, except to keep order on the estate or demand rents. Your Sebastian wants to impress.'

'Not mine, Brigid. Not mine.'

'Not yet, lass. But you watch yersel' tonight because they'll all be watching you.'

Deirdre laughed, 'I'll be on my best behaviour.'

Later, Deirdre would remember this moment, when she had really intended to do just that.

The entrance hall was filled to bursting with all the new arrivals milling around uncertainly together. Two of the lads from the village ceilidh band were setting up in the corner in front of the grandfather clock. Rory, the fiddler, was tuning up and Chas, the accordionist, was adjusting the height of their microphone. The stairs to the upstairs level had been roped off, but the double doors to the kitchen were latched open, food set out on the scrubbed pine table, drinks on the counter.

Brigid moved into the kitchen, and surveyed the chicken legs, slices of ham and salmon terrines, the pork pies and the bowls of salad, the individual portions of sherry trifle, slabs of fruit cake, and the plates of cheeses and homemade breads. She nodded at one of the servers and began to fill her plate. Deirdre poured herself a glass of sparkling water and went looking for Sebastian. She found him in the study talking to a trio of crofters, who were grumbling about the size of the open grazing land on their side of the hillside. Sebastian was wearing trews and a waistcoat in a bright blue tartan pattern, which she did not recognise at first, but which seemed familiar. He looked up for a moment, smiled at her and continued with his discussion. She returned to the kitchen. Glasses of wine had been laid out on trays. She helped herself to a prosecco. In the hall, the musicians had already started playing.

She looked around at all the faces, all the people she knew and recognised from her village and the surrounding area. Several were wearing their clan kilts or jackets or sashes. Most of the older folk were there, anxious to see what the inside of Carlyle House looked like under new management.

But there were very few young people, classmates from her school. She spotted Emily Gunn, however, clinging tightly onto Tom Mackay's arm. Tom had already left school and was working in the foundry in town. Emily was quieter than usual, her conversation a mere whisper in the surrounding hubbub. She waved as soon as she saw Deirdre, who considered – for a brief moment – crossing the hall to join them, when she was rescued by the arrival of Cathel and Ellen.

'How's your da?' Cathel asked.

'I don't know,' Deirdre looked away.

'You haven't been to see him then, in the hospital?'

'No.'

'Do you know when he's coming back?'

'Everything is alright on the farm, isn't it? There're no problems, are there? If you need any help, I can come over.'

'No, no, everything's just fine. I was wondering, that's all.'

'I don't know when he's getting out. Anyway, I'm staying with Brigid now.'

'Yes, I know. You told me,' he paused. 'What really happened, Deirdre? Was he drunk again and …?'

Ellen pulled Cathel closer and turned back to Deirdre.

'You're looking very glamorous tonight, Deirdre. That red velvet is perfect on you, and those garnets are gorgeous.'

Deirdre smiled, 'Thanks. All Brigid's idea.'

The music seemed to get louder, the rhythm faster.

'Are we going to do some reels, or what?' Cathel turned to Ellen, 'I want to take my lass out on the floor and whirl her around a couple of times, show her off a bit.'

'I think it's Sebastian's privilege to start that, isn't it?' Ellen winked at Deirdre.

'Of course. I'll go and break him loose from all those old crofters and their grumbling.'

But when Deirdre returned to the study, Sebastian was no

127

longer there. Instead, she found him in the kitchen, talking to Janet and Maud Munro, who were smiling and giggling at something he had just said.

Sebastian looked up as soon as he saw Deirdre.

'These ladies are looking resplendent tonight, don't you think Deirdre, in their new lacy shawls? I just told them the colours were a perfect match for their twinkling eyes.'

Deirdre smiled, 'Yes indeed, Mr Carlyle, they are,' she paused, 'but they're calling for the dancing to start in the hall, and they won't start without you.'

'I'm not sure I'd know how to keep up, let alone lead anyone in a Scottish reel, if that's what you're suggesting.'

'Och, Mr Carlyle,' Deirdre made a mock bow, 'you're far too modest. Besides, you have me to teach ye! And we'll start with an easy one, won't we ladies?' she turned to the Munro sisters. 'An eightsome reel!'

She grabbed his hand and pulled him after her into the hall, where a great cheer went up.

'Well, she's a saucy one to be sure,' Janet said in a raised voice, when she noticed Brigid nearby.

'Aye, that's as maybe, Janet,' Maud Munro answered. 'But I'm thinking she's got the right, looking as she does tonight.'

'I'm not sure it'll turn out well. What do you think, Brigid?' Janet turned to face Brigid. 'He's twice her age at least.'

'May and September,' Brigid paused. 'Or perhaps May and July.'

'What are ye talking about?'

'I saw a film once – a romance between an older man and a younger woman. He was quite a lot older, but it seemed to work out alright.'

'Is that what you're calling this, a romance? Well, well, we'll see, won't we? Let's away, Maud, to see how the dancing lesson is going.'

128

Janet linked arms with her sister, and strode off, leaving Brigid with a smile on her face.

By the time Brigid had poured herself another glass of wine and moved out into the hall, the eightsome reel was well underway. Three sets of dancers were whirling and twisting around each other, setting to their partners and pulling hand over hand in their circles. Onlookers were lined up around the sides of the hall. Others crowded at the doors to the kitchen and the study. All were clapping their hands and tapping their feet, and whooping as the dance progressed. The shouts and the music, and the warm smiles of everyone in the vicinity was infectious. And, it was impossible, Brigid thought, not to be drawn to the magical combination of Deirdre's self-assured presence, her gleaming red hair rising and falling as she moved to the steps of the dance, the garnets glinting in the lamplight; beside the unabashed enthusiasm of her partner, who was completely at her mercy. Even Sebastian's missteps as he turned in the wrong direction, or leaned forward to take the hand of the wrong partner, were the source of good-humoured comments from the sidelines.

So, amidst the noise and the warmth and the bonhomie, nobody noticed the front door open until the final eightsome chains had been completed, each partner had bowed to the other, and the music died down. Only then did they feel the cold outdoor air creep into the room and see the shadow of James McIntyre fall across the floor of the makeshift ballroom.

'So, this is where I find ye, my daughter, on the day they tell me I can come home from the hospital. No fire in the hearth, no light in the window. I had to go doon to the pub to see the notice in the window, about the party at the house of the sassenach laird.'

The room fell silent. Rory's bow poised in mid-air, dancers still clasping their partners, arms in readiness for the next reel. Everyone stared at James, a large white bandage wrapped around his head, a plaster across the bridge of his broken nose.

Sebastian stepped forward, his hand firmly in Deirdre's.

'It's good to see you, Mr McIntyre. Will you join us? Have a drink and a bite to eat?'

'I'll no' be mixing with the likes of you, Carlyle. You and your people have taken everything from us highland folk. And,' he paused, noticing Sebastian's hand, 'you'd best be letting my lass go. She's none of yours, nor ever will be.'

Janet whispered in her sister's ear. Brigid moved into the light.

'This is all your doing, woman, isn't it? Taking my girl away with your nasty talk, my Máire barely gone to the other side. Ye'll rot in hell for this, see if you don't.'

Deirdre pulled away from Sebastian.

'That's enough, Da. This has nothing to do with Brigid. We both know that.'

'She's poisoned your mind, lass. What harm is there in a father wanting a little affection from his own wee lass when he's grieving?'

More people had now crowded into the doorway from the kitchen, the clatter of plates and the clinking of glasses abandoned as they waited and watched. James looked around at his audience and then turned back to glare at Deirdre.

'And I'll no' have you cavorting in public. I can see fine that's what you've been doing – all tarted up. Sweating too, I wouldn't doubt! A regular hussy, now that your ma is not here to mind you. So ye'll come with me *now*, girl.'

'No, Father. I'll not be coming home with you.'

'Indeed! There's no-one here'll dare stop me. You're still my daughter, and there's an end to it.'

'It's too late for that. I'll not come home again, not tonight, not ever. Do you want me to tell everyone why? To tell them what really happened?'

There was an audible intake of breath as her words hung

130

in the air.

As James made a move towards Deirdre, his hand raised, Brigid stepped between them. For a moment, James' hand stopped in mid-air and then he roughly pushed Brigid aside. She staggered back, her feet losing traction. Only Cathel's quick reactions prevented her from falling and smashing her head on the parquet floor.

'No, Mr McIntyre,' Sebastian raised his voice, as he also stepped forward. 'You've just shown your true colours, hitting out like that, and threatening more! You're not fit to be called Miss McIntyre's father. You've forfeited that right. Everyone here can see it.'

'Miss McIntyre is it now? She's no longer my wee girl Deirdre. That's the truth of it, isn't it? You've claimed her, as your right. She's for *your* bed. The laird will have his way, with the land *and* the women.'

'You can say what you like about me, sir. But you'll apologise here, now, both to your daughter and to her aunt.'

'I'll no' apologise to my kin, nor to the auld witch either. I'll awa' hame to my own hearth, for now. But this is not the end. I'll be getting the law to sort you all out. And it'll not be that Constable Mackenzie, who you've got in your back pocket either, with his lying reports of what happened to me in my own house.'

And, with that, James turned and left, slamming the door behind him, as a final blast of cold air was suddenly sucked into the room.

Chapter 26

Meghan

As soon as Cathel opened the door, it was as if I'd returned to Christmases past, before my father died, when we all still played 'happy families'. An only child, I'd enjoyed visiting aunts and uncles, playing with cousins, existing for a few hours in places where chaos and noise were acceptable. The farmhouse was all of this. Aromas of roasting meat, and a pudding – rich with fruit and rum – steaming on the stove. A medley of popular songs playing at low volume from speakers set on either side of the fireplace. A Christmas tree in the corner, with flickering, coloured lights reflecting on the ceiling above. Brennan and his younger brother, Craig, racing up and down the stairs, chasing each other with robotic plastic figures, emitting warnings of death and destruction to all who opposed them. The years had taken all this away. Names and faces lingered, but my extended family had all drifted apart, too busy with our own lives and our own new friends to keep in touch.

Cassie sniffed the air, alert and excited. She watched the boys, tail wagging. She sidled up to Ellen, who was stirring the gravy in the kitchen. And, from a distance, she eyed the old man who sat motionless, in an armchair in front of the fire, in the other room. James McIntyre looked up briefly as Cathel took me over to meet him; and then nodded and turned away. His eyes seemed glazed, uncomprehending. Cathel smiled and led me back into the kitchen to sit with Ellen.

As the meal progressed, I noticed McIntyre's pale eyes staring at me from time to time. I wondered how he felt as a guest in his own house. Perhaps, like me, he was remembering how it used to be. What was uppermost in his memory now? Disappointment and regret, or happier days, filled with love and laughter? Could he still distinguish between them?

The remains of Christmas pudding and brandy butter were already congealing on our plates, and Cathel had gone to uncork another bottle of wine, when I volunteered to pull a cracker with the old man. I leaned across the table, a red and gold paper offering between us.

'Who did you say you are then?'

His eyes held mine, as if weighing up the possibilities.

'I'm Meghan, Meghan Bell.'

'You remember, James. You met her earlier,' Ellen leaned over and patted the old man's hand.

'Aye, I remember well what yon Cathel told me. But that's no' her name.'

'Yes, James, it is,' Ellen paused. 'Remember. I told you she's staying in the *bàthach*. We converted the old byre into a rental cottage.'

'Well, she has you all fooled then.'

'How's that?' Cathel had returned to the table.

'This here's my girl, my Deirdre.'

'Oh no, James. You know that canna be.'

'I know what I see with my own eyes, boy.'

'I'm Meghan,' I repeated. 'I'm living in …'

'You're still holding with that story, are ye? Is that what the auld witch told you to say?'

Ellen turned to Cathel, and mouthed, 'Stop him now!'

'Brigid is dead, James. She died many years since.'

'Well, none too soon, my boy, if you ask me. Nothing but a troublemaker that one. Filling my girl's head with all kinds of nonsense, suggesting …'

'James, please, enough of this. Let me get you a wee dram.'

'I'll take the dram, but no' before … You disappeared, girl. I didn't know where you were.'

'Deirdre didn't disappear. She left. But this is Meghan, remember? Meghan.'

'Did ye ken, Cathel, where she was all along? What business was it of yours to keep a daughter from her father?'

'James, we don't need to do this now. It's over. Deirdre's gone.'

'Over? Over, you say, when she's sitting across the table holding out that … that thing.'

'James, you know that canna be.'

'Och, man, you've lost it,' James laughed. 'I knew you'd return, girl. You've a duty to look after me, like your ma told you.'

'Mr McIntyre, my name is Meghan. I'm staying in the barn.'

'What need have ye of the barn, when this is my house? You have your own bedroom here, upstairs. And you can keep your da comforted at night.'

He leaned across the table and grabbed my arm. I pulled back quickly, scraping my chair on the tiled floor as I stood up, but James tightened his grip. He dragged me forwards so that I fell across the table, ramming my chin onto the wood. Still he held on. Cassie, who had been sitting quietly in the corner, leapt up barking and baring her teeth. She clamped her teeth round James' ankle and began to tug him away. James let out a yell and tried to stand up to kick her away. But as he loosened his hold on my arm, his knees gave way, and he collapsed onto the floor. Craig started to cry. And Cassie ran to hide under my chair.

*

Half an hour later, James was sitting on the sofa, cradling a large tumbler of whisky, his bandaged ankle elevated on a cushion as he stared into the flames of the fire. Brennan and Craig were upstairs playing a new video game, and I was sitting at the table with Ellen and Cathel, each of us with a whisky. I still felt a little shaky.

'I'm so sorry,' Ellen began. 'I had no idea he'd assume you were …'

'Perhaps I shouldn't have pulled away so suddenly. Perhaps I should have gone along with his illusion.'

'It's nothing to do with what you did, Meghan, or didn't do. He's obviously confused. This may be the last year we can bring him here, Cathel.'

'Aye, maybe so.'

'But what happened to Deirdre? Why did she leave?'

'She left her father's house, this farmhouse, because …' Cathel hesitated. 'Because he was trying to mess with her, after her ma died.'

'And she left …' Ellen smiled, 'because she fell in love.'

I remembered the cottage which Ellen had shown me on the Carlyle Estate, where Deirdre and Brigid had once lived. The blackened shell where Ellen had said 'they were not inside' when it burned down.

'With the laird of Carlyle House?'

'Aye, that was the beginning, wasn't it, Cathel?'

Chapter 27

Deirdre

In the silence that followed, Cathel's arm still round her shoulders, Brigid clutched at her chest.

'My pills, son. In my handbag. On a chair in the kitchen.'

A few minutes later, lying feet up on the sofa in the study, a glass of water in hand, she smiled weakly at Deirdre.

'I'll not be going anytime soon, child. It's just my angina. The pill will do it while I rest.'

'Dr Ferguson's here, Brigid.'

'I'm not needing a doctor. He knows that.'

'Well, I'm here now anyway,' Ronnie Ferguson laughed. 'I nearly had a turn myself out there. I'd forgotten how much fun the eightsome was, but also how much energy was needed to keep going until the end. If you don't mind, my dear, I'll just listen to your heart and then sit here for a wee bit and catch my breath.'

Outside, in the hall, Maud Munro turned to her sister.

'What a terrible man! No wonder the poor wee lass left home. I'm surprised that our Máire lasted so long living in that house.'

'Aye, it would seem that something's really wrong there,' Janet replied.

'I think we've misjudged her, Janet. She's become such a beauty too.'

'Maybe so, maybe so. He'd surely be tempted by such a lass in his own house.'

'Och, don't even say that, Janet. That's a wicked thought.'

'I say things as I see them, sister. But the lass is well out of it, I'd say. Let's away in and sit with Brigid a while.'

'I think not. We'd best not be bothering her now. You'll just start asking questions and upsetting the woman.'

'I wouldn't.'

'Aye, we both know you would. We'll go get ourselves another trifle and a glass more of the bubbly wine.'

As the two sisters returned to the buffet in the kitchen, others remained in the hallway, awkwardly waiting for the musicians to resume playing or wondering if the party was over and it was time to leave. Sebastian clapped his hands from the study doorway, and everyone drew back, making space.

'I'm so sorry for that interruption. But ...'

'Nay, man, that was none of your doing,' someone called from the back.

'I hope you'll all stay a little longer. Mrs Macleod, Brigid, is resting and is no worse for wear I believe. Neither she nor I, nor even her niece, Deirdre, would like this to spoil your evening. It's still early. There's plenty of food and drink for you to enjoy, and I'm sure that Rory and Chas here have plenty more reels they're waiting to play for you.'

Rory played a quick riff on the fiddle.

'And you, sir, will you be trying out some more of those fancy steps of yours?' Another voice called out from the darkness.

There was a peal of laughter from the crowd.

Sebastian smiled, 'If my teacher will join me, I'd be delighted to provide you with some more entertainment.'

'You're the perfect host then, man.'

Someone started a rhythmic clapping, and several others joined in.

Sebastian turned and went in search of Deirdre.

*

137

The mood had changed. When they had arrived, Deirdre had noticed eyes turning in her direction. She had seen herself in the hall mirror as they prepared to leave Brigid's house. The schoolgirl had disappeared. A rather handsome young woman had taken her place. And this was to be the night when Sebastian would take her hand and show everyone how they were, how they could be, together. But most of the guests were of her parents' generation and older, and were wary of the new uppity lass in their midst. She could see it in their eyes. She could only be sure that Cathel and Ellen were on her side, and Brigid, of course. But when she heard the music and envisioned herself dancing with Sebastian, all her doubts vanished. She would throw caution to the winds and be herself. What could possibly go wrong when the rhythms and the sounds of a highland ceilidh were in full swing? It was in her blood and it ran in the veins of every generation who had ever lived here.

But after her father's outburst, there was another murmur filling the rooms of Carlyle House. Some were shocked and curious; others were sympathetic, but also curious. Sebastian had become the local hero, authoritative and amiable at the same time. Deirdre, on the other hand, had become a pawn in the male world where might was right. It was not a role she wanted to assume. She had stood up for herself, spoken honestly of her feelings and resisted her father's demands. But, in the end, it was Sebastian who had won.

So she sat with Brigid in the study, holding her hand, wondering about her own next move, watching as the old woman finally fell asleep at the fireside.

'Come, Deirdre. Let's get some food in you, another drink or two, and join the others in some more of those reels you promised me,' Sebastian stood beside her, his hand reaching forward.

'I'm not sure I can, not now, after ...'

'You mustn't let them see you care.'

'Why not, when I do?'

'It's a sign of weakness. You're a strong young woman,' he paused. 'That's what I loved about you, from the beginning.'

'But what will happen now, to me, to Brigid?'

'Let's worry about that tomorrow. You can both stay here tonight, out of harm's way. I'll take care of you. I want to. I think you know that.'

Deirdre smiled. But, she wondered, would she lose control of her own life by handing herself over to Sebastian's care? Influence, age and gender were all on his side. Before her mother's death, the future had looked very different.

Tomorrow, in the light of a new highland dawn, she would climb up the hillside to the Eagle's Nest and talk to her friend. Tonight, however, she was hungry, and she certainly needed another drink. And, out there, the music was calling. She even imagined she could hear the skirl of the pipes.

Chapter 28

Deirdre

As they drove back into the village the next morning, Deirdre at the wheel of Brigid's new car, Sebastian following in the Land Rover, there were very few people out and about. Some were still in bed, sleeping off the aftereffects of the previous night's festivities. Others had returned to their regular Sunday routines – some to the kirk, Marge and Fergus readying themselves for their midday openings, and a few crofters checking on their animals. The temperature had dropped again overnight, fields covered in a thick layer of frost. Snow was forecast for the next few days. Out at sea, a mist was hovering on the horizon, the water glassy and still.

Over breakfast, Deirdre had told Sebastian about Iolaire. She had not really intended to, only mentioning that she was going for a walk when she returned to the village. Brigid had smiled and nodded. Sebastian had been curious. And so, he had piled more peat onto Brigid's fire while he waited for Deirdre to change into warm clothes, before they started the climb up the hillside together. It would be an opportunity, he had said, to talk about her plans for the future now that her father had returned and was spoiling for a fight.

They skirted the McIntyre land, taking a wide route around the village, outside the fence which closed off the village's common grazing land from the surrounding moorland. Deirdre strode confidently ahead, jumping the

140

streams which trickled down the hillside and avoiding the boggiest ground, with Sebastian following her lead.

When they reached the slope leading up to the eyrie, there was no sign of Iolaire.

'Has he gone for the winter?'

'He's never flown far away, even in winter. After I returned him to his nest, I came each day to visit, sometimes fed him by hand. Eagles mate for life and like to return to the same nest each year to breed. Let's sit and wait for him.'

They found two large rocks to rest on, Brigid's house barely visible in the crystalline landscape below.

Sebastian sighed, 'What a view!'

Deirdre smiled, 'Iolaire stays for me too. We understand each other.'

'You believe that, don't you?'

'And you don't?'

'I think we interpret nature in our own way. We see what we want to see, draw conclusions to make them fit our preconceived ideas and desires. We do that with people. Why shouldn't it be the same when we look at the natural world?'

'You say that, believe that, because you're a townie at heart. And,' she hesitated, 'because you only trust what you can see with your eyes, or have read about in books or heard on the radio or TV.'

'This is what Brigid has taught you?'

'She was the one who helped me understand that I too have the gift of *an dà-shealladh* – second sight. My mother called it ungodly and wicked.'

'And how does this gift work exactly?'

'I dream.'

'We all dream, and sometimes we even remember our dreams. They're supposed to help us put all the good and bad things, which happened to us previously, into our subconscious. They allow us to move on with our lives.'

'Yes, but my dreams, our dreams, happen.'

'Happen? As in the future?'

'Sometimes not exactly as I first imagined, but yes.'

'For example?'

'Okay,' Deirdre laughed. 'You sent me roses for my birthday.'

'You liked them, didn't you?'

'Yes, but let me tell you the whole story. After I saw them, I wondered if you'd picked them from your own garden at Carlyle House. Although, Brigid told me it was the wrong time of year. But still, I was curious.'

Sebastian laughed, 'I remember.'

'Yes. But then, a few weeks later, you had Archie laying out the garden with lots of rose bushes.'

'But where does the dreaming come into it?'

'The night of my mother's funeral, the first time Da came into my room and touched me …'

'He did this before?'

'Yes, but that's not what I'm trying to tell you. That night, I'd met you earlier, down at the beach.'

'You weren't too keen when I found you …'

'Right. Well, after that, before Father got home, I had a dream. I was all dressed up, walking down a long hallway. It was a party, lots of people nodding and smiling at me. I recognised the tartans everyone was wearing, except one I'd never seen before. But now I see it's the same one your trews were made of last night.'

'The Carlyle – from the Borders. That is odd.'

'Yes and, in my dream, I also looked out one of the windows. There was a huge rose garden, rows and rows of bushes laid out in the moonlight, sheltered from the sea by a stone wall,' she paused. 'I'd never been to Carlyle House before, ever. Nor even down the road to Annanside Bay. When I told Brigid my dream, she said your grandfather had planted a beautiful rose garden, just like the one I'd described. But, when he inherited it, your father let it go to wrack and ruin.'

'It could all be coincidental.'

'Okay. So, tell me about the roses you sent for my birthday.'

'What about them?'

'How did you choose that particular bouquet?'

'I rang a florist in town and told them I wanted some flowers for a girl on her birthday. The assistant asked me your age so, eighteen roses. She suggested white roses, for innocence.'

Deirdre laughed, 'And the orange rose?'

'She also asked me if I liked you? She didn't ask me my age, or she might've misinterpreted my answer.'

'She didn't mention the meaning of an orange rose then?'

'She might have. I don't remember. I simply said you were the most beautiful girl I'd ever seen and you had gorgeous red hair,' he grinned. 'I didn't tell her you were a feisty little madam, or goodness knows what colours she would've added to the bunch!'

Deirdre playfully punched him in the chest and laughed again.

'Orange represents passion.'

'Not so innocent then!' he paused. 'So how does this all work? You dream you're at a party where you see my tartan and a rose garden in the moonlight. Later, I send you roses for your birthday, you go snooping around my back garden, and I decide to clean up the place.'

'The details matter. The connections linking past, present and future.'

'If you're trying to tell me we were meant to meet, I'll go along with it.'

'But you still don't believe, do you?'

'There's only one thing I know for certain …'

'And that is?'

'From the first moment I saw you, even when you scolded me at the pub for interrupting your mother's wake, I was in awe. I'd never felt like that before. I knew it was foolish – there was no reason to think you'd even look twice at me. But I couldn't get you out of my head.'

Sebastian leaned forward and took both of Deirdre's hands in his own.

'Marry me, Deirdre. I'll look after you, protect you from your father, give you anything you ask for.'

'But I haven't even finished school yet.'

'No, I know. And that's important to you, I understand. But if we just agreed to get engaged, for now. You could be safe. You could stay with Brigid, if you'd like, at one of the cottages on the estate. And I'd have you near, knowing that one day, we could be together as man and wife.'

'And what if, later, I change my mind, or you do?'

'I'm not a man to change my mind. And I'll do everything in my power to make you happy, so you don't either.'

'I don't know what to say. You've …'

'I've spoken too soon, haven't I?' he smiled. 'But what of your dreams, Deirdre? They told you I'd be coming along. So, in this world where you say you – and Brigid – have second sight, at what point do you consciously follow them? Or do you just wait and see?'

Deirdre suddenly turned and pulled away from Sebastian.

'Look!' she said, pointing up the hillside. 'There's Iolaire!'

Sebastian laughed, 'Saved by the eagle!'

The bird swept down in freefall, his sharp staccato calls echoing around them, golden-patched wings extended, head forward, focused on the scene below the eyrie. Deirdre raised her arms overhead and waved them from side to side, as Iolaire negotiated the air currents with his flight feathers. Sebastian ducked as he felt the beat of the eagle's wings close overhead, stirring the air, talons stretched below, readied for landing, or snatching prey. And then the bird rose again, made two circles overhead, before settling on the rocks above.

'Iolaire,' Deirdre said, 'this is my friend, Sebastian. And he has just asked me to marry him.'

The bird cocked his head to one side, as he usually did when Deirdre started a conversation, and listened.

Chapter 29

Meghan

Cassie and I walked downhill, away from the farmhouse and our cottage, away from the old man whose fading memories still haunted him.

I had never known Deirdre – never even seen a photo of her. I could only imagine how she must have looked, only just turned eighteen and already irresistibly beautiful. From our first days here, in the village pub, Liane had forbidden Dougal to speak her name. At the pageant, it seemed that Cathel had wanted to say more about little Aileen's song of the shipwreck and the broken-hearted Annie who longed to join her lost lover. But Ellen had quickly changed the subject, and I'd begun to wonder why. Was Deirdre also broken-hearted when her lover, the laird, had disappeared?

Deirdre had fallen in love, moved onto the laird's estate. Presumably to be near him, but also to get away from her father. James McIntyre was a strong man. I could still feel his vice-like grip on my arm. How much more powerful he must have been when he was younger, when he and his daughter had lived together in the farmhouse. And how much more frightening. But why had Sebastian set fire to the cottage where Deirdre and Brigid had lived? Also, falling in love with the laird of Carlyle House, according to Ellen, was 'just the beginning'. Where had their lives taken them? Where and how had it ended? There were so many strands to this story, half-told from the perceptions of bystanders.

Deirdre had apparently died. But where was Sebastian Carlyle now? Had they met up secretly and gone away together as James believed? Ellen had said Sebastian did not wait for Deirdre. So, what had happened before or after their supposed elopement to make him abandon her? And how had she died? In an accident? Had she been murdered?

I was afraid I'd never know the answers, afraid that the truth had been buried with Deirdre and Brigid, and perhaps Sebastian also. I had to know the whole story. Deirdre's life had started to dominate my imagination. I vowed, then and there, to start my research on what had happened to Sebastian. He, at least, might still be alive. I would make it my first project for the New Year.

*

For several days after Christmas, a biting wind blew inland, sweeping the village and the hillside with bitterly cold Arctic air. Each morning, I walked through the village with Cassie and stood on the clifftop watching the waves crashing below. I found the waves hypnotic, calming, reassuring. Here, I could feel the wind on my face, snuggled into the warmth of my anorak. Even Cassie had a little winter coat of her own.

It was an escape from the house and the sudden changes in temperature which I had associated with an unseen presence. Lately, it seemed these occurrences were less frequent, less obvious. Perhaps I really had imagined everything. Perhaps it was merely a phenomenon caused by the cold wind, which found cracks and crevices in the walls of the old stone barn, seeking the vacuum left by the warmth of the logs burning in the fireplace. Even Cassie seemed less alarmed, now only occasionally huddling closer to me on the sofa for warmth when the drift of cold air passed by. After all, what did our being here have to do with anything which might have occurred in a barn many years ago? As for the guidebook being moved on my bedside table and the bed linens being

147

out of order … Perhaps, I'd been careless in my bedmaking or in returning the book to the nightstand before turning off the light the night before. I'd become noticeably more casual about life since I'd arrived in the village, less of a neatnik. Richard would've been delighted.

*

New Year's Eve saw me down at the pub, eating a late supper, perched at the bar beside Dougal once again. Everyone, it seemed, was waiting for the Hogmanay celebrations to begin. Ellen had told me about the bonfires, which would be lit all along the coastline just as the old year turned to the new. But Dougal, already a few drinks in, was quieter than usual, sometimes lost in thought; and I felt the need to break the silences.

'Why the bonfires, Dougal? Is it an old or a new tradition? And is it local?

'Och, it goes way back. A wee bit Celtic, a wee bit Viking. Like *Samhain*, it's all about the sun and the light.'

'*Samhain*?'

'The Day of the Dead – Hallowe'en celebrated the Druid way. People die, and their spirits cross to the other side, the dark side. At *Samhain*, we remember them and call them home.'

'Ellen said Brigid used to celebrate Hallowe'en very differently.'

'Aye, because it wasna a time of silliness to her or to many of us older folk. It meant something. It was about family, ancestors.'

'What was Brigid like?'

'She was sae bonny, and I really wanted ….' he looked away briefly. 'She was a wee bit older than me, and I was shy …'

'You, shy?' I laughed.

'Aye. And she went off and married yon other feller.'

148

'So, what did you do?'

'I joined the navy, went around the world. I thought aboot moving to Australia. But I could never settle awa from the Highlands. And I could never settle on another girl, either,' he paused. 'It wasna just that she was pretty. She was an' all that. But she was different, clever, knew all sorts of things that many never know,' he paused again. 'Some called her a witch.'

'Like James McIntyre?'

'Aye. And others too. But she was never afeart of their talk,' he lowered his voice. 'Like the lass Deirdre. They were close, those two, turning their backs against the unbelievers.'

Liane walked up to our end of the bar.

'What are you two talking about then?'

'I was asking Dougal about the bonfires,' I answered quickly.

'A great tradition – lighting fires, looking forward to spring. I love seeing the wee lambs again. Will you be staying for that?'

'Oh yes,' I smiled. 'I'll be propping up your bar, with Dougal here, until summer.'

'Well, that'll be good for business at least. But don't you go believing everything this old blether tells you.'

*

Outside, the wind was cold and gusty. But it had blown away all the clouds, and an almost-full moon shone overhead. The sea was choppy and erratic, and it glinted and sparkled in the moonlight. I remembered so many New Year's Eves, crowded into small rooms, drinking too much, dancing with strangers, and kissing everyone as the bells tolled midnight. But, tonight, I was amongst families and neighbours, people who had known each other for generations. I was a stranger here; but I did not feel out of place or alone as I had so often before.

149

In the darkness, without warning, a hand grabbed mine. Instinctively, I pulled back, startled. I looked down and saw little Craig.

'Hello, Meghan,' he said. 'Are you afeart of the dark?'

'No, not now that you're holding my hand.'

'Me neither,' he said. 'But I've lost Mum and Dad, and Brennan in the dark.'

'We'll just wait together then … until they find us.'

A huge crowd had gathered, and there was an air of excitement as people chanted the traditional countdown for the bonfire to be lit. In the distance, all along the coast, other villages lit their own bonfires, shining beacons in the night. Faces glowed in the firelight. There was laughter and squealing as the fire crackled and tiny burning splinters of wood were carried on the wind, drifting skywards and dying slowly as they fell. Each blackened ember, each fading flame a faint memory.

As we walked back to the farmhouse, guided by Cathel's torch, Craig skipped along beside me, swinging my arm with his as he continued to hold tightly onto my hand. The new year felt like a new beginning. I had come here to isolate myself from people. And now I realised, before, I'd made my life too complicated and cluttered my mind with expectations, instead of appreciating each day, each person, each experience. From now on, I promised myself that I'd stand on firm ground, taking each day in my stride, one challenge at a time.

Everyone was going to my cottage for the first dram of the new year, and I'd left the outside light above the front door switched on. It was motion-activated. As I let go of Craig's hand and moved towards the door, the light came on, but the door was no longer a bright, glossy white. The outline of a man's head had been painted in black across its surface, huge branching antlers sprouting from a mass of shaggy locks. The paint was still wet, dripping onto the doorstep. For a moment, I stood staring at it. Half-man, half-beast, he looked angry, disdainful, and terrifying. Behind me, I heard Craig screaming.

'The Horned God,' Ellen said quietly.

Chapter 30

Deirdre

'So, what did you tell your Mr Carlyle in the end, lass?'

'I didn't tell him anything. I don't even really remember what I said to Iolaire. It felt odd talking to him, with Sebastian sitting beside me and listening.'

'Perhaps Sebastian understood you a little better, after.'

'He said so, but ...'

Overnight, the sea mist had crept onshore, closing in on the village, hiding the familiar, creating ghostly outlines in the half-light. Even Brigid's front gate was invisible from the kitchen window. Only the muffled bleating of the wintering flocks in the fields beyond reminded Deirdre that life continued as usual outside the cottage walls. She briefly wondered how her father was coping alone and then dismissed the thought. She could shelter in place with Brigid in the village for a day or two; but soon daily routines would be restored. James would return to his regular nightly visits to the pub. And Brigid's cottage was just next door. It was a threat she could not ignore.

'I can't stay here, can I, Brigid?'

'Nae, lass, I think that it'd not be safe, not in the long term. I'm an old woman, and I can't protect you from a violent man when the drink's in him.'

'So, I should accept Sebastian, agree to get engaged, move to a house on the Carlyle Estate?'

'What do you really feel about the man? You said he'd do

anything for you. But he's not just offering you alternative accommodation, he's offering you his life, *until death do you part*. And you, you'd be promising the same. It's no' a promise to be taken lightly, lass. It has consequences.'

'I could move away, to the city, like you did. I could get a job, find a place to live, take night classes.'

'Aye, you could do all that. But you'd find the city a cold place alone.'

'You could come with me.'

'I'm old, Deirdre. I want to spend the last of my days here, surrounded by the sounds of the hills and the turning of the tides. I want to remember how it was when my Iain and I were together. I don't want to die hearing the traffic pass outside my window.'

'I'm sorry, I shouldn't have asked.'

A log shifted in the fireplace, orange flame turning blue as the last of the carbon was exhausted. Below, the peat glowed steadily.

'I really do like Sebastian. He makes me laugh and we talk a lot. And my dreams told me he was coming, didn't they?'

'Aye, it would seem so.'

'But?'

'He's offering you his love, and his passion too. What will you offer him, when he holds your hand at night and looks for love in your eyes, when he takes you to his bed and wants to feel the passion in your body?'

'I've never been touched like that except by my da. And that was horrible.'

'Of course! That's not love. It goes against nature. But I was never frightened or unwilling with my Iain. You won't be either, with the right man.'

For a few moments, the only sound in the room was the hiss of steam as flames took hold of the topmost log, and the logs below settled lower onto the peat.

153

'Sebastian's really quite attractive, isn't he? And he's not made a pass at me this whole time. He makes me feel safe. Perhaps,' she smiled, 'being a little older, he'll have learned a few bedroom tricks and it'll be fun.'

Brigid laughed, 'Oh, lass, you were always the one with the answers!'

*

As the first flakes of snow swirled downwards, clearing away the mist falling in the fading light of the afternoon, Deirdre called Sebastian and agreed to accept his offer of accommodation. She and Brigid would spend Christmas in the village, and then move into a cottage on the Carlyle Estate as the new year turned. She would need time, she said, to consider the bigger question of an engagement.

The following morning, they awoke to a whiteout. The heaviest snowfall in more than a decade had made all the roads impassable. Power and communication lines had collapsed. Villages were cut off. Farmers and crofters struggled to feed and shelter their animals.

As the days of isolation strung out, Sebastian began to make plans. And Deirdre waited each night, in her sleep, for a sign which would lead her to make the right decision.

Chapter 31

Deirdre

As soon as the world had been restored to some semblance of normality with the beginnings of a thaw, Sebastian called. Deirdre could hear the excitement in his voice as they spoke; but she was still unable to give him the answer he wanted. Instead, she talked of the practicalities of the move – how she would collect everything she needed from the McIntyre farm, the daily school run, and how the new household would function. Sebastian laughed and promised to take care of everything.

Christmas came and went. Deirdre spent the season with Brigid and Fergus and his family. Sebastian had flown south to stay with friends. And, once or twice, Deirdre's thoughts turned again to her father. Despite everything, she had loved him and still worried about him. But Brigid reminded her that there was no going back, only the future to look forward to, her future to consider.

*

And then it was New Year's Eve, the night of the village Hogmanay celebration and the lighting of the beacons along the coastline.

Above the beach where Deirdre first met Sebastian, a small pillar of rocks had been erected, a pit at its centre filled with dark, compacted peat and covered with fresh kindling. It would not be lit until midnight. Despite a partial melting

155

of the snow, the temperatures continued to drop each night below freezing point; most of the villagers planned to hunker down indoors until the last minute. Each family prepared their own traditional Hogmanay meal. For some, like Brigid, it was bowls of steaming cock-a-leekie soup. For others, haggis or meat pies, mashed neeps and tatties. In each household, it was a time for sharing memories and food, and toasting everything and everyone with tankards of beer and large drams of whisky until the time came for them to leave the warmth of their own firesides.

As she walked down the road to the cliffside, arm-in-arm with Brigid, Deirdre could hear Rory playing the pipes, the strains of the music drifting across the moors, fading in and out with the gusting wind. And, as the last few minutes of the old year ticked away, Deirdre looked around. Most people had formed groups of family, friends, neighbours. But no-one stood alone. And no-one looked like Sebastian or her father.

The countdown began, the beacon was lit and the flames caught the kindling quickly. A shout went up, and Rory began to play the familiar introduction to *Auld Lang Syne*. Everyone knew the words, swaying to the music as they sang. A group of children from the local primary school stood with their teacher beside the beacon and sang the Gaelic words. Deirdre took Brigid by the hand and joined the group.

The song ended and people moved around, shaking hands, some hugging each other, others calling to friends to join them at their house.

Deirdre looked out across the shoreline and saw beacons lit on other cliffsides and other hilltops. Every Hogmanay beacon held a promise. Since the time when the Vikings had occupied this land, generations had taken this moment to look forward to the return of the sun, and the spring equinox. A time when day and night were in perfect balance, light and dark in equilibrium. It brought the renewal of life in the glens and moors, the hills and the mountains, and the arrival of lambs and calves in the fields below the village.

But tonight, Deirdre could feel the cold wind on her cheeks, the stinging in her eyes. She had expected Sebastian to be here. She had wanted to relax, feel the warmth of his hand in hers as she had done up at the Auld Village at *Samhain*. In three more days, she and Brigid would be living in the promised cottage on the Carlyle Estate. He would be near at hand every day and every night. But would it be forever? For her forever? If he had come tonight, she would have felt surer, safer. His absence felt like desertion. Brigid hugged her closer. And Deirdre knew that she felt it too.

Chapter 32

Meghan – January 2018

It was more than an hour before Ellen could persuade the boys to go upstairs to bed. And then only because I'd agreed to let Cassie sleep on Craig's bed.

Brennan wanted to believe it had been a joke and suggested the possibility to Cathel. His eyes locked on his father's as he spoke, seeking reassurance that it was as simple as that. Craig had hunkered down on the sofa beside Cassie. But when Ellen insisted I spend the night at the farmhouse, we all sensed this was more than a Hogmanay prank.

I clicked on my mobile, but there was no signal.

'The internet's down, again. You can't look it up tonight, Meghan.'

'Who is the Horned God, Ellen? And why would someone paint him on my front door?'

'Some kind of Celtic guardian, I think. As for why someone would …'

'Not a good sign, that's all I know. All those Celtic gods aye had two sides to them.'

'Meghan doesn't want to hear that, Cathel.'

'I'll paint over it tomorrow, and it'll all be forgotten.'

'But, if it's a threat, it won't be over, will it? I'd even begun to believe I'd been imagining things.'

'What things?'

'An intruder. And a … I don't know … a presence in the house, watching me.'

'Did you know about this, Ellen?'

'Meghan thought it might be the spirit of someone who died in the cottage. As the cottage had only ever been a barn, I told her it was unlikely.'

'But now, what do you think?'

'There's a big library up at Carlyle House, Meghan. Sebastian's father was a great collector. Do you remember, Cathel, that time we went up there for dinner with Deirdre and I found that book on old farming methods?'

'Aye. So, there'll be books on ghosts and gods too. No serious collector would want to miss out on those, would they?' he laughed.

'Do you think we could go up there and look?'

'I haven't been there for a while. But if the internet's out ...'

'Go in the morning, the two of ye. It'll probably help if I get the boys to help me paint the door. But remember to come home before dark, in case the Horned God is waiting for you both in the shadows.'

*

It was around eleven when we reached the narrow road which led to Carlyle House. A hard frost had settled on the landscape, small white diamonds glistening on the heather and the grass at the roadside. Ellen shifted down and took the bends carefully.

Today the sun was pale and watery, and a mist hovered over the shoreline. Carlyle House seemed to float in the mist, insubstantial and unanchored. And yet its walls rose tall and straight above the dank air, still dominant, still a compelling monument to its past.

The door groaned and creaked on its hinges as Ellen pushed it open. Inside, the air smelled of damp wood and dust. The pendeloques of the small chandelier overhead tinkled briefly as the outside breeze caught them. Ellen switched on the light and shut the door. In the corner, I noticed a grandfather clock, the hands stopped at nine-fifteen. The staircase leading upstairs was roped off.

'When was he last here?'

'Sebastian disappeared fifteen years ago,' Ellen hesitated. 'I don't know when he left, or if he even did. No-one saw him go.'

Ellen opened a door on the right of the hallway and led me into the study. Four high shelves of books expanded on either side of a large stone fireplace, gold-embossed spines gleaming in the subdued artificial light. Piles of logs lay heaped on one side, with ashes and half-burned embers left in the grate. A large mahogany desk sat at the windowless end of the room, a stand with letterhead stationery on one side, a green-shaded banker's light on the other. Pens lay on a leather writing pad, which also bore the Carlyle crest.

'What do you mean by "if he even did?"'

'The last time anyone saw him was on the cliffs with Deirdre. They were having an argument. But there was a lot going on that day. There was an accident out at sea and the coastguard was called in.'

'And that was it?'

'At first, I came regularly to the house – once a week or so – to check in with Sebastian, as I used to. But he was never here. I thought he'd just gone off, back south perhaps, and expected me to carry on for a wee bit. I waited a week or two and then contacted his solicitors. A few days later, they called and told me I had a permanent job on the estate if I wanted it. And I accepted. I collected the accounts, the appointment diaries and logs, all the office files and some reference material, and moved into the empty cottage, which had been fixed up as a rental property. I'd no need of all this space. It was simply a matter of connecting the landline and I was set. The gamekeeper saw to the routines of the estate, making the bookings for the shooting and sorting out the fishing licences.'

'And you haven't heard anything from Sebastian since?'

'My only contact is Tom Brady at the solicitors. His instructions are always "on his client's behalf".'

'But you've been back here from time to time?'

'I try not to come to the house more than I have to. This is going to sound silly, and I never said to Cathel …'

'My lips are sealed.'

'Every time I've come back alone, I think I hear noises upstairs, as if someone's moving around up there.'

'You think Sebastian might still be here?'

'It sounds crazy, doesn't it? I mean, how would he live here alone all this time? But, every time I see a Land Rover passing, I wonder if it's him. I imagine he never really left. It's foolish, but there's something about this big empty place …'

'I understand. Let's get this over with; see if there are any books which mention our Horned God and go home. I'd feel a lot better if I knew what I was up against. Perhaps,' I added laughing, 'we might even find some of Sebastian's old photo albums, a diary with all his secrets written in code!'

'Until he disappeared, I always thought he was a decent sort of a man. He did a lot for the crofters, made a point of meeting everyone. But no-one knew anything about him before he turned up after his father's death and took over. Then, less than a year later, he just upped and left.'

'So, probably didn't leave many clues behind?'

'I've never found anything personal, no. But you're welcome to look.'

The lowest bookshelves were very organised and sectioned by topic. We started there, each of us working our way up on either side of the fireplace. There were books on local history, farming and estate management, hunting and angling, some of which had large glossy photo pages. Higher up, on one side, there was a series of what looked like

161

first editions of Dickens. At the other side of the fireplace, a mix of other classics in hardback and a few contemporary paperbacks. Dust had settled everywhere, and my hands were soon coated black. Ellen was still working her way up the other side of the bookshelves, so I pulled over the small library stool to my side to reach the books on the top shelf.

There were three books on Celtic traditions at one end. I collected all three and climbed down to look at them under the desk lamp. But, as I switched it on, the bulb flickered and exploded. Glass scattered across my hand and onto the desk.

'Are you okay?'

I nodded, 'I think so.'

'I told you,' Ellen laughed, 'this place! I think it's the damp. It gets into everything, especially the wiring. But you've found something?'

'Looks promising,' I smiled and carefully swept the splintered glass to one side.

Together we bent over the desk. The first book was a calendar of the Celtic year, the four annual festivals linked to the passage of the Earth in relation to the Sun, including *Samhain*, which Dougal had told me about. Another was an almanac with advice for farmers and fishermen on the weather, and tales of good and bad omens. Apparently, lambs with black faces were considered bad luck, but I'd always thought they were particularly beautiful.

Finally, there was a book entitled *The Celtic Way – Gods and Myths*. As I pulled the book towards me, I noticed a folded piece of paper wedged between the pages. It marked the page where there was an exact likeness of the Horned God which had been painted on my front door. And, in bold type at the top of the page, the name *Cernunnos*. There were several paragraphs on the suggested derivation of the name and its evolution over the centuries. But it was the final paragraph which caught my eye and which I read aloud –

Cernunnos is believed to be the lord of life and of death. He is a guardian of nature, protecting the forests and the moors, and watching over the wild creatures who live there. But he is also the god who comforts and sings to the souls of the dead, and guides them to the other side.

Ellen unfurled the bookmark. It was a sheet of the Carlyle letterhead, the crest, centred at the top, with the name *Sebastian St. John Carlyle* in dark blue script below.

'He marked this page?'

'Anyone could have marked it, Meghan.'

'But who else, apart from you, had access to the study? A cleaner, perhaps?'

'No cleaner.'

'Let's take the three books and go home. We can talk about it there.'

'Any secret diaries, intimate photos of past liaisons?'

'No, sorry Ellen, none at my end.'

'Nor at mine. Shame!' she added, smiling.

As Ellen disposed of the broken glass and replaced the bulb in the library, I stood at the foot of the staircase and listened. There were no sounds of footsteps, or creaking floorboards, only a muffled whistling of the wind down the chimney in the library. And, as we left, a final tinkling of the crystals hanging from the chandelier.

Outside, the sea mist had moved inland, and visibility was down to a few metres. Ellen drove slowly, headlights at fog setting, but the twists and turns of the narrow road were difficult to follow. I knew she was worried about the sheep, and I kept a lookout on my side. What we did not expect, however, was to meet another vehicle. We were surprised, therefore, to see headlights approaching at speed. Ellen swerved and pulled over to the side, one wheel suspended over the ditch on my side.

'Did you see?'

'Damn maniac!' I was still clutching the armrest.

'I mean, was it a Land Rover? Was it him driving?'

'It could have been anything or anyone. I was just focusing on living to see another day.'

Chapter 33

Deirdre – January 2003

As promised, three days later, Sebastian arrived with one of the estate vans and loaded up the larger items. Brigid drove behind him out of the village, Deirdre sitting beside her.

Their new accommodation was a small single-storey stone cottage, a little further along the main track leading past Carlyle House and nearer to the beach. Set at an angle to both the ocean and the slopes of the dunes, it was sheltered from the worst of the weather. Nevertheless, all the windows of the main rooms had unobstructed views of the sea. Both the bedrooms looked over the sandhills and up to the hillside beyond.

But, as Sebastian unlocked the door and stood to one side to let Deirdre go in, she noticed it. Underlying the smell of new paint, there was another odour, more pungent and old.

'Sorry about the strong paint smell,' Sebastian smiled. 'I've had the windows open for more than a week since Archie finished whitewashing the place. I hope neither of you are allergic.'

'There's another smell too. What's that?'

'The cottage has remained closed up … since my mother's time. Old cottages, you know. I'll start to unload, shall I? And you can tell me where you want everything.'

As Sebastian walked back to the car, Deirdre turned to Brigid.

'What did he mean "since my mother's time?"'

'I didn't know he'd give us this cottage. I should've asked.'

'Why? What's wrong Brigid?'

'Sebastian's mother, Jenny Carlyle, lived here until her death. His father, Malcolm Carlyle, was what they call nowadays a control freak. He ruled his household with an iron fist. Sebastian left home early – boarding school, university. He was lucky. But Jenny, she had a nervous breakdown. Malcolm moved her out – into this cottage apparently. He didn't want her around. A few months later, she was dead.'

'Dead? What happened?'

'There was talk of suicide, or worse. Nobody ever knew the truth. Natural causes, they said. It was all hushed up. Malcolm knew all the right folks.'

'So why did Sebastian give us this cottage?'

'Because,' said Sebastian, who now stood in the doorway clutching a suitcase in each hand, 'it's the best – and biggest – house on the estate, apart from Carlyle House itself. And you've got unobstructed views of the sea and the hills. I thought you'd like it. Is there something wrong?'

'Your mother died here!'

'I imagine that people have died in most of the old houses in the Highlands. Your mother died in your farmhouse, didn't she, Deirdre?'

'Yes, but ...'

'I didn't think it would matter to you. I'm sorry if I was insensitive,' he paused. 'If it makes you feel uncomfortable, you and Brigid can come up to Carlyle House. I thought you might like a little privacy, for now at least. A place to call your own.'

'No, no, we'll settle just fine, Mr Carlyle,' Brigid smiled. 'We'll keep the windows open for a while longer as you suggest. It's probably just the damp, as you said.'

But later, when they were alone, Brigid told Deirdre that she had also noticed the smell of death lingering in the walls.

They would go the following day, she promised, up to the Auld Village and cut some sprigs of the rowan tree which grew outside her great grandfather's house, to hang over the front door of the cottage and above the fireplace in the sitting room.

'The starlings will have eaten all the red berries!'

'Aye, it's too late for those. And for the green leaves. But we can take some small branches, make wreaths, add rosemary and thyme. It'll be enough. We're together here, as your mother would've wanted it. There's no need to be afeart, lass.'

But Deirdre was afraid, tossing and turning most of that night, expecting she knew not what. In her own house, she had been afraid of the living, not the dead. There had been no lingering miasma of death after her mother had been carried away from the McIntyre farm. Just the ache of loss and loneliness. But in this pristine cottage by the sea, sheltering below the sand dunes, there was no mistaking it.

Chapter 34

Deirdre

When they awoke the next morning, Deirdre's head was throbbing, and she could see that Brigid was tired.

'You need to rest today, Brigid.'

'Nay, lass, we need to go up to the Auld Village, for the rowan.'

'You don't need to drive all the way over to the village and make the climb. I'll walk up the hillside here, behind the house. Perhaps there'll be another nearby.'

'Will you know it? It's wintering now, so look out for some brown seed pods hanging or fallen.'

As she closed the door behind her and looked along the beach below the cottage, Deirdre stood for a few minutes, breathing deeply in the brisk air outside the confines of the cottage. She could taste the sea salt carried in on the wind. Huge waves crashed inshore, some already encroaching on the footprints of the dunes. Perhaps the move had been a mistake. She did not know exactly what she had expected when she first agreed to Sebastian's suggestion, but it had not been this. The reality of their isolation, in a strange, possibly haunted place where death had left its imprint, was unsettling. She could not survive it alone, and Brigid already seemed tired and unwell. But moving into Carlyle House was a step too far.

Just beyond the cottage, she found a well-trodden path through the dunes and began to climb. Clumps of thick

168

marram grass intruded on the path as she moved inland, giving way to flatter, wetter land beyond. And then the heather-covered moors, their blooms now winter-brown. She crested the first slope and saw it – a small stone enclosure, set firmly on flat ground, in the shadow of the rising hillside behind.

As she approached, she could see graves laid out meticulously – small headstones at one end of each raised mound. Clustering to one side, there were four rows, four headstones in each of the first three rows, only three in the fourth. Access to the small cemetery was through an iron gate set in the back wall. If the original designers had intended to keep the gate intact by sheltering it from the onslaught of the gales coming from the sea, they had not taken account of the salt-laden air. The gate was rusty, one of its hinges rotten and broken. It hung lopsidedly, and Deirdre had to lift the whole contraption to gain access.

A gorse bush had taken root in a corner at the unoccupied end of the graveyard. Wilting thistles and stinging nettles and dock leaves spread across the ground where grass had refused to grow. The headstones were simple, unadorned blocks of stones. Each carried only a first and last name, without text and without dates. Every surname was Carlyle. There was one exception. Nearest to the wall, in the fourth row, the wording simply read Carlyle Child (Male). Immediately, in front, there was Jayne Carlyle. And, in front of that, Malcolm Carlyle.

The Carlyles, who had claimed their right to the Big House, and their families – individuals who had once loved and been loved – had been defeated by time. Only the wind cried as it disregarded the guardianship of the stone walls and crept around the graves.

Deirdre turned away, closing the gate firmly behind her. She wondered if this was where Sebastian would lie at the end. And, if she married him, would she too be expected to lie in this lonely place beside him? This was not how she would like to be remembered.

A sickly sun had crept over the hillside, eliminating some of the shadows below; and she began to climb up between the rocks. She had come to find a rowan tree, and her task was not complete. Brigid was depending on her. Sparse clumps of heather still clung to life in the crevices between the rocks. But soon, the landscape became bare scree, the loose rocks slipping away under her feet as she tried to gain traction. She sat down to catch her breath, wondering why she had continued to climb when she knew that no rowan tree could grow in this ground.

She decided to make the descent down the other side of the slope, and then work her way back around below the clearing and the Carlyle graveyard.

The other side of the hillside had been eroded by the melting snow, and small rivulets had made their own courses downhill. And here, there was more vegetation. A few small pine saplings had taken hold, leaning back into the shelter of the rocky hillside, green mosses at their feet. But just when she thought of circling back to her starting point, she saw the rowan. It was unlike any she had ever seen before. Perched on a huge boulder, its roots had disappeared between fissures in the rock. It had grown at an angle to its host, but had survived and prospered for several years. Even if Deirdre had not seen the brown seed pods, she would have recognised the familiar domed-shape of the bare branches splaying out from its trunk.

Before leaving the cottage, she had taken a small knife and some string with her in her jacket. Now, because of the tree's precarious foothold, it was not difficult for Deirdre to find footholds in the fractured rock and cut off some of the smaller branches. She bundled them together with the string and, flinging them over her shoulder, turned for home.

But she had miscalculated the descent. Circling back to

the front of the hillside, she arrived again at the clearing and the cemetery.

Magnus sensed her arrival, even before she noticed Sebastian standing outside the enclosure. The dog growled once and then grew silent as he recognised her. Sebastian's head was bent, whether in thought or reverence, Deirdre could not discern from a distance. But surely a lonely figure in a barren landscape.

Shrouding his eyes against the low shards of sunlight, he turned and swept his hand over the stone wall.

'A grim reminder of one's mortality, don't you think?'

'Your family have certainly made it so.'

'You don't hate the idea of loved ones buried deep in the earth, rotting for eternity?'

'We all die, Sebastian. But we can remember the dead with love and respect, honour their lives. This place …'

'I know, this place is bleak, soulless,' he paused. 'My mother's here, Deirdre.'

'Yes, I saw that.'

'She's not buried beneath the floor or behind the walls of the cottage. She was a good person, a caring mother.'

'But troubled.'

'And that's what you and Brigid felt at the cottage yesterday?'

'Perhaps. But there was something else, as if she'd been snatched away too soon, even unwillingly.'

'You're implying her death was not from natural causes?' he paused. 'My father was a bitter man; and not happy with his lot in life. He liked to have his own way; and relieved his frustration by taking his anger out on those around him. My mother took the brunt of that, especially when he was threatening me. But there was never any suggestion he'd been involved in her death.'

'Did you ever fight back, try to protect your mother?'

'I was a child, Deirdre. I never believed he'd do her

serious harm.'

'And now, what do you think?'

'She lost a child, got depressed; my father couldn't deal with it. He moved her out of the house and into the cottage. And she died there. That's all there is to it.'

'We're being troublesome, aren't we? I warned you, that first night on the beach, you wouldn't understand our highland ways. We can leave, go back to the village. You and I … we don't have to go on with this. Perhaps it's better if we call it off now, before it's too late.'

'Oh no, Deirdre, please don't say that. I could never give you up.'

'But what if I don't, if I can't, feel the same?'

'Then I'll spend the rest of my life keeping you close until you are convinced. We're meant to be together, Deirdre,' he smiled then. 'Besides, I've arranged a party.'

'You just had a party.'

'Yes, but this one's for us. A celebration of our engagement.'

'Our engagement? But I haven't agreed …'

'I know, I know. But I thought it'd look odd if you and Brigid were living on the estate, and we didn't have some kind of understanding. It could be misconstrued.'

'I see. So now you're protecting my reputation! And who've you invited to this celebration?'

'It'll just be a small dinner party. A few friends from London will be coming and …'

'You already told your friends about me?'

'Of course. How could I keep you a secret?'

'And who else?'

'My sister, Meredith, and her husband, Tristran.'

'Will there be anyone I know?'

'Brigid will be invited, of course.'

'Anyone else?'

'I thought you'd prefer to keep it low-key.'

'Those who know me in the village are not invited. How will that be construed?'

'I thought we'd make a formal announcement in the local paper.'

'Oh, Sebastian!' Deirdre sighed.

'I can ask Cathel and Ellen, if you like. But I thought they might feel uncomfortable.'

'Don't you mean *iochdarach*?' Deirdre spat out the word.

Sebastian raised his eyebrows, 'No need to translate!'

'It means inferior! They might feel inferior, rubbing elbows with all your fancy friends and family.'

'I've upset you, and all I wanted to do was make you feel special.'

'If you wanted to make me feel special, you could've returned in time for the lighting of the beacons at Hogmanay.'

'New Year's Eve? I didn't think it was that important or that you'd be expecting me. It was just a few more days. And I wanted to go shopping before I flew home – to buy you a beautiful dress for the party.'

'For a party that you didn't discuss with me, for an engagement that I haven't agreed to!'

'I'll just cancel everything, make some excuse.'

'And what will all your friends think then?'

'It doesn't matter what they think, what anyone thinks. I thought it'd make you happy. And I thought by moving here ...'

'That I'd agreed to everything? I needed a refuge, someone to turn to.'

'And that's what I want to be for you. I'd planned the party for next month, Valentine's Day. It's not too late to cancel it. Is that what you want me to do?'

'Yes! No! I don't know! Right now, Sebastian, I just need to get back to Brigid. She wasn't feeling well, and I've already been away too long.'

'Let me walk you back, at least.'

'I'd rather go on my own,' she leaned forward and patted the dog on the head. 'Magnus, take this man for a walk. You both need some good highland air.'

Chapter 35

Meghan

The black *Cernunnos*, daubed on my front door, had certainly been a threat; completed in the night when no-one was around. And a driver had nearly run us off the road down to Annanside Bay in the fog. There was nothing down there except a beach and Carlyle House. Whoever it was, had known the road well, not slowing down when they saw our headlights. I'd spent so much time concerning myself with the unseen presence in the cottage, my supposed sightings of Deirdre. Instead, perhaps I should have been worrying about the real threats in the here and now.

After the frost and the sea mist, the snow had arrived. The sky was grey with large flakes which fell relentlessly for two days. The new year had turned, and Sebastian was still out there somewhere. Now was the perfect time for me to look for him.

I looked up the online *Who's Who* – under the Carlyle family, who had inherited the Big House and their associated Scottish properties. Sebastian, born April 22, 1964, was the son of the Rt. Honourable Malcolm Carlyle and Jayne (née Robertson). Malcolm Carlyle died in 2001, and Sebastian had inherited the estate. So, he was thirty-eight when he met Deirdre, twenty years her senior. He also had a sister, Meredith, who was born ten years later in 1974. Sebastian had been educated at Eton and Oxford.

There was no mention of him in the annals of Eton,

175

but the Oxford student magazine *Cherwell* had one photo of him in the winning coxed-4 boat in a regatta in 1984. A slight figure with fair hair, he sat at the rear of the boat – the coxswain – waving his cap with the rest of the crew. But his face was turned away from the camera.

Then I started trawling through the national press from 1985 onwards, when I would've expected him to graduate. One mention only, in the *Tatler* magazine, eleven years later. Meredith married Tristran Compton in 1996. There was a picture of the bride with her brother, Sebastian, in the garden of the Compton family home in West Sussex. Sebastian stood with his arm around his sister's shoulder, smiling broadly. Fair-haired and tanned in a pale grey morning suit, he was – I had to admit – quite a catch. A paragraph underneath mentioned that Sebastian Carlyle had recently relocated to the City of London from Hong Kong, which was soon to be handed over to China.

And then an obituary in the *Daily Telegraph*, eight years later in March 2004, listing the death of Tristram and Meredith Compton killed by an avalanche in the Swiss Alps. They had no children.

Facebook had started in 2004 – the real beginning of social media – but there was no mention of anyone who could have remotely been Sebastian Carlyle. And I searched every possible spelling and nickname, and alias which I thought might have been used.

I had come up empty-handed. There wasn't even a living relative whom I could chase down.

As soon as snow was forecast, Cathel moved the sheep into shelter down the hillside. The cows were in the open-sided barn. We could see steam rising from the warm straw at their feet, the chickens hunkering down nearby. Cassie had long ago lost her fear of the farmyard; and, on a good day, had taken to following the hens round the yard in a good-natured game of chase. But now, nothing moved in the village. For two days, I only ventured out when I took Cassie for her potty breaks. We carried the snow indoors with us, large puddles collecting in the entranceway as we dripped and melted. Outside, it fell hour after hour, erasing our footprints as if we'd never been there.

And I thought about Deirdre. Her memory lingered in the village, but the life she'd led, and why and how she'd died, had long ago been buried with the past. It had almost become taboo to mention her name. Whatever had happened to Sebastian, wherever he had gone, wherever he was, mattered less than why I was still haunted by Deirdre. Like me, she had sought the comfort and reassurance of an older man. And, perhaps, like me, it had turned out to be a disappointment, an illusion. Was this why I felt so connected to her story? In the here and now, we were both in limbo. It was the future which was important, finding a way to move forward, finding a way for both of us. I couldn't – I wouldn't – let go until the whole story had been told.

*

On the third day, we awoke to a clear sky and bright sunshine. Living in the city, I'd never seen the magnificence of a snow-covered landscape. It had merely been the stuff of Christmas cards. But today, there was a reassuring serenity to the white expanse below, a stillness which wrapped the village up from one side of the valley to the other, enveloped the hillsides and stretched to the mountains in the distance, like white icing on the tiers of a wedding cake. The snow was deep, drifts accumulated in the bends and banks of the road below.

Ellen tromped across the farmyard mid-morning. The snowploughs wouldn't make it into the village until the next day. This meant the boys were off school and wanted me to go outside with them to build a snowman.

The four of us rolled and moulded balls of snow,

177

balancing them precariously on top of each other. The snow was soft and difficult to control. Ellen worked with Brennan, and I with Craig. Coal and carrots were fetched from the kitchen, small pieces of firewood from the fireplace, until two lopsided snowmen stared at each other across the farmyard. Cassie barked, whether in alarm or excitement, we couldn't decide. I threw the first snowball in her direction. She leapt up, trying to catch it. Then the boys started lobbing more snowballs at each other; and we took sides. We laughed and mocked each other, dodging and slipping our way across the farmyard. Cassie ran from one team to another, sliding to an uncontrolled standstill as she leapt up to catch the balls flying overhead.

I'd lost contact with my fingers. My face stung with cold, my nose numb. My boots and coat were sodden. And I felt exhilarated. I'd forgotten how good it felt to be silly. I'd forgotten how good it felt to laugh and scream and not care how you appeared to other people. I had, quite simply, forgotten how to feel alive. Whatever had happened in the past, whatever my life would be like when I returned to the city, whatever threatened me in this wonderful place where people had welcomed me unquestionably, I was ready for it.

'Come and get me!' I yelled to no-one in particular.

'Run and hide then, Meghan! Run, run, run!' Brennan shouted back.

*

It was nearly a week later, with the roads gritted and salted, that I drove into town to do a few errands. Afterwards, too tired to cook a meal after my day out, I walked to the pub with Cassie for supper. Dougal was there as usual, propping up the corner of the bar, and I joined him. I smiled as I realised I'd turned into one of the regulars.

Maybe, I thought, this would be a good opportunity to see what else he could tell me about Deirdre and Sebastian, and perhaps *Cernunnos*. But I'd hardly sat down when Liane came over.

'Have you told her then?'

'Nae, she's just sat down. Perhaps you'd like to do the honours, Liane.'

'Told me what?'

'There was a man in here the day, looking for ye. His name was Richard something, wasn't it, Dougal?'

'Richard Wellesley?'

I could feel my face redden, my heartbeat quicken.

'Aye, that was it,' Dougal smiled. 'He said you'd gone off without leaving a forwarding address …'

'And that his calls never seemed to go through to your mobile.'

'And he said that you'd posted a picture on Facebook of the New Year's bonfires. So, he knew you were here. Perhaps that wasn't such a good idea,' Dougal smiled again.

'So, you told him I was here.'

'Nae, lassie. Why would we be wanting to do that? If you hadn't told him where you were, it was because you didn't want him to find you. Liane said you'd been here and left,' he winked.

'And Dougal told him you'd mentioned going on to Spain.'

'Spain?'

'I told him you'd left before the snow arrived. It was too cold up here in the winter. You'd fancied a villa in *España*.'

'And he believed you?' I laughed.

'Of course,' Liane smiled. 'We stick together around here, don't we, Dougal? If a girl wants to leave a man, it's her business.'

'I can explain.'

'Och, no need for that, lassie. It's none o' our business. But I did notice he was wearing a wedding ring, and you're not.'

179

'What'll you have for your tea then, lass?' Liane passed me the menu. 'There's a good shepherd's pie on tonight.'

Just then, Fergus came in from the back. He looked at me.

'Well, here you are then. And me thinking you'd left already.'

'I didn't go anywhere.'

'Och, well I know that. But that yon fella was thinking you had, after speaking to these two conspirators here.'

'He asked you too?'

'Of course. He was checking up on their story.'

'You didn't tell him, Fergus, did you?'

'That you were still here? Nae, of course not. I told him I'd seen you here once or twice on the beach walking with that dog of yours. He seemed surprised you had a dog. I told him it was a fierce wee beastie, not to be trifled with either.'

'And?'

'I told him you'd left a few days back and to go and bother other folks,' he paused. 'I don't like folks who poke their noses into other folks' business.'

Dougal smiled.

'A gullible soul, that man of yours.'

'He's not my man, not anymore, Dougal.'

'That's as we thought.'

I looked from one to the other, tears welling up.

'I don't know how to thank you. You barely know me and yet you lied for me.'

'Less about the lying, lassie. That's a sin around here. Let's just say we can manage a good cover story, when we've the need.'

'And we know how to protect one of our own,' Liane added. 'We girls need to stick together,' she patted my hand. 'It'll be shepherd's pie then?'

'And a dram of your best all round,' I added. 'With my thanks.'

Dougal laughed.

'Have you got any more of these pining ex-lovers looking for you, lassie? Cause, if you do, Liane here'd better start stocking up on more of the good stuff!'

Chapter 36

Deirdre

Sitting beside Brigid in the cottage, recounting her conversation at the Carlyle cemetery, Deirdre remembered each step she had taken, each challenging word she had exchanged with Sebastian since their first meeting nearly five months earlier. At first, it had been an exciting game. And later, yes, he had become her refuge. She had pulled all the strings until they had drawn so tight that now she, too, was entangled. Brigid had warned her to be careful, to be sure. It had been a fantasy of her own making, and it had spiralled out of control. Sebastian's version was reality, the version she had chosen to ignore. And she could not imagine a way forward or a way back.

Brigid listened quietly as she wove the rowan wreaths, carefully choosing each small branch, twisting one around another, weaving in sprigs of rosemary and thyme, and tying them all together with strips of thin red ribbon she pulled from her sewing basket.

'What shall I do, Brigid?'

'There's only one thing to do, if you've decided you don't want to marry this man, if you really don't want to spend the rest of your life with him. Tell him the truth. I hope it's not too late for that.'

'But he said he'd never give me up, that he'd spend the rest of his life trying to convince me.'

'People say a lot of things when they're in love, child.

182

Most learn to move on. I don't know Sebastian well. I only know he's the laird, and a Carlyle. And his father wasna an easy man to get along with.'

'He talks about being with me for eternity.'

'That's a long time.'

'I told him that!'

Brigid laughed, 'Of course, you did, lass. Of course, you did.'

'So, we can go home, back to your cottage?'

'Not until you've told him the truth. This isn't the time to run and hide because he'll surely follow you. And be sure to let him down lightly. Dinna hurt his pride.'

For the next few days, Brigid drove Deirdre to school each morning; and then spent the rest of the day at her own house in the village. And, each night, they returned to the cottage beneath the dunes at Annanside Bay.

*

It was the night of the first full moon of the new year, the January moon, the Wolf Moon, when Deirdre had her dream. It was a Saturday. It was the day Deirdre had promised herself she would go up to Carlyle House and speak to Sebastian.

When they awoke that day, there was a light snow drifting lazily across the windows of the cottage. The sea was calm, and the familiar gusting wind had died down. A stillness had settled on the landscape. Deirdre had expected, had wanted even, the day to be blustery. It would, she thought, have been a reflection of her inner feelings, the elements in tune with her mood. The winds here were always a salve to her soul; today, she had wanted them to soothe her conscience. So, she waited, delaying her confession.

As hour succeeded hour, the snow continued to fall relentlessly on the landscape, until hills and dunes and beach were all blanketed in white. Even the sea, tides turning, seemed lost in the swirling white mist. Just before the light finally left the sky, Deirdre opened the door and stood on the doorstep. Silence had settled in around the cottage, and the moon, the full moon, was rising. Tomorrow, she promised herself. Tomorrow, she would give Sebastian her answer.

It was late when she finally left Brigid and went to bed. Yet she lay awake for a long time, watching the moon cast long shadows across the floor of her bedroom. She had never closed her curtains at night, even as a child.

As a cloud passed over the face of the moon, and the room, for a few minutes, was plunged into blackness, Deirdre fell asleep.

She was running, running in the darkness. For a few moments, the moon slipped out from behind the clouds, and she could see her footsteps had left deep imprints in the virgin snow. But, as the moon disappeared again, she realised she did not know the path she was on, nor even if it was a path. Perhaps she was running across a treacherous part of the moors, where she might never be found. Behind her, there were footprints, her footprints, but she was frightened to turn back. Shivering with cold, she stood quietly, listening, hoping to hear something, anything, which would guide her forward in one direction or another. But, out in the frozen landscape, nothing moved, every living creature had gone to ground. Now she wished, more than anything else, that she had not decided to run. She could not even remember why she had done so. It would, surely, have been better to face up to what had made her so afraid than to die out here alone. Even now, she could do so, just follow her own footprints back. It was then, as she stood motionless in the darkness, that she saw a light up ahead, swinging from side to side as it appeared over the crest of the hill. And a voice called out, a man's voice –

'Follow the light. This is the way home.'

Later, when she awoke, she remembered the man's voice. She did not know or recognise him, but his voice had made her feel safe. She had not been afraid to follow him. If her dreams were real – and she did not doubt it – then this was the man she was destined to find. He would take her to a place she could call home. Sebastian had been good for her in so many ways, but now she was afraid she would lose herself in his world, stifled by his vision of who she could become under his tutelage.

If she had to wait a lifetime to find this man, then so be it.

Chapter 37

Deirdre

In the early morning sunshine, the snow crystals on the bedroom window seemed to glint like jewels. And, outside the walls of the cottage, the wind had turned, carrying warmer air across the shoreline from the south.

Deirdre climbed the track behind the cottage. It would be easy now to speak to Sebastian. Her mood had changed, her courage restored. He would understand that their brief relationship had been impractical on so many levels.

She imagined how she would feel if the man in her dream held her in his arms and kissed her. She wondered what it would be like to lie naked and unashamed beside a man whose voice, as in her dream, had made her feel so safe. Surely, with him, she would be able to look into his eyes and let him see into her soul.

As she was making the final turn up to Carlyle House, she saw Sebastian walking towards her, a large box under his arm.

He laughed, 'Great minds! I was just coming down to see you.'

'I can't do this, Sebastian. I can't agree to get engaged, marry you, none of it. I came to tell you that.'

'I understand.'

'You do?'

'Of course. I've been moving too fast, pressurising you. I can wait.'

'Wait?'

'Yes, give you space to get used to the idea. I'll wait until you leave school.'

'But I don't want you to wait. I want you to understand that this won't work, not for me, not even for you.'

'You're young. In time ...'

'This is my time, Sebastian.'

'Of course, it is. I do understand how you feel. But do you understand how I feel?'

'I never meant to deceive you, Sebastian. But I realise now that my way of behaving, talking, might make you think ... You once called me a feisty little madam. That's who I am, who I've always been. You're a good man. You deserve better.'

'You're all I want, Deirdre. All I've ever wanted. And I can't, I will not let you go,' he held out the box. 'This is the dress I promised you. Wear it, wear it for the party.'

'For the party? Didn't you hear what I said? There will be no engagement.'

'Take the dress anyway. It's yours. I bought it for you.'

He thrust the box into her hands.

'It won't change my mind.'

'We'll see. I can be very persistent.'

Deirdre turned to leave.

'And I've done something else for you, to make things easier at home. It was going to be a surprise. I was going to tell you later at the party, but now seems like a good time.'

Deirdre stopped in her tracks.

'What home are you talking about?'

'I spoke to your father.'

'You did what?'

'Yes. I told him we were planning on getting married. And, as a goodwill gesture, I'd give him his croft and all the land he works, freehold. At no cost to himself. On condition that he raises no objections to our union and keeps his distance.'

'And he agreed? Well, of course, he did. Traded his daughter for the land! Was he drunk or sober at the time?'

'It was difficult to tell. But now he has the official deed.'

'Oh, well, that's alright, isn't it?'

'I thought it'd help.'

'Help who exactly? Well, you, of course! This is why it would never have worked between us.'

'Because I'm trying to make your life easier?'

'Because you're trying to take control of my life, and you don't even realise it.'

Chapter 38

Meghan

January merged into February. The snow melted, rain fell, and overnight frosts clung to the hillsides and the roads. And then, one day, we awoke to sunshine; sunshine whose warmth penetrated the layers of my padded anorak and was carried on the breeze across the valley as Cassie and I took our morning walk. I had laid the spectre of Richard's pursuit to rest. There had been no more threats, either real or imagined.

Now all my thoughts were of Deirdre. Perhaps, that's why she came to me again, in the hills, when we were all alone. She was there to remind me of the promise I'd made to uncover the truth – the truth of her life and her death.

*

With the possibility of spring on the horizon, I decided it was time to explore more of my surroundings. I'd been fascinated by the sandy beaches, the dramatic cliffs, and the moods of the ocean. It had been a novelty, so different from city life. And I had loved celebrating the village festivities associated with Christmas and the bonfires of Hogmanay. My diary brimmed with the details, my evolving paintings trying to capture the colours and the moods of each experience.

Behind the farmhouse, there were hills to climb, and the arrival of a warmer day was a perfect opportunity to explore. My guidebook talked of a place called the Eagle's Nest –

189

Iolairean a'Neadachadh in Gaelic. Each year, for as long as locals could remember, pairs of golden eagles had nested on the cliff face. They built their eyrie and laid their eggs in time for hatching in mid-March. And, beyond the nesting site, in the next valley, there was the Auld Village, which had been abandoned since the time of the Highland Clearances in the 18th century, when villagers had been forcefully evicted from their homes by their new landlords.

I packed a lunch; Cassie and I then set off up the hill, following the route the guidebook had laid out. There was no-one at home in the farmhouse. Cathel was working with the pregnant ewes in the valley below. I could hear him whistling to his two sheepdogs as he herded the flock to new pastures. The boys were at school. Ellen had told me she was busy finalising the account books for the end-of-year tax filing, and would be working all week in the cottage on the Carlyle Estate. Nobody saw us leave.

The climb was steep, and rocks hidden under the heather made treacherous footholds. Cassie, with her nose lower to the ground, was able to negotiate them more easily. But when we reached the stream which crossed the land, it was Cassie who hesitated. The melted snow had filled it with a rushing torrent and it was impossible to know how deep it had become, nor how far it stretched on either side. With Cassie in my arms, I made a leap at the narrowest point, dreading the possibility of twisting my ankle if I miscalculated the width of the chasm or our combined weights. I landed heavily on the other side, slithering to a stop and clutching at the old heather stumps.

Further up, outside the fence-line, the land levelled out and heather gave way to an expanse of moss and thin spiky grasses. This was the bogland which I'd read could be treacherous for the unwary. We skirted round the area carefully, and reached another slope. Very little grew here on the rocky ground; just a few tufts of grass and sparse sprigs of heather nestling by the large boulders and scrubby trees.

As I crested the top of the hill, I saw a vast heap of twigs piled wide and high on the top of a sheer rock face – the eyrie, and moving around on top, a large golden eagle. I tethered Cassie below the crest, stroking her head as I tried to soothe her into silence.

I heard him before I saw him, the male circling above, his short shrill cries piercing the silence. He was quite a bit smaller than his mate who sat on the nest. And he was alarmed by our arrival. Cassie froze, seemingly aware that she was in the presence of a powerful enemy. The eagle made a steep dive towards us, wings folded, and then soared up again, wings flapping as he reached the top of his climb. I sat down near Cassie, just a little above her, a shield against attack; and watched, entranced, as the male repeated his flight pattern over and over again. I pulled my small camera from my backpack slowly and began to take pictures. I wished I'd brought my phone to take a good video. I don't know how long we sat there nor how many times the male swooped down and soared up again. But I stayed there long after I'd finished taking my pictures.

In the far distance, I could see the coastline and the horizon beyond. I had no concept of the time, but the sun already seemed a little lower, the sea a dark green in the glow of it. I untied Cassie and we made a long detour around the cliffside, down and around the hill, out of sight of the nesting pair. There was still time to reach the Auld Village, if we hurried.

A *lochan* – as my guidebook had called it – was on our route. It was our landmark to find the village. It lay in a small dip in the landscape, still and crystal clear. We started along the rough path which skirted the edge. Cassie padded down the slope and drank from the water, reminding me I was thirsty, and hungry too. I'd forgotten to eat my sandwich to give Cassie her lunchtime snack. I found a boulder to lean against, facing the warmth of the sun, and sat down to eat. There was little to no wind, and the sun was comforting. I closed my eyes for a moment. It felt wonderful to sit quietly, alone in the wilderness, breathing in the pure highland air. Cassie walked around the water and nosed her way into the tall reeds which grew at the far end of the lake. The last thing I remember before I fell asleep was watching the reeds swaying as she moved into the water.

I woke suddenly, startled into wakefulness. The air was a little chillier; and the sky had mellowed to the orange-tinged glow of late afternoon. Cassie had fallen asleep too, her head resting in my lap. She stirred briefly as I stretched my legs. Much of the lake was in shadow, but a few rays of sun still traced their way across the water. It was too late now to walk on to the abandoned village. At this time of year, night settled in quickly in the Highlands; and we had at least a half an hour's walk back down to the cottage.

I looked at my reflection in the water. My hair had grown longer since my arrival. Going to the hairdresser had not been on my list of priorities, but I didn't know I looked so gaunt. I was sure I'd probably put on a few pounds, eating Liane's fish and chips and cottage pies at the pub. I tried a smile, but my reflection didn't smile back. Cassie got up and stared into the water, but she didn't seem to have a reflection at all. Instead, she barked and leapt back. I looked at the face in the water and realised it wasn't mine. The cheekbones were higher, the hair more luxuriant, the face more beautiful than mine. But it was the eyes which held my attention, focused, locked on mine.

In that moment, I saw Deirdre there in the water. She'd been here all the time, living and breathing not far from the village where she was born. She hadn't died all those years ago as I'd been told. And now, too late to save her, I'd found her body. I waded in and thrust my hands and arms below the surface until I could feel the pebbled bed of the lake, tearing

192

up the pond weeds as I scrabbled around. But each time, my hands came up empty. The last rays of the dying sun were sinking below the lip of the hill. Without its brightness, as I climbed out of the water, the *lochan* seemed deeper and darker. Behind me, the water settled; and I knew, without looking, that Deirdre's face had already disappeared.

Chapter 39

Deirdre

Brigid was sitting at the kitchen table drinking tea when Deirdre returned to the cottage.

'Such a beautiful day, child. Come sit with me. I've been watching that magnificent seagull out there over the bay for a while. The power and control in his wings, swooping down to catch his prey, and then soaring up again. He seems tireless.'

'Persistent?' Deirdre snapped back.

'You spoke to the man, and he wasn't happy?'

'He understood! But he refused to take no for an answer. He keeps insisting that I go to the party, wear the ridiculous dress he bought for me and pretend we're just postponing the official announcement until I'm ready!'

'He's just saving face.'

'I wish I believed that. He's made an agreement with Father.'

'What agreement?'

'He's given him the croft and the land. Da's paid nothing, but it's his, freehold, forever. In exchange for me, apparently!'

'We'll call Cathel. Ask him to come over during the week and help us move back to the village.'

'Last night, Brigid, I had a dream. I was running away. It was night and I was lost in the snow. A man came out of the darkness, carrying a light. He told me to follow the light, and he'd show me the way home. It was *an dà-shealladh*. I know it was. This is the man I must wait for, Brigid, not Sebastian. This man made me feel safe.'

'I wondered this morning, when I saw you. You seemed lighter in spirit, happier. But this is also dangerous, lass. If you do find this man and go with him, Carlyle will not forgive, nor will he forget.'

*

It was only later, alone in her room, as the now waning moon rose again in the sky, that Deirdre opened the box Sebastian had given her. She would not be wearing the dress to any party, but it was surely her right to look at it and then leave it behind in the cottage. A final gesture to Sebastian that it was all over.

She pulled the dress from its tissue paper and laid it across her quilt. The emerald green silk sparkled in the lamplight. She held it against her cheek and felt its smoothness. Surely there would be no harm in her trying it on? She took off her nightgown and slipped the dress over her naked body. The bodice was tight-fitting, pleated velvet with tiny seed pearls sewn down each pleat line. The silk sleeves billowed out from the shoulders and were caught in velvet cuffs. The silk skirt floated around her ankles as she moved. Then she noticed the other smaller box, nestling in the tissue paper. Inside, a long silver chain with a large pendant cross, set with emerald and topaz gemstones; two pendant earrings to match. She brushed out her hair until it swept across her shoulders, and put on the jewellery. And she looked at herself in the mirror.

She no longer resembled the girl she had seen nearly five months earlier in her mother's mirror. In the dress Sebastian had given her, she saw a beautiful woman wearing expensive clothes, extravagant ornaments; the colour of the silk a perfect match for her eyes. This was the Deirdre whom Sebastian saw. He had known, always known, this was who

195

she could become. He had chosen his gift with care, knowing the moment would come when she would see herself through his eyes. He loved her completely, unashamedly and was prepared to go to any length to prove it.

Her eyes filled with tears, which ran down her cheeks and made dark stains on the silk sleeves as she tried to brush them away. Perhaps, if Sebastian had grown up in the Highlands, he would have understood. Perhaps, if he were less privileged. Perhaps even, if he were still a young man. The Deirdre he had fallen in love with, the one she saw in the mirror tonight, was not the real Deirdre. She wanted love to make her feel like Iolaire as he soared overhead, catching the air currents, weightless. She wanted to run across the moors like the deer and lie hidden in the heather. Or simply to rest in the warmth and shelter of the dunes and listen to the motion of the tides. Wherever she went in life, she knew she would return, like Brigid, to the hills where she had been born, to a small stone cottage nestled beside the sea. If she had accepted Sebastian's offer, she knew she would have withered and died in Carlyle House. No amount of caring and kindness could have saved her.

As she turned away from her reflection, she saw a glimmer of light outside. At first, she thought it might be Sebastian walking Magnus on the beach, familiar torch in hand to mark his way. But this light flickered and moved as if stirred by the wind, red and yellow and white sparking from its core. It was a fire. Someone had built a bonfire on the beach.

Chapter 40

Deirdre

Standing in the open doorway, Deirdre looked out over the sand and watched the flames of the small bonfire buffeted by the breeze. The smell of burning driftwood wafted inland; the sound of the cresting waves creeping relentlessly forward, moon and ocean synchronised in their never-ending tidal dance. Three figures crouched beside the fire, mere shadows, outlines in the moonlight. They seemed frozen, motionless, soundless; Deirdre wondered if she was imagining them. She listened for their voices, but from where she stood, she could hear nothing.

Was this what her dream had promised, meeting a stranger on the beach beside a bonfire? Was this the light that she had been called to follow? She hesitated now, knowing that stepping there, outside into the night, following the firelight, might really take her to the place her dream had foretold and where she might be changed forever. If her dream was realised, would she welcome the consequences? And if it was not, would she find herself spending the rest of her life searching?

As she stood there hesitating on the doorstep, a sudden gust of wind caught her silk skirt, and the door of the cottage slammed shut behind her.

*

The three men stood up as Deirdre ran along the sand

towards them. And, as she drew nearer, Deirdre could see the fear in their eyes.

'I am sorry,' the taller man stepped forward. 'We did not want to intrude.'

Deirdre stared. His words were heavily accented, his English stilted. But this man, the one who had spoken, was the one she felt sure had spoken to her in her dream. It was the same voice. And, for a moment or two, she took in the pale complexion, the dark hair and beard and moustache. She had not imagined how he would look. He certainly did not look like anyone she had met before.

'If this is a private place, we did not see the notice.'

'It was the fire, I saw the fire,' she stuttered.

'And that is not allowed?'

'No. I mean yes, that is allowed.'

'This is the first time we have been here. We did not know if it was permitted.'

'I had a dream last night ...' she laughed then, conscious of how strange her confession might sound to complete strangers.

The three men remained standing; fear now turned to confusion.

'Can I sit with you beside your fire?'

'Of course. And we have some good whisky, if you would like. But perhaps that is not allowed?'

'No, that isn't allowed. But I won't tell anyone.'

Deirdre hitched up her skirt and sat down cross-legged.

'I am Andrik. These are my brothers, Arron and Jan.'

'And I'm Deirdre.'

'Deirdre,' Andrik echoed. 'You live in the Big House.'

'No,' she smiled. 'I've decided not to live in the Big House.'

'You are running away!' Arron sat back down on the sand, smiling. His hair was lighter than his brother's, and his chin bore only the slightest suggestion of stubble.

198

'Not exactly. But I am leaving.'

'We did not expect to find a princess on this beach in the middle of the night.'

The third brother had spoken. His fair, curly hair crowned his head in an unruly mop. Deirdre imagined him as a cherubic child, getting into all sorts of mischief and always being forgiven.

'Jan, she did not say she was a princess.'

'Oh, yes, Andrik,' he smiled. 'Only a beautiful princess would look and dress like Deirdre, and run away in the middle of the night. She is being chased by a *bogle*. That is a ghost in Scotland, is it not? At sea, they have told me many stories about them.'

Deirdre laughed then.

'So, Andrik, you're the oldest brother, Jan is the youngest …'

'And I am in the middle,' Arron added.

'And you're sailors?'

'We are trawlermen. We catch herring. Our uncle, he has the boats,' Andrik sat down beside Deirdre. 'Drink with us.'

Deirdre shook her head.

'We will not tell anyone.'

For the first time since her arrival, Andrik smiled. The firelight softened his features, melting the sharp contrast between his pale complexion and dark hair. And now she could see his eyes were the palest blue. Deirdre found herself unable to look away. He leaned in towards her as they talked, listening and watching, reading her with his eyes.

A shadow crept across the moon, and the fire seemed to shrink a little in the darkness. The onshore breeze had picked up, and she shivered. Andrik put his hand out and touched her arm.

'You did not come out ready for the weather, without a coat, and without shoes. Please take this.'

He removed his leather jacket and wrapped it around her

shoulders. His coat was still warm, but Deirdre could not shake the chill in her bones. In the distance, she imagined crashing waves on the headland and a storm brewing on the horizon. At the heart of the fire, blue flames battled to survive the wind.

Arron stood up, collected some fresh wood from the nearby pile, and stacked them carefully on the bonfire. Jan refilled the men's paper cups with whisky.

'*Nazdrave*!' they said together.

Arron and Jan swallowed their whisky, but Andrik passed his cup to Deirdre.

'Please, just a little to keep out the cold.'

She took a deep breath and swallowed. The burning liquid hit the back of her throat and she coughed.

Jan laughed. 'If you are leaving the Big House, where will you go?'

'Back to the village.'

'And the *bogle* will not find you there?'

'It isn't a *bogle*, Jan. It's a man who wants to marry me.'

Andrik put his hand on her arm again.

'And you do not want this?'

'No, I thought maybe once I did. But, now? No, I don't. And I'm a little afraid he'll never leave me alone.'

'In this village, he will certainly find you,' Jan had spoken again.

'Yes.'

'Then you must come with us.'

'And what would I do? I don't even know where you live.'

Andrik stood up and held his hand out for Deirdre.

'Perhaps we can walk a little? It will make you warmer. And we can talk.'

Deirdre took his hand and together, in the shelter of the sand dunes, they walked along the beach. Andrik told her that the brothers came from Eastern Europe, and now they

200

shared a house near the harbour in the city. He told her about the fishing trips they made with their uncle's trawler fleet. As he spoke, Deirdre imagined the anonymity and freedom she would have in this city, where Sebastian could not find her. And she could be with Andrik, get to know him.

So, Deirdre told him about her life in the village and the laird who wanted to marry her. And she told him her dream, of *an dà-shealladh*. In the silence that followed, she wondered if he had misunderstood her words. But he pointed back to where his brothers sat beside the bonfire, and said, 'So this is destiny? You believe this?'

'You think I'm a little crazy, don't you?'

'No. I think it is a wonderful idea – to meet someone that you have dreamed of. And,' he paused, 'I think now that you should definitely come to the city with us, to a place where we will keep you safe from this laird, as you say.'

'And, if I come with you, and Arron and Jan, I can go anywhere, do anything, leave if I want to?'

Andrik laughed, 'I promise we will not be kidnapping you. We ... I am only offering you a seat on the back of my motorbike tonight, and a place to stay until ...'

'Until?'

'Until you are happy and do not have to run away again.'

*

Deirdre took off the dress which Sebastian had given her. The silk skirt was dark with wet sand, which still clung to the hem. She shook it, and the grains scattered across the stone floor. When Brigid saw them in the morning, she would know where she had been; and she would remember Deirdre's dream. There was no need to leave a note, a note which would make Brigid complicit in her escape. Deirdre folded the dress back into its box, carefully placing the jewellery back in place. She dressed quickly in jeans and a jumper and warm jacket, threw a few personal items in her

backpack, and closed the door of the cottage quietly behind
her.

*

The brothers turned their bikes around and started up the
track to the main road, Deirdre seated behind Andrik.

Deirdre looked up at Carlyle House, its pale walls casting
shadows on the moonlit beach, a single light burning in an
upstairs room. Sebastian was still awake. Perhaps, he had
been watching her on the beach. He would have seen the
bonfire and been curious. And perhaps, he had heard the
motorbikes start up and had seen her leave.

Chapter 41

Meghan

Deirdre had come back to find me. I was more intrigued than concerned about this possibility. Was it merely chance that had linked us? Surely, it had been more than coincidence, my simply being in the right place at the right time? I'd begun to believe she'd waited and watched for me. I didn't believe in heaven and hell, and was not convinced there was anywhere where souls existed after death. But I'd always found the concept of limbo – the place where restless spirits wandered between this life and the next – rather troubling.

Both Deirdre and Brigid were deemed to have second sight. I wasn't quite sure how it worked, but I couldn't believe that living in the village, in the old byre on the farm where the McIntyres used to live, would suddenly give me the ability to see into another dimension. Yet the memory of her face reflected in the water kept returning to me, those proud, defiant eyes staring directly into mine. If I'd been a better artist, I thought, I might even have tried to draw or paint her image. But I knew I could never have done her justice.

*

It was a day or two later, on one of our walks, when I met Dougal coming out of the village shop.

'Off along the cliffs again, lass?'

I nodded and smiled.

'Is she drawing you there, to her special place?'

'Whose special place?'

Dougal looked around quickly and took my arm. Neither of us spoke as we crossed the common ground and turned to walk further along the cliffside. Far below, the water was in perpetual motion. There was no beach here, no visible ebbing tide. The waves crashed into the rocks without regard for the waxing or waning moon. It ate its way through the granite and the sandstone, carving arches and leaving sea stacks in its path. The moods of the ocean depended only on the wind and the landscape it had created for itself; surging and fuming, each minute of each day a little different from the one before.

'She loved this place,' Dougal smiled. 'That was why she chose to die here.'

'She chose to die? She killed herself?'

'You didn't know? I thought at least Ellen would've said.'

'What happened? Why? She was so young, and so beautiful.'

'She could've had any man, any life. Instead, she went for that Carlyle fella. You know about him, right?'

'Sebastian, yes.'

'Aye, Sebastian St. John Carlyle, the laird,' Dougal spat out the words in disgust. 'He wanted her. But the silly wee lass couldna make up her mind, and ran off to the city with the bikers.'

'Bikers?'

'She met them on the beach, and left. Shacked up with the three of them, Fergus had said.'

'She moved in with three bikers?'

'Aye, and the gossip was something terrible. A few months later, she was back, wanting to get back together with the laird. She hitches a ride on a fishing boat and walks through the village, bold as brass. Goes to stay with Brigid for the night and waits for her man to come and find her,' he hesitated. 'Now I'm all for young folks sowing their wild oats, so to speak,' he laughed, 'but we're a small community, and the kirk doesna abide with that kind of thing … at least not out in broad daylight.'

'And did Sebastian come and find her?'

'Aye, the next afternoon, he comes roond. They meet on the cliffs, along the path from the village, in plain sight of everyone. And they talk and argue for a wee while. The laird is not happy, made to look the fool in front of everyone. He doesna stay long.'

'And Deirdre?'

'She sits by hersel', crying and all. And then there's the accident out at sea. The coastguards are out with boats and helicopters. Everyone's upset. It's how many folks make their living, and we're remembering kinfolk who've gone down too.'

'The minister's prayer, and the song at the Christmas pageant, I understand. So, Deirdre, what does she do?'

'The next day she throws herself off the cliffs right here and … well I dinna have to paint you a picture.'

I looked over the edge of the cliff and wondered how it must have felt to fling yourself over the edge, knowing that your body would be smashed on the rocks long before the water closed over your head. Did Deirdre have time to regret her decision on the way down, when it was too late? I, too, had felt the power of the ocean beneath my feet, and the draw of the waves urging me down. It was a compelling experience, but a deadly temptation.

This wild and beautiful landscape held the power to touch you, reach down deep inside, evoke an emotional response. For me, it had become a sanctuary. Perhaps for Deirdre, who had lived here all her life, the sea churning below the cliffs had offered another kind of refuge.

Chapter 42

Deirdre

Deirdre wrapped her arms around Andrik's waist and followed his lead as he leaned into the turns of the road. The swaying of the bike and the warmth of Andrik's back was soothing for a while, until she saw the village. It clung to the hillside, nestling on the slopes and sweeping down to the shore beyond.

The journey she was undertaking, the decision to leave, had been rash and unplanned. She considered asking Andrik to take her back to Brigid's cottage. Her life was there, everything she had always loved and treasured. Her days spent exploring the moors and climbing the hills were ingrained in her soul. Her nights listening to the rise and fall of the waves on the beach below the village eased her in and out of each new day. Her memories were all locked into this small space and time. The people there would protect her. They would understand. They were not living in medieval times. No-one could take away her freedom with impunity. Her father had been appeased – he had accepted his thirty pieces of silver. But Sebastian could not really harm her, could he? He might not forgive or forget, as Brigid had said. But, in the end, he would have to accept her decision and move on. He was a civilised man, a man of the world.

And then she remembered Iolaire, her friend and confidant. Tonight, in the dark, he too would be resting in his eyrie. But as the sun rose, he would look for her again and wonder at her disappearance. In her heart she knew she would return to the village one day. But the lifespan of an eagle, especially in the wild, was not long. She might never see him again. As they made a turn around the next bend in the road and the village faded into the darkness, this felt like the most terrible loss of all.

Yet now, she had found Andrik, the man whose voice she had heard in her dreams, whose body she now clung to in the cold night air. He was the man whom she had been destined to meet. She believed this. Brigid had taught her to trust *an dà-shealladh*. In her dream of Carlyle House, she had been confused, walking alone down a long hallway with no end in sight. In this other dream, she had heard Andrik's voice, and it had made her feel safe. So, she would move forward slowly, taking one day at a time. To resist destiny was to play the fool and to spend your life in a torment of regret. She leaned her head against his back. And, as his arm reached for her and pulled her closer, she knew the day would come when the hills and the shores of the Highlands would call her home, to a place where she and Andrik could live in peace.

They travelled inland for a while, along a narrow road hemmed in by tall firs, before skirting a small coastal hamlet, houses sleeping in the shadows. And then they swerved away from the ocean and up into the hills. The air was crisp and clear. In the distance, snow-covered mountains glistened in the moonlight. The sky was filled with tiny, glittering sparks of light. The road climbed steeply, twisting and turning back on itself. There were no houses up here, no people. A young stag stood transfixed at the roadside. A pair of mountain hares dashed into the undergrowth, pursued by the sleek red body of a fox. Then, in the distance, a narrow loch, the ruin of a stone *shieling,* a summer shelter for crofters and their flocks, abandoned now.

Arron signalled to the others that he wanted to stop, and they all pulled over. A rock had become embedded in his front tyre.

Andrik dismounted, 'Are you tired? You are perhaps not used to riding a motorbike?'

'I ride a bicycle.'

'Much more exercise to ride a bicycle,' he laughed and, for the second time that night, held his hand out to her. 'Shall we walk down to the water while we wait for Arron?'

They climbed down the grassy slope, already damp with the overnight dew. A small pebbly beach lay exposed in the moonlight. Deirdre picked up a small stone and skipped it across the water. It bounced two, three times before sinking. Andrik chose another, and his skipped further, longer. She chose another. He chose another. They laughed and jostled each other. Concentric circles radiated across the water, each one empowered by the next, a rippling kaleidoscope of light. And, in the middle of the loch, stretching to the opposite shore, a perfect reflection of the night sky, the illusion of stars floating on its surface.

Andrik turned and pulled her towards him. She froze for a moment, alarmed by the suddenness of his action. Andrik drew back.

'I am sorry. I did not mean …'

But, as she felt the cold air rush in to fill the space between their two bodies, she suddenly felt as if she could not breathe, as if she had lost a gift she did not know she had been given. A minute longer, and it might be gone forever.

'No, Andrik. I want you to kiss me. I want it more than anything I've ever wanted.'

And, as they kissed, Deirdre knew she wanted more, much more. There was nothing she would not give Andrik. She would abandon everything she had known to be with him. Her life until now seemed like a shadow. Whatever happened tomorrow or the next day or for the rest of her life would not erase the memory of how she felt at this moment. She knew – they both knew – this was only a beginning.

Her body ached now in anticipation of what would be. She imagined, once again, how it would feel to lie naked beside him, their bodies wrapped around each other, his hands caressing and exploring each secret part of her. But she was afraid too. The reality of their eventual lovemaking might not be as she imagined. Instead, a bestial fumbling in the dark, an ordeal to be endured. She remembered her mother's tears in the bedroom next door. But, worse still, was the thought that Andrik would change his mind and abandon her; or even die at sea, as so many others had done, always just a hair's breadth from the other side. Whatever the future held, she determined to store each detail of this night – when anything seemed possible. A memory for the time when he might disappear.

Chapter 43

Deirdre

She awoke alone, in an unfamiliar place; her last memory of resting her head on Andrik's shoulder as they pulled away from the loch. A chink of light slipped past the ill-fitting curtain at the window, illuminating bare stone walls and weathered beams overhead. Outside, the noise of traffic passing, clips of unintelligible conversation, a foghorn in the distance. And, although she lay in a double bed, there was only one pillow. Andrik had not slept beside her. Her jeans and jumper lay carefully folded on the wooden sea chest at the bottom of the bed.

She rose, found the bathroom, and splashed warm water on her face. There were two more bedrooms in the small hallway, each door open, each room empty, clothes strewn on unmade beds. At the end, one larger room – a kitchen with blue-painted kitchen cabinets, a small gas stove and fridge, a dining table and four chairs, a sitting area with a sofa and two armchairs, a TV and a small wood-burning stove. And an alcove porch with a coat-rack laden with yellow sou'westers, rubber boots paired below and a heavy front door leading directly onto the street.

A small potted plant shrivelled on the windowsill, with a folded piece of paper propped against it, a single initial – *D* – handwritten on the outside –

We have gone north to catch fish. Maybe three or four days. There is food in the cupboard and the fridge, and money in

210

the drawer below the kettle. Please eat and spend as you need. I am thinking of you as I go. Please wait for me.
Andrik
P.S. I am sorry I did not know how to write your name. There is a key in the drawer. Always lock the door.

This was not how Deirdre had imagined her first day. She had looked forward to lazy days with Andrik, walking the streets together hand-in-hand as he showed her the city, discovering new places, learning about each other. He had not told her he would be going to sea so soon. And she had not asked him. Now she was quite alone. If Sebastian had been here, he would have taken her out, shown her all the best sights. And yet, Andrik had gone. But that was exactly why she had left Sebastian and refused his offer of marriage wasn't it? Because he always took charge, led her where he thought she should go. Andrik had trusted her to be able to look after herself, explore the city in her own way. He had given her the freedom to leave or to stay; only asking, hoping she would wait for his return. He had made no assumptions, no conditions. His trust made her want to prove she was capable of anything.

*

The city was blanketed in a thick sea mist. She could see the breakwater stretching away from the harbour, lit by pale lights seemingly suspended in mid-air. Boats shifted on their moorings, bumping against the harbour wall. A woman passed with a baby muffled in a pushchair. Another opened her front door and looked along the street, as if expecting a visitor. A delivery van careened around the corner and disappeared down a side lane.

Deirdre wondered when Andrik and his brothers had set out to sea. She could still hear the intermittent call of a foghorn – whether from a lighthouse or a ship, she could not tell. Already, like so many before her, she found herself

211

worrying about a man out at sea.

She had thought of walking the length of the harbour, perhaps finding a stretch of beach, some hills to climb beyond. But now, with the fog, she knew she could lose her sense of direction. It was safer, she decided, to explore the city, take account of landmarks – street names, shops, cafés – and find her way back down to the harbour.

A maze of small cobblestone lanes led uphill. Some had remained residential, terraces of two-storey houses fronting directly onto the pavement, a vase or a figurine on the windowsill, rooms hidden behind lace curtains. Others had branched out, catering for the stream of tourists who poured into the Highlands each year. Signs advertising Bed and Breakfast vacancies swung over front doors. Bubble-windowed cafés displayed cake stands with freshly-baked goods inside and linen tablecloths on round, rickety tables. Small second-hand emporia offered tourist almanacs on racks in their doorways; broken pottery and pewter mugs, old maps, and yellowing paperbacks stacked inside their dark interiors. As she crossed the road which paralleled the harbour, the lanes expanded into narrow roads with clothes boutiques and shopping bazaars overflowing with cheap gewgaws for visitors to buy and take home, only to be abandoned later in some dusty corner of their house.

Finally, she arrived at the main street. A department store, two or three chain stores and chemists, grandiose old hotels and quaint pubs offering locally brewed beer and whisky and gin, chalked menus set outside, and larger tourist shops with upmarket merchandise for the discerning traveller. Local buses and luxury coaches and taxis, rental cars, bikers and cyclists; all competed with pedestrians for passage here. Despite the cold and damp and fog, the street was noisy and overcrowded. Diesel fumes pumped heat into the air.

Deirdre turned away, finding her way easily downhill and back to the relative quiet of the harbour. She walked the length of the breakwater and sat on the end of the wall where she could look out to sea, her feet swinging over the side. She thought about Brigid, and Sebastian, and what they had said to each other. Perhaps, he had not yet discovered she had gone.

'Mind yersel' lassie. There'll be a deal of spray coming yer way when the tide turns.'

Behind her, a man was carrying a pile of lobster pots up the breakwater steps. His boat lay at an angle, caught on the shingle below, stranded there by the low tide.

'That'll be wonderful,' she laughed. 'Perhaps, I'll just wait for that then.'

He smiled, 'Don't say I didna warn you.'

In the distance, the foghorn continued to send out its alert.

For a while, she sat listening to the cries of the seagulls squabbling over scraps of sea life stranded by the tide, as she waited for the waves to return. She heard the boats shifting as the water pulled and pushed them with each ebb and flow. Was the tide coming in now back at the village? She did not know how far they had travelled the night before. Perhaps at home, on the beach below the village, it was already high tide.

Reluctantly, she returned to the cottage. A steady drizzle had arrived with the turn of the tide, and although it cleared the fog as it fell, the damp had seeped slowly inside the collar of her jacket and soaked her jeans.

She had three more days to wait until she saw Andrik again. But how long would he stay with her? And what would she do in the meantime, and every time he left to go to sea again with his brothers? She had absolute freedom now. Or did she? She could not leave knowing how she felt about him, believing she understood how he felt about her. And yet, she could not stay here, always waiting for his return.

Chapter 44

Meghan

Dougal had completed the story. Deirdre had killed herself because Sebastian would not, could not, bring himself to take her back. But why had he disappeared, leaving his estate for more than fifteen years? Because he was angry? Or because he regretted not swallowing his pride, accepting Deirdre's apology and taking her back? And where was he now? Perhaps he really was still nearby, living under the radar at Carlyle House. If he'd been the one who broke into my cottage, what was he looking for in a building which was no more than a byre when Deirdre was alive?

If that really was the end of the story, why was Deirdre still here? Was she waiting for Sebastian to change his mind? Was she expecting me to find him and bring him home? I could start my research all over again, but I knew I'd done everything, looked everywhere; in the end, the outcome would be the same. I had no idea where he was and no way of finding him.

*

I am not by nature someone who frequents graveyards, delving into the past by looking at headstones, imagining lives lived long or cut short. But I awoke a couple of days later and decided that the final step for me – perhaps to lay Deirdre's story to rest – would be to visit the cemetery which stood on the hillside above the village. I would find

214

Deirdre's grave.

Cassie and I walked through the village as usual and then took the left turn away from the cliffs, past the campground and the small grey-stone church, and up the hill to the cemetery. The graves were enclosed inside a low stone wall; but it was unlike cemeteries I had seen before. Staggered up a steep grassy slope, the graves were sparsely separated from each other. There were no ledgers here – the stones which lie flat on the ground covering the whole grave. Only headstones, jutting out of the ground, the names and inscriptions facing away from the sea and up into the hills. The ground seemed very unstable, sandy and loosely packed, held together against the weather by the sod alone.

The fancier monuments were on the upper part of the hill, nearest to the gate, their heavy headstones listing at strange angles, their supplementary madonnas and angels and urns barely holding on to their plinths below. I criss-crossed the ground here, looking for the name Carlyle, expecting to see generations of lairds maintaining superiority, even in death. But there were none; instead, I found a scattering of the Sinclair and Sutherland, Mackenzie and Gunn families.

Further down, clustered on one side, there were many with the name Mackay. Their headstones were simple, names and dates and beloved relationships. Some had died at birth, a few in old age. Too many had died at sea, losing their lives in youth and early manhood.

And then, as I moved across, I saw the name Brigid Macleod beside that of Iain, her husband. *Beloved mother & wife*, it read. *Ne'er chastened.* This, I thought, must be James McIntyre's auld witch and Deirdre's mentor. Nearby, Máire McIntyre rested. James, I imagined, would be laid to rest beside his wife. But there was no sign of a grave for Deirdre, not here beside her mother nor near Brigid.

Another missing link, I thought. There was always some element of Deirdre's story which left more questions and prevented closure.

Standing at the bottom of the graveyard, I heard the waves in the distance, and smelled the decomposing seaweed on the beach far below, wafted inland on a stiff breeze. I could understand why they'd decided, centuries earlier, to bury their dead here. The location spoke of the vastness of eternity, the empty air between the high land where the dead were buried and the valley of the living below. Here, the sky seemed much closer, heaven nearer at hand. But to me at that moment, it felt like abandonment; a hill-climb away from everyday life and the memories of the living, a landscape where only tough grasses grew and where the wind whispered its secrets around the disintegrating headstones.

As I turned to leave, I was distracted by a movement at the furthest corner of the cemetery, away from the lych-gate. There was a small copse of trees outside the wall, which I hadn't noticed when I arrived. Cassie started barking, but all I could see were branches swaying crazily in a sudden downdraft.

We left the graveyard and walked towards the trees. Despite all the foliage, there really were only two trees there. Yews, I realised. The trees of immortality. Since ancient times, they'd been planted around gravesites. Every living part of the tree – bark, leaves and berries – is extremely poisonous. These two were relatively young, probably less than twenty years old, so their trunks had not yet acquired the gnarled and twisted look often seen in older trees. But they were already taller than me, their leaves full and green, their branches reaching out towards each other, stalwart supports against the elements.

Grass and heather grew under the trees. On one side, the ground lay unspoilt, the purple heather blooms already in bud. But on the other, the turf had been cut into rectangles and looked recently disturbed, with some of the subsoil scattered on the grass. Cassie started snuffling at the ground and, before I could stop her, had pulled one of the rectangles loose. I leaned over to replace it, and saw a wooden plank immediately below where she had removed the turf. I rolled the rectangle a few inches and dropped it back into place. It clattered onto the plank with a hollow echo. I moved along what I assumed was the top end of the plank and rolled back the next roll of turf, hoping that I was wrong. There wasn't another plank, but a continuation of the same piece of wood. I knew even before I tapped on it that it, too, would sound hollow. Here, outside the cemetery, in the shadow of the yew trees, I knew it was a wooden coffin. Just a few inches below the disturbed turf, there were bones, bones which Cassie could smell.

Someone had taken great care to conceal the coffin, but it was in shallow ground. Perhaps, it had only recently been laid here, and they intended to return to dig a proper grave. Or, if it had been here for years, they could have made plans to return from time-to-time. If that was so, it was a gruesome thought, the desecration of a grave by a bone collector.

I shuddered to think these might be Deirdre's remains. Was this what everyone in the village was afraid to admit – that Deirdre had been buried in unhallowed ground or that they knew there was a bone collector in their midst? But who felt they had the right to disturb her final resting place, and for what purpose? If I had really seen her, perhaps she wanted me, an outsider, to help her. Perhaps, Dougal had only told me a part of the story. If so, this was much more terrible than I could ever have imagined. After all these years, was Deirdre still not allowed to be left in peace?

Chapter 45

Deirdre

Andrik did not return for five days – twenty tides. And, when he did, Deirdre was not there.

*

While she waited, she decided to tidy up the cottage, change sheets, do laundry, dust and scrub. And she searched for signs of Andrik's identity. In the bedrooms, she found only clothes and toiletries. But in the sitting room, there were nautical magazines organised in date order, and a clutter of paperback novels piled on top of each other at the bottom of a bookshelf. A copy of *Moby Dick* and a range of Hemingway novels, a *Complete Oxford English Dictionary*, a well-worn Bible; and another apparent religious text, written in a script Deirdre did not recognise, were arranged above. Beside them, some shells and quartzite rocks, glass floats in a wire basket. And, on the top shelf, a silver-framed family portrait; babies cradled, small children seated on the ground, men and women, old and young, all posed and staring ahead. She thought she recognised a small dark-haired Andrik in the group but could not find Arron or Jan.

Outside, the rain continued to fall steadily, but the city and the harbour were sheltered from the fierce winds she was accustomed to at home. So, each afternoon, she walked across the city, hidden beneath the hood of her anorak, exploring the streets and lanes and alleyways until she could distinguish the character of each neighbourhood. She heard the squeals of children at breaktime playing in the yard behind their school, and knew that two hours later, a crowd of mothers and fathers would be waiting outside the gates to take them home. A few streets away, young men hung out around street corners, watching and waiting as cars cruised by, catcalling her as she passed. Men hurried in and out of the bookies, tossing betting slips onto the pavement and lighting-up cigarettes as they left. She saw faces passing in buses, friends exchanging greetings, youths flirting with giggling girls. She watched shopkeepers hand-cranking shutters over shop fronts at the end of each business day. She saw couples, arm-in-arm, hurrying into cafés and pubs as darkness closed in.

And she counted out each day, measuring its advance by the tides. Four times a day, the tide turned, two low tides and two high. Six hours each, with a twenty-five-minute lull after each high tide. Three days until Andrik's return, twelve tides and three hours or less. But twelve became sixteen; and sixteen became twenty. And each afternoon, she walked further and further across the city until, on that last day, she went as far as the motorway and the bridge which led north to her village.

*

Dusk had overtaken her when she returned to the harbour. She saw the lights on in the cottage, and she began to run. The front door stood open, Andrik was there waiting. Inside, the room was warm, the fire stoked high.

'Where have you been? I thought you had gone.'

Slowly, Deirdre pulled off her anorak and pushed past him to hang it on the rack.

'No, Andrik, I stayed. It was you who left, you who didn't return when you said. I went out. I can do that, can't I?'

'Of course, I am sorry. I did not mean ...'

'And Arron and Jan, where're they?'

'They have gone to the pub. We have been home many hours now. But I waited here for you.'

'Waiting's not too much fun, is it?'

'You are angry. I am sorry. Perhaps you do not want to stay here anymore.'

'Oh, Andrik. I want to stay, I really do, but …'

'This is not as you expected. But now, we are here for more than a week,' he hesitated. 'Please, can I hold you like before? Perhaps, love you a little?'

And so, that evening and night and into the next morning, they loved each other, and made love. Deirdre was lost in an ocean of emotions and physical sensations she could not have imagined or explained. As each wave ebbed and flowed, she moved with the swelling tide. She soared skyward with Iolaire. She was breathless as she climbed the hillsides, feeling the strength of the rocks beneath. She lay back in the heather and was warmed by the midsummer sun. She had come home.

Chapter 46

Deirdre

They left their room and explored the city together. Clouds still hovered overhead, but the rain held off most days. Deirdre showed Andrik places he had never seen before, explained the people he had never noticed. And Andrik took her along the coast and up into the hills on the back of his motorbike. Every day made a new memory. She compared what she saw with all the experiences and places she had known. But she did not tell Andrik. As if by mutual consent, the past was not explored or explained, only the present mattered.

He told her the brothers all worked together on the same trawler. Their uncle had named it *Purvi*, meaning 'The First'. It was his oldest ship, the one he had bought to start his fleet, and he had given this to his nephews.

'But when the currents are fast, and the wind blows hard, the boat rolls and pitches. You can hear the wood creaking below decks, like the bones of an old woman complaining of the cold.'

Deirdre smiled, 'She's an old woman you know well.'

'Yes. But this time, out there on the sea, in the darkness and fog, I was afraid. I have never been afraid before.'

'Why were you afraid this time?'

'Before, I was ready for the sea, for my death if it was destined. Now I am not ready to die. I have been given too much. You have filled my heart and my mind. I began to

221

wonder if I had imagined you.'

'Well, you didn't,' she kissed him on the cheek.

'No. Arron and Jan told me not.'

'When you were away, I watched the sea too. Each day, I counted the high and low tides.'

'You are a perfect lady for a trawlerman to love.'

'But I'm also afraid for you. You said you'd return after twelve tides, but you were gone for twenty.'

'We found many shoals. We could not leave. We were lucky, even though …' he paused, '… even though Jan told the other men you were a runaway princess with beautiful red hair.'

'Oh.'

'You know?'

'It's an old seaman's superstition – it's bad luck if you set out to sea after you've seen someone with red hair,' she smiled. 'But apparently not this time.'

'No, definitely not this time. And not for me, ever.'

*

Each morning, Deirdre found herself counting the days until Andrik would leave again. Arron and Jan came and went, their existence reflected only in abandoned coffee cups, unmade beds, and sometimes, in muffled conversations she heard outside Andrik's room in the night. They did not bring girls home; although, some nights, she noticed the silence in the house and realised they were sleeping elsewhere.

But, when the final morning arrived, the day she knew the brothers would be leaving again, she regretted the week she and Andrik had spent together. They had shared so much and yet so little. The immediacy of their love had consumed them. They had forgotten to travel through their past lives, discover what had brought them to this place, why they had bonded so easily. Deirdre wondered now about Andrik's life before he had met her, the girls he had known, the trail of love affairs he may have left in his wake. He had given her his full attention for a week. But a man like Andrik, in his twenties, with his dark, brooding good-looks, had not been a virgin when he had taken her to his bed. Of this, she was certain.

The room felt cold, the sun still below the horizon. She pulled the covers up around her chin and moved in closer to Andrik, clinging to the warmth of his body. Instinctively, he stretched out his arm and drew her in. It was a familiar gesture, one she remembered from the first time they had kissed beside the moonlit loch.

In the half-light, she watched him, as she had done every morning since his return, his eyes opening slowly, searching her face, reading her mood.

'I am so sorry to leave again. I, too, am sad.'

'How long will you be gone this time?'

'We must go further to find the herring.'

'So, how long?'

'A week, maybe more.'

'And you want me to stay, waiting for you?'

'And you do not?'

'I want to be with you. But when you're not here …'

'Soon, it will be better. My uncle will find an investor, buy better sonar, and then we will outrun all the others and get to the fishing grounds first.'

'But you will still go away, leaving me alone.'

'You must decide what you want to do. I will always love you.'

'Will you?'

'You are now, to me, the only girl.'

She laughed then.

'I knew I wasn't the first.'

'We do not look back, only forward now. Remember. That is the plan.'

'That is the plan.'

'And you too, you must make a plan, your plan. What did you want to do before, before we loved each other?'

'Go to university, get a job, travel. I wanted to leave the village and do something!'

'Now you have left the village. What is next in your plan?' he smiled. 'What will you study at university?'

'I've always loved history and music. I'd like to do both.'

'So, you are an ambitious lady! I like that. And then you will become many things?'

'Yes, I will … I can become many things.'

'And we'll do many things together. You have made a perfect plan for us both.'

Deirdre laughed and hugged Andrik.

'I have, haven't I? Because now we're together, we can do anything.'

*

In the silence that evening, Deirdre knew Andrik had understood. She could not sit alone, always waiting for his return, her life suspended between their days and nights of lovemaking. Their love would sour if she only lived through him, waiting and anxious. Sebastian had believed, had told her, that it would be enough. But he had not really understood.

Chapter 47

Meghan

I could not forget finding Deirdre's open grave. The reality of what I'd seen had shocked me. To be consigned to an unmarked grave, isolated and alone outside the churchyard and subject to disturbance by someone who might still hold a grievance against her, seemed to be the stuff of horror fiction.

I knew there was only one person I could speak to confidentially, but Ellen always seemed to leave before I woke in the mornings and was usually tied up with the boys and Cathel in the evenings. I'd wait until we could speak alone. But I couldn't sit around the house, or the village, waiting. I had to get out, breathe in some good highland air, and walk out the tension I could feel building in my shoulders.

When we'd arrived – nearly seven months ago – I'd taken the coast road north. But now, with the arrival of spring, and my greater confidence in finding my way around and being able to tackle the protocols of driving on single-track roads, I decided to take the hill route. I had no desire to go as far as the city; just reach the outskirts of the first little hamlet.

In the distance, the mountains still held onto the last remnants of the winter snow, hidden from the warmth of the sun in the deep crevasses etched each year into their slopes. But in the glens, new life had begun. Cathel had birthed most of the lambs in his flock already, and I watched in delight as

225

they gambolled in the fields below the cottage. They were still relatively unafraid of strangers and sometimes nosed their way through the fence as Cassie and I walked past. But they'd not yet been let loose in the hills, where they would still be prey for foxes and buzzards and eagles. Instead, the one-year-old sheep – hogs, Ellen had called them – were roaming the hills.

The road was quiet, and I only met one logger and a couple of delivery vehicles on my route, which switched back and forth, following the contours of a wide stream hidden amongst the trees. Steep bracken and heather covered hillsides stretched up on the other side of the road. I'd brought a packed lunch and my drawing pad and camera, and was looking for a suitable place to set up camp. When I saw the ruined *shieling*, overlooking a long narrow loch, I knew I'd found the perfect spot.

I sat for a while, stretched out on the travelling rug, my back leaning against a large boulder near the water. Some geese landed on the loch, causing a commotion amongst a family of paddling ducks. Small brown butterflies competed with the honey bees for nectar from swathes of blue and white, and yellow flowers. And, faintly in the distance, I heard the baaing of sheep.

It all seemed so perfect, so unspoilt. I couldn't understand why Deirdre had run away from this incredible place, a place replete with superlatives. Sebastian had probably been her first love, an older man, but still a man with status and prospects who loved her too. What could have driven her to run away to the city with some bikers? Was she looking for adventure and excitement? She certainly regretted her decision after only a few months. She'd had her fling, realised the grass was not greener on the other side, and changed her mind. But when she returned, he had rejected her, and she'd lost hope. If her mother had been alive, if her father had been a different kind of man, if she'd listened to

Brigid, perhaps she would've still been alive.

She'd been so beautiful, so young. If she'd just waited for her life to turn around, she would've found love again; the memories wouldn't fade, but there were always new ones to make. I, too, had felt desperate. Only after I'd decided to leave Richard, did I finally realise the futility of my past expectations. He'd taken, and I'd given, until I was drained and exhausted. Coming here had been a wonderful release.

Many years earlier, I'd been at a friend's funeral. He'd locked himself in his garage, the car engine running, and listened to the soundtrack of *La Bohème* as he drew the carbon dioxide fumes deep into his lungs. The ex-love of his life was not at the funeral, only his grieving mother.

The note on her wreath laid outside the crematorium read simply –

See you in the next life, my son.

A single mother, she had devoted her life to him. And, at that moment, her loss seemed so much greater than his. No-one can see what's in another's heart and understand their pain. But I had determined to move on, look for new horizons, start again. And I'd begun to see that this was the perfect place to do so.

I walked up into the hills with my backpack, Cassie exploring every bush and boulder, ears pricked, tail wagging. I ate my sandwich, took photos and sat for a while with my sketch pad. And as I looked, I realised that I could never capture the changing moods of the landscape below. Even the camera, with its wide-angle lens, was inadequate.

*

A couple of days later, Ellen came round for a late-night drink. She'd been to a parent-teacher evening at the school and was glad to leave Cathel to put the boys to bed. She looked tired, and I was reluctant to start the conversation and

227

reveal what I'd discovered.

'So, how was it?'

'What?'

'Your wee walk to the Auld Village?'

She took a sip of her Scotch.

'I didn't make it,' I hesitated. 'I saw her at the *lochan*; and then I found her grave.'

'You're talking about Deirdre?'

'Yes. So, you know?'

'Of course, I know it's Deirdre you're on about. You've been asking a lot of questions. Dougal told Cathel, who told me. It's a small place, Meghan.'

'And?'

'Can we start from the beginning? You said you saw her? She's dead. You know that, right?'

'Yes. Dougal said. But then I saw her. Or at least, I saw her reflection in the *lochan*. I fell asleep in the sun, and when I woke, she was there, staring up at me.'

Ellen smiled.

'You woke from a wee nap. It was just a dream then.'

'If it was a dream, it was very real. I waded into the water. After you talked about hearing things at Carlyle House, I thought she might still be alive. But, when I saw her face there, I imagined she'd been murdered recently and was lying under the water.'

'But she wasn't?'

'No, no, she wasn't.'

'And then you went up to the cemetery and found her grave?'

'Well, yes, and no,' I hesitated again. 'This is why I wanted to talk to you, alone.'

'Go on.'

'Her grave wasn't in the graveyard.'

'It wasn't in the graveyard? I don't understand.'

'It was outside, under some yew trees. Why?'

'I don't know. Everyone's always buried in the cemetery.'

'And the coffin wasn't buried. It was just under a pile of turf.'

'That's the highland way.'

'No, I mean, it wasn't buried properly. It lay just an inch or two, immediately below the turf. Either it had only been put there recently … or someone wanted to get into it from time-to-time.'

'Someone wanted to get into it?'

'There was dirt all over the grass, as if it had been disturbed recently. Cassie started digging, and the whole lot came away,' I stopped. 'You didn't know she wasn't in the cemetery? I thought you and Cathel …'

'When she died, Brigid said there was to be no funeral, and no mourners. She and Fergus handled all the arrangements. It would be a private, family affair, she said.'

'And what about her father, James, wasn't he included?'

'He was furious about everything. Called her a brazen hussy and refused to have anything to do with it,' she took another sip of the whisky. 'Of course, with the dementia, he's forgotten all that now.'

'And you didn't ever go up there to see for yourself?'

'No, perhaps we should have. But Cathel and I … No, there's no excuse. We didn't. I've never been to the village cemetery. Cathel's dad and my grandfather are buried up on the hills behind our family farm.'

'So, nobody knew where Brigid and Fergus had taken her?'

'I'm not sure if anyone knew or didn't. Nobody's ever said anything. Deirdre's departure and return, what happened … There'd been so much gossip in the village, most of it very cruel. She was gone. Sebastian was gone. We all wanted to move on too. But if the grave is, as you said, that's criminal. Who'd be doing such a thing after all these years?'

'It was so sad and horrible.'

'And it was definitely Deirdre's grave – you saw the marker?'

'Well, no. It was unmarked. I just assumed. There was no headstone for her in the cemetery. I mean, who else could it be?'

'I don't know, Meghan. I'll talk to Cathel quietly. There might be a simple explanation.'

'A simple explanation for digging up someone's grave?'

'Until we know for sure who or what is buried up there, we'd better keep it to ourselves.'

'Okay, I agree. Thanks,' I paused. 'I never went as far as the Auld Village, the day I saw Deirdre in the water. But I'd still like to go, if you'd come with me.'

'You're afraid to go alone?'

'Past the lake, yes. I know this sounds foolish, but I think Deirdre really did come to me there. It's as if she wanted me to find her grave, lay her to rest properly. I wouldn't have gone up to the cemetery if I hadn't seen her face in the water that day.'

'Maybe so, lass. You've been seeing or imagining a lot of things since you got here. Perhaps, like Brigid and Deirdre, you've discovered you've got the sight.'

'And you've been hearing noises at Carlyle House.'

Ellen laughed, 'Aye, so I have.'

Chapter 48

Deirdre

Deirdre climbed the hill above the shopping centre and walked along the main road to the City College. Going back to school, finishing her classes with giggling teenagers like Emily Gunn was not part of her plan. At the college, she could fast-track her last few months and apply to university. She had grown into a woman with a secret lover. Her life now would be her business and hers alone.

Even though it was only early spring, the sky was cloudless, the tree-lined driveway leading to the main entrance of the college dappled by the overhead sun. It was a perfect day for a new beginning. All she had to do was wait for her old school records to be emailed to the Registrar's Office, and for them to confirm her registration.

But as she walked away, down the hill back to the cottage, she could not shake the image of the village, where tongues wagged, and no-one could keep secrets.

*

Day followed day, week followed week, punctuated by Deirdre's hours in the classroom and the brothers' return. There was a balance now between her need for self-determination and her physical and emotional attachment to Andrik. She maintained two separate identities. It was easy to listen to the confidences of the others, her fellow students, and keep her distance. She had only ever confided in Brigid.

231

And, some nights, she wished she could do so again. Brigid was a valuable ally, but she was also old and vulnerable. A word here, a hint there, would be enough to put her in an impossible situation. Although Deirdre was eighteen and old enough to leave home without her father's permission, the police might be persuaded to believe that she had been kidnapped by a motorbike gang and was in danger, especially if Sebastian had seen her on the beach below Carlyle House with Andrik and Arron and Jan.

*

It was late April when the skylark alerted her to the possibility that she was being watched.

As the days grew longer and the sun climbed higher in the sky, Deirdre spent each dry afternoon outside in the garden behind the cottage. She left the musty silence of the college library, preferring to take her books and a mug of tea outside to study. A small flagstone patio was bordered on one side with what had once been a vegetable garden, only a latticework of stakes and the resurgent growth on some unearthed sprouting potatoes remaining. An expanse of untended grass, interspersed with March's growth of thistles, dandelions and wild poppies, expanded beyond the patio to the slatted fence at the bottom of the garden and the cobbled alleyway beyond.

She had intended to clear the weeds. But, one day, she noticed a male skylark hovering above the overgrown grass and trilling excitedly. Nearby, on the fence, the smaller female feigned indifference for a while, but remained watching the performance. Within a few days, the nest building began. It was unusual for them to build their nests so near the coast, but they had found a perfect, sheltered place.

The female had already started her vigil on the nest when the brothers returned home in mid-April. Deirdre warned them to keep away from the nest; she and Andrik sat

232

quietly each afternoon watching the male as he flew in and out of the garden, sometimes standing sentinel on the fence and sometimes foraging for insects in the tall grass or the abandoned vegetable patch.

Deirdre waited in anticipation of the eggs hatching and the frenzied activity of both birds as they sought to feed their fledglings. She was alone again when that day arrived.

And she was alone two days later when the male skylark flew up from the nest in alarm, diving down and soaring up again in the alleyway beyond the fence. The slats in the fence were old and dry and had crept apart over the years. Deirdre had not noticed the fractured shadow of a stranger behind the fence until the skylark raised the alarm. But, as she looked up from her book, the shadow moved quickly away.

During the days which followed, Deirdre expected to see the shadow return. She planned to challenge the stranger, warn him off. But he did not return. Instead, she became wary of her surroundings, the people she passed in the street, the idlers on street corners. She noticed faces, faces she had seen before which she could not place; cars cruising past the cottage and on her journeys to and from the college. She changed her routines, took circuitous routes to familiar places, slipped in and out of shops she had no need to visit. She double-checked the lock on her front door each time she left the cottage and searched all the rooms for signs of disturbance each time she returned. She slept with the light on.

At home, in the village, she would have easily discovered the source of her fears. But, here in the city, there was a transient population, an unfamiliar busyness which made her restless and uneasy. And Deirdre had decided from the outset to keep herself apart from the curiosity and prying questions of neighbours and fellow students who might have offered her a sense of security, when Andrik and Arron and Jan were

233

away. The arrival of the skylarks had centred her for a while, focused her attention on the things she knew, the annual evolution of the natural world. But they also reminded her that every living creature was at the mercy of another, that each had to beware the enemy who was always watching and waiting for their moment to pounce and destroy them.

Chapter 49

Deirdre

She had not decided whether to tell Andrik about the shadow behind the fence. Out at sea, he needed to be mindful of his own safety, not worrying unnecessarily about hers. Besides, she reasoned, the stranger had not come back again; at least not when she was at home. And she had not seen anyone following her when she was walking outside in the city or along the harbour and the pebbled beach beyond.

When he returned, Andrik did not notice her uncertainty because he came with news of his own.

'Our uncle has found an investor. We – you and me – will be together more. We will find the fish more quickly.'

'That's wonderful.'

'My uncle does not yet know the name, but the solicitor says we will meet very soon. He, too, is from Scotland. Perhaps, you can come with us?'

'I think you'll manage very well without me.'

'Perhaps, it would be a nice place to visit where this investor lives?'

'Perhaps. But I've got my exams.'

'And you are working on your plan.'

Deirdre laughed then.

'Yes, I'm working on my plan.'

For days, the brothers spent their mornings sitting at the kitchen table, looking at catalogues of the latest fishing equipment – radar and GPS systems, sonars and echosounders – and checking availability and prices. Andrik drew up lists and forwarded them to his uncle. Deirdre had never met Uncle Georgi. She imagined an old man, with a beard and moustache like Andrik, wearing a flat cap. He was their grandmother's brother and had emigrated to Scotland between the world wars. She wondered how much he understood about modern technology, and the nature of his agreement with the new investor.

Andrik and his brothers left again before the proposed meeting was arranged. They had been home for more than a week. Although Deirdre and Andrik spent time together most afternoons and evenings, they had both been preoccupied, she with her studies and he with his plans for his uncle's fleet. Their lovemaking was urgent, as if time was passing and they had too little of it. She longed again for those lazy mornings when they had made no plans. It would be different, she promised herself, when everything settled back into a routine, when there were not so many unknowns on the horizon.

*

Deirdre completed her last exam, and ran home through the rain and the blustery wind. She could hear the waves crashing over the breakwater in the harbour and thought about Andrik out at sea, hoping the brothers had found a safe place to ride out the weather. She had planned to work in the back garden, clearing the weeds, cutting the grass, planting some seeds in the vegetable patch. It was safe to do so now. The young skylarks had already flown, the nest abandoned. She hoped they, too, had found shelter from the storm.

She lit the fire and piled on some peat logs for a slow burn, brewed a fresh pot of tea, and sat for a while staring into the flames, which were being buffeted by the downdraft in the chimney. Cradling her mug in her hand, she remembered sitting with Brigid in the cottage on the Carlyle Estate. It all seemed so long ago, that other life. More than three months had elapsed since her night-time flit on the back of Andrik's bike. She hoped Brigid was safely back in her cottage in the village. She hoped Sebastian had reconciled himself to her decision.

Despite the season, the light had faded quickly with the dark rainclouds overhead, and she laid back on the sofa and closed her eyes, contenting herself with the dim glow of the fire. She was half asleep when she heard the knock on the door. She knew no-one in the city who would visit, nor was she expecting any deliveries. Cautiously, she peered out into the half-light, but whoever was on the doorstep was hidden by the front door overhang. She considered ignoring the visitor, but the knocking started again, louder this time. She picked up the fire poker and turned the key in the lock, standing back a little as she pulled the door towards her. The man pulled back the hood of his anorak.

'Let me in, lass,' he said, 'it's pissing rain out here and I'm soaked through.'

It was Fergus.

Chapter 50

Meghan

Ellen and I skirted round the hillside, avoiding the nesting eagles in their eyrie, and found the path which led past the *lochan*. The water sparkled in the early afternoon sun, crystal clear, non-threatening. I could clearly see the rocks and algae on the bottom, under the shallow water along the edge. There were no bodies lying there, no faces staring up at me.

We crested the hill; below, in a small glen, were the houses of the Auld Village. I counted eight houses, mostly ruins now, clustered together. More than two centuries earlier, the people who lived here had been driven from their homes. For the conquering Southerners who had taken control of the land, they had become an unnecessary burden. It had been more profitable and simple to replace them with sheep.

The houses had been simply designed as two-roomed buildings with a fireplace in the larger room. They reminded me of the cottage where I was staying in the village. The people who lived here, I imagined, had the same sense of community, each one looking out for the other. If there had been secrets or personal tragedies here, they too, would have kept them hidden from the outside world.

'That was the house where generations of Brigid's family once lived,' Ellen pointed to a house where a large rowan tree leaned against a crumbling chimney breast, a pile of balanced rocks nearby. 'She used to bring Deirdre here.'

238

'And the cairn?'

'Sometimes cairns are used to mark trails. But here it was more likely a memorial to the past,' she smiled. 'Deirdre probably laid a few of the rocks herself over the years.'

The houses were sheltered by the terrain from the worst of the wind. But even today, in the stillness, I could hear it whispering around the fallen stones, prowling through the gaping holes which once held doors and windows, and stealing down the chimney beside the cairn.

'Can you can hear it?'

'The wind?'

'Aye, the wind ... and the voices. There are always voices in the wind up here. It's a sad place.'

Grass and weeds had taken over inside the houses and the surrounding area; and a rabbit poked his head out of a hole nearby. He froze when he saw us standing there. None of us heard the eagle overhead. We only saw the shadow briefly as he spread his wings for the final few moments of his dive, his talons stretched out below. The rabbit let out a terrified scream as he was carried up into the air and over the hill.

'Oh, my god!'

'Aye, that was scary, wasn't it?' Ellen laughed. 'It might even have been Deirdre's eagle.'

'Deirdre had an eagle?'

'When she was a wee 'un, she rescued an eaglet up at *Iolairean a'Neadachadh* – the Eagle's Nest. It had fallen out of the nest when the adult birds were away. She returned him to the nest, and visited him every week until he was fully fledged. Later, Cathel told me she believed he was a friend, perhaps her best friend. For years, until she died, she'd go up to the eyrie and talk to him. He even flew down into the village to see her once or twice.'

'But, after all these years, is it possible he's the same eagle?'

'Perhaps. Eagles can live a long time. Not so long in the

wild, of course, but still a long time.'

'Have you talked to Cathel about the grave?'

'Aye, I have. He's been up there to the cemetery and seen what you saw. He's going to ask Fergus where he and Brigid buried Deirdre. But he's got to find the right time. It's not something you can ask over a pint in the pub. He thinks Dougal might know something too.'

If it was Deirdre's eagle we'd seen a moment ago, had he followed us up to the Auld Village? Was it possible he knew I was trying to find her? It seemed so unreal, and yet so much had seemed strange recently. I didn't believe in fate, not really. But I didn't believe in coincidences either. The butterfly flapping its wings in the Amazon theory, or the six degrees of separation, were both about relationships. Everything was connected to everything else, everyone to everyone else.

'Do you think, Ellen, it would be alright if I added a stone to Deirdre's cairn?'

'That would be perfect, lass. And I'll add mine to yours.'

I chose a large flat stone which lay under the rowan tree and wedged it carefully on one side of the cairn. Ellen lay a smaller one next to mine, and patted my arm.

'We will find out what happened to Deirdre, Meghan. I promise. And we'll do right by her memory.'

Chapter 51

Deirdre

Deirdre stared at Fergus.

'What's happened? Is Brigid okay? How did you find me?'

'Well, lass, if you let me in out of the rain, I'll answer all your questions. But, yes, my mither is well.'

'Of course, sorry, come in.'

Fergus shook off his wet jacket, and hung it on the rack beside the sou'westers.

'I see you weren't expecting visitors,' he gestured at the poker, which Deirdre was still holding.

'Not when I'm alone.'

'You're alone? Why did you not come home?'

'I'm only alone when they're out at sea,' Deirdre smiled. 'But come and sit by the fire and take a cup of tea.'

'Perhaps something a wee bit stronger, lass. Neither I nor the heater in my van can keep up with the drive over the hills on a day like this.'

For a few minutes, neither spoke. Deirdre filled a tumbler with whisky, and Fergus stirred the fire with the poker she had laid on the hearth. He continued to stand with his back to the heat. She sat in an armchair, perched forward, the earlier comfort of the sofa abandoned.

'How did you find me, Fergus?'

'It wasna that difficult to follow your trail. He knew where you were before ...'

'Sebastian?'

'Aye, the same.'

'He sent you? If so, you've had a wasted journey because I'm not going back to him.'

'He sent me, yes. But not so that he can have you back. He says he understands.'

'He's said that before.'

'Aye, but now he knows you're with Andrik.'

'He even knows his name?'

'Aye, of course,' he paused, taking a draught of his whisky. 'Carlyle's a canny man; and a man with money who knows people. There's nought folks like him canna do in this world. But that's what made him so appealing to you, wasn't it, lass?'

'So, what does he intend to do, now that he's found me, knows where I live and the name of my lover?'

'He's decided to help you all. He's put some money into the trawler fleet.'

'He's Uncle Georgi's investor? I thought he was going to invest his money in the estate, not a fishing fleet.'

'He's an opportunist.'

'And, this time, what does he hope to gain?'

'He intends to make money from his investment, of course. And ...' Fergus paused again, '... he wants to prove to you there are no hard feelings.'

'And you believe him?'

'I'm only the messenger, lass. But I'd say he meant it.'

'And he sent you all this way to deliver this message?'

'He wanted me to ask you something else in person.'

'Of course he did!'

'Don't be hard on him, lass. He's a man who had expectations. He fell in love with the most beautiful lass in the Highlands. You made him believe you might marry him. And then you ran away in the middle of the night.'

'Because he wouldn't take no for an answer. So what

does he want you to ask me now?'

'To come back with Andrik and his brothers for a visit. He wants to see you, talk to you again, make everything right. He wants you to feel free to visit your home, see Brigid. He doesn't want you to be afeart.'

'When someone tells you not to be afeart, it makes you wonder if perhaps you should be.'

'You think too much, lass,' Fergus laughed. 'Will I tell him you'll come?'

'No. But I'll talk to Andrik.'

*

Fergus had been anxious to return to the village before closing time, and had not stayed long after that.

Deirdre spent much of the evening in front of the television, barely noticing what channel or programme she was seeing. Later, she tossed and turned in bed, remembering the village and all the people who lived there. She had become accustomed to the city and the daily routines of her life. Andrik's arms had always been there, waiting to wrap her in their cocoon of warmth and safety. Not since their first night together had she felt the ache of separation from the life she had left behind.

But now, suddenly, she realised how much she missed the sounds and the silences of home. The rippling trill of the curlew circling over the moorland and the newborn lambs calling for their mothers. The silence which shrouded the glen as the haar mist rolled inland, muffling movement and sound like a heavy blanket of snow. The clicking of Brigid's knitting needles as they sat by the fire and talked. She longed to make the breathless climb up the hillside to watch and wait for Iolaire, to listen for his call and feel the sweep of his wings overhead, to open up her heart. To sit by the rowan tree in the Auld Village and listen to the songs of the past carried on the wind, meandering through the crumbling remains of her great grandfather's house.

As Fergus drank his whisky, intoning his words with their highland inflections, she had remembered all this and so much more.

She had abandoned everything and everyone she knew to be with the man she loved. She did not regret the choice, only that she had been forced to make it so suddenly and so completely. Fergus had offered her a passage home. With Andrik at her side, with Arron and Jan, perhaps she would not need to be afraid.

Chapter 52

Deirdre

In all the months she had stayed in the city, Deirdre's dreams had only been pale reflections of her new life. She had floated on clouds, lost her way down dark alleyways, encountered strangers, and worried about exams where all the answers eluded her. But, since the night she had met Andrik and his brothers on the beach below Carlyle House, she had not *seen* into the future. She did not awake in the morning, believing that what she had seen in the darkness would later be realised.

Last night had been different. At first, she tried to convince herself that Fergus's arrival had simply stirred up suppressed memories. But the vivid colours of the dream and the emotions they had evoked were so powerful she could not easily put them aside. In her heart she knew, if Brigid were here, she would tell her to take them as a warning. It was *an dà-shealladh*.

In her dream, she was standing on the hillside above her father's croft, looking into the sunset, a magnificent display of colour and light, reds and oranges, pinks and purples. The sea was calm, mirroring the kaleidoscope from horizon to shore. In the middle distance, a large boat drifted slowly across her line of vision and out to sea. For a minute or two, it stood out against the horizon, a dark silhouette against the brightness. Moments later, it seemed to be consumed by the glare of the setting sun. Shading her eyes, she watched the

245

sun sink below the distant hills. The boat had vanished. Only a maelstrom of swirling currents marked the place where it had been. And, behind her, she heard the wind moaning as it wrapped itself around the crags and swept her up in its embrace.

The dream reminded her of the old island myth of the struggle between the *Mither of the Sea* and *Teran*. But it was all wrong. At this time of year, the *Mither* subdued *Teran*, banishing him to the bottom of the sea. The balmy weather of summer brought calm waters and safety out at sea. It was only as the days grew shorter and the nights longer, when winter winds blew down the hills and into the glens and storms raged out at sea, that sailors were truly at peril. In her dream, *Teran* had won, sucking the ship and its occupants down into the depths. The outcomes of her dream and the myth were twisted, misshapen, reversed. It was this, more than anything, which made her believe she had foreseen a terrible disaster. And Andrik and Arron and Jan were trawlermen, out at sea all the time, in every kind of weather.

*

For three more days, she was haunted by her dream. Three days waiting for Andrik to return. And when he arrived, he was breathless and excited.

'The investor has agreed to supply Uncle Georgi's fleet with all the latest technology.'

'The investor's name is Sebastian.'

'No, it's Carlyle.'

'It's Sebastian. Sebastian St. John Carlyle.'

'You know him?'

'He's the man who wanted to marry me, the man I ran away from.'

Jan laughed, 'Uh-oh! Sounds like trouble.'

'You did not tell me his name.'

'No. We agreed only to look forward, make plans for our

246

future together. You decided the past was better forgotten.'

'Why would this man, the man you left, now want to invest in Uncle Georgi's business? Is he a man of the sea himself?'

'No, Arron. He's a laird, a landowner, from the south.'

'You do not have to concern yourself with this, Deirdre. It is our business,' Andrik paused. 'Our ship – the *Purvi* – will be the first to have the new equipment installed. When it is done, we are to sail north to meet Carlyle and demonstrate to him how it all works.'

'You can't go.'

'What do you mean I cannot go?'

'I had a dream. The *Purvi* will sink.'

'This is what you dreamed?' Andrik laughed. 'It is because you are afraid of this man.'

'And because Fergus …'

'Who is Fergus?'

'He's the owner of the pub in the village. Three days ago, he came to visit. Sebastian discovered where I lived and knew your name. He wants me to go back with you to tell me he has no hard feelings and that I shouldn't be afraid to return home.'

'So, you will come, and we will all be together. You will not have to be afraid.'

'I'm not afraid for myself.'

'Well then, do not worry for us. Your dream is just a dream.'

'Like the one I had the night before we met at Annanside Bay?'

'Perhaps just a coincidence.'

'You don't understand, do you, Andrik? I have *an dà-shealladh* – second sight. Sometimes, in my dreams, I can see into the future.'

Andrik laughed, 'You say sometimes. It is perhaps your imaginings. After the future happens, you think of how you dreamed and make a connection.'

'Not this time, Andrik, not this time. Please believe me. Please don't go.'

'Of course we will go. It has been arranged. Our uncle has signed the agreement. If your dream has made you afraid, you do not have to travel with us.'

'Ask yourself, like Arron said, why would Sebastian want to invest in the fleet? He knew where I lived, where I live with you and your brothers. He knew your name.'

'She is right, Andrik. What does this man really want?'

'Arron, now you, too, are worrying. It is not good to go to sea and worry.'

'I think we should listen to what Deirdre says. She knows this man. We do not. We can find another investor.'

'It is done. It is not our business to question Uncle Georgi. We must only do what he asks. He is the one who pays our wages,' Andrik paused. 'I will not believe in this second sight, this dreaming.'

'What about *Baba Vanga*, Andrik?'

'Who's *Baba Vanga*, Arron?'

'A blind mystic from our country, who died just a few years ago. They said that she could see into the future, Deirdre, like you.'

Chapter 53

Deirdre

Deirdre moved around the house slowly, touching each surface, remembering the times she had spent in the cottage, with Andrik and alone. They were leaving. And she was travelling on the *Purvi* with the brothers. Despite her fear, she had decided to go with them. Whatever disaster the dream might have foretold could, perhaps, be avoided if she were there to see Sebastian, talk to him. Brigid had told her once that such things were possible, hadn't she? She could not let Andrik and his brothers go without her. And yet, as she heard Andrik close the front door behind them and turn the key in the lock, she knew that the cottage and her life there would be changed forever when – or if – she returned.

*

The sail north went smoothly, the ship hugging the coastline. For this trip, only the three brothers were aboard. There were no other crew members. Arron was at the helm in the wheelhouse, Jan sitting beside him. The new instrument panel with its shiny dials, the latest software and digital monitors, and GPS screen, had been installed and all were working well. Only the fish-finding sonar, which would sweep horizontally around the trawler in search of shoals of fish when they were several miles from shore, was still untested. They would use that when they set out on the first day of their sea trials.

Andrik was up on the deck with Deirdre, his arm around her waist.

'Carlyle's investment will change everything. When all of Uncle Georgi's fleet is fitted out, we shall be rich. We can buy a house, you and me. We can get married and make many babies.'

'After I've been to university.'

'Yes, of course. We have agreed. You must complete that part of your plan first.'

Andrik laughed and drew Deirdre closer. She laid her head on his shoulder, felt his warmth, the strength of him.

The trawler cut a determined swathe through the waves. Ahead, the sun glittered through a prism of light as it caught the spray over the foredeck, the ship dipping into the troughs of the biggest rollers. Overhead, a flock of seagulls followed their progress, swooping down into the swell which rose and fell in their wake, hoping for an easy catch. Nets and equipment were all stowed and tidied away. The decks had been swabbed, and the handrails revarnished. Below deck, the galley was gleaming, the cabins spotless. Deirdre had been given the VIP tour. It was all ready for Sebastian's inspection.

And then the familiar skyline of the Highlands came into view. Deirdre told Andrik the names of the two highest peaks, and the legend of *Gleann am Falach* – the Hidden Glen – between them.

'For centuries, people walked through the Hidden Glen. It was a shortcut to the villages and towns on the other side. And then along came cars and lorries and buses. People wanted a proper road through the glen. It was only going to be single-track, but it was never completed. Each day, the construction crews dug and bulldozed a stretch of the road. And the next morning, when they returned, huge boulders lay across the area they had cleared. The engineers were stumped.'

'Stumped?'

'Confused. These were boulders they had not moved or seen the day before. For several years, the council promised to complete the road. Some of the old folk said it was where the devil walked at night, searching for lost souls. In the end, it was abandoned. The track's only used by hillwalkers now. Most locals avoid it if they can.'

'And you, too, believe this?'

'I believe, Andrik, there are many things we do not understand.'

'And these things, like your dreams, make you afraid?'

'Fear makes you cautious, alert to the possibility of danger. It can sometimes save your life.'

Andrik turned towards Deirdre, cupping her face in his hands.

'I think you are the most wonderful and beautiful lady in the whole world. So I, too, will be cautious and alert. I believe we were always meant to be together. I know now I cannot live without you.'

'And I,' said Deirdre, 'know I can't live without you.'

But, as she looked out to the headland and the familiar cliffs beyond, Deirdre felt the wind caress her face, and tasted her tears mingling with the salt in the air. She closed her eyes and drifted slowly with the motion of the boat. Only a few months earlier, she and Sebastian had sat together on the deck of his small motor boat. He, too, had professed his love for her, offered her a new life. She had not been able to look him in the eyes and tell him how she really felt, because her needs then had been different, more practical. But, if he had really felt about her, as she now did about Andrik, how could he have so easily forgotten? How could he now be offering her forgiveness and the freedom to live her life without him when he had said he would keep her by his side for eternity?

Chapter 54

Meghan

The beach was at the bottom of the hill, a narrow strip of sand and smooth round pebbles which disappeared with each tide, a picturesque backdrop to the car park. Although it was already mid-May, a couple of days and nights of stormy weather had blown inland and had kept Cassie and me from our usual walks. When the sun came out, we were both excited to go outside and breathe in the warm, clear morning air.

Every day since Ellen and I had visited the Auld Village, I'd expected to hear that Cathel had spoken to Fergus. But each time I asked, she said he'd not found a suitable opportunity; and my mind would not let go of all the questions I had about Deirdre and the disturbed gravesite up on the hill. Going to this beach, below the cemetery, had been the solution. I didn't want to look into the darkness below the squares of sod. Being nearby, however, seemed to salve my conscience as if to let her know I'd not forgotten. As Ellen had said, I'd begun to feel as if Deirdre and I could communicate, as if I, too, had the sight. Perhaps, thinking that was enough for me to find some answers.

The tide was out when we arrived. Seaweed was strewn across the beach, and some had even been tossed onto the tarmac of the car park by the storm surge. I remembered our first walk on the other beach, the day when Cassie had found the bone, the day I'd seen Fergus beachcombing in the distance and I'd hurried away, afraid of meeting a stranger.

Fergus was no longer a stranger. Along with Dougal and Liane, he'd kept the secret of my village hideaway from Richard, pretending that I'd already left. And he knew where Deirdre had been buried. It was only a matter of time before Cathel spoke to him.

I took off my shoes and socks and waded into the cold water with Cassie. The beach sloped very gently, and it didn't take long to get used to the temperature in the shallows. Small shoals of minnows flitted below the surface, sweeping away like dark shadows as we approached. We walked the length of the beach until we reached an area where black basalt boulders stretched out into the water. As we turned back, I noticed a familiar figure climbing up the path from the car park. He looked as I'd seen him all those months ago, bent over, walking slowly, a large wicker basket on his back. It was Fergus. I didn't think he'd seen us, hidden by the rocks from the hillside above. But I had seen him. It was definitely Fergus, and he was climbing the hill on his way up to the cemetery.

I hesitated just long enough to ask myself a question. I'd follow him, that was certain. But should I just watch from a distance and report back to Cathel and Ellen? Or should I seize the moment and talk to him myself? And then I smiled as I asked myself another question. What would Deirdre want me to do? The first time I'd met Dougal, he'd told me Deirdre had been *tappet thrawn* – wild and headstrong. I'd told him I could also be that way … under the right circumstances.

I dusted off my feet and put on my socks and shoes. Just enough time, I estimated, for him to get to his destination and for us to remain hidden as we approached. As I started on the climb up the hill, I held Cassie on a short lead and prayed she wouldn't betray us by barking.

Fergus skirted the wall of the cemetery and made his way round the back to the graves beneath the yew trees. For a few minutes, he stood quite still, and I wondered if he'd come here to say a silent prayer in her memory. But, if that was his only motive, why had he not also noticed the disturbed ground over her grave? He turned away briefly from us and looked out to sea. By the time we'd reached the cemetery gate, he'd laid down his basket and was carefully rolling back the loose sod. As he levered up the wooden board below, Cassie lunged forward, snatching the lead from my grasp and barking loudly.

Fergus let go of the board, which fell back crookedly over the void below.

'What the hell are ye doing here?'

'I could ask you the same question, Fergus.'

'You followed me?'

'I was walking on the beach when you arrived,' I hesitated. 'But I came here a couple of weeks ago. I saw what had happened to her grave. It's been you all along, hasn't it?'

'What business is it of yours what I do and don't do? You're just an incomer. No, not even that, a tourist. And you think you can interfere in something that's none o' your business?'

'Ellen said only you and Brigid knew where Deirdre was buried, that no-one else was invited to her funeral. And now you think you've got the right to interfere with her remains? That must be a criminal offence, even up here in the Highlands.'

'This here's not Deirdre's grave. I wouldna ever touch that.'

Chapter 55

Deirdre

They had expected to moor in the shelter of Annanside Bay, and had been told they would meet Sebastian and discuss the sea trials over dinner at the Big House. Deirdre had wanted Brigid to meet Andrik. But none of their expectations were met. Instead, as they rounded the headland, Fergus called on the ship-to-shore radio. Sebastian had been unexpectedly called away and was not sure when he would be back. They were to moor overnight in the deeper water, nearer to the village, and start the sea trials the next day without him. Fergus would collect Deirdre in the dinghy so that she could spend the night with Brigid in her cottage.

*

Fergus said nothing as they left the ship, only nodded as she climbed down into the dinghy. Deirdre had wanted to stay with Andrik, but he had convinced her to spend the night with Brigid as they might be making an early start in the morning. Now the dinghy bounced up and down on the incoming tide as Fergus pulled alongside the jetty below the village.

In the warmth of an early summer evening, a few of the regulars were drinking outside The Piper. The Munro sisters – Janet sporting a large floppy sunhat – were sitting in their front garden waiting. Marge Ferguson was taking in the newspaper stand outside the store, getting ready to close up. Nothing had changed. And the word was out; Deirdre McIntyre had come home. Everyone stared at her as she walked up the hill from the cliffs to Brigid's house. Deirdre held the gaze of each of them, her head held high, smiling unabashedly as she passed.

Brigid, too, was waiting for her, the front door open. Deirdre stood on the front step of the cottage for a moment and looked back down the hill. Brigid continued sitting in her armchair at the unlit fireside.

'Come here, child, where I can see you.'

Deirdre turned quickly, ran in and knelt at the old woman's side.

'How are you, Brigid?'

'All the better for seeing you, lass. I missed you. But you shouldn't have come back.'

'I didn't have a choice, really, did I?'

'If you think you can change things, you canna.'

'You told me once I could, I thought if I spoke to him. But now he's not here.'

'He never intended to be.'

'But Fergus said ...'

'My Fergus is a worried man today. There's something wrong, and he'll not speak of it.'

'He didn't say anything to me on the way over. It wasn't like him,' Deirdre hesitated.

'Should I go back to the ship, tell Andrik we need to leave?'

'Even if he'd listen to you, child, it will change nothing. You know that, don't you?' she smiled. 'But tell me about your man, this Andrik, and what you've been doing in the city all these months. I was worried when you left. I hope he's made you happy? Is he a good man?'

The light had almost faded from the western sky when they finished talking. Brigid had prepared a pot of Deirdre's favourite beef stew, and they had eaten it as they talked. And then there seemed nothing more to say. Brigid had reiterated what Deirdre had thought since the night of her dream, and in the succeeding days. Sebastian's promises, relayed through Fergus, did not ring true. Something was wrong. After all he had said, what could have been so important to take him away today, with no mention of when he might return?

'I'm going to walk down to the cliffs, Brigid.'

'And look for your man?'

'If he's still awake, perhaps …'

'You do what you must, lass. You do what you must. But I'll away to my bed.'

Light and noise spilled from the windows and the open doorway of the pub, but the cold night air had persuaded the late drinkers inside. Deirdre heard the clink of glasses, the hum of conversation, the shouts from the players round the billiard table as someone sunk another ball. In the darkness, she passed by unnoticed.

She followed the familiar slope and the twists of the road down to the cliffside, where she could look across the bay to the anchored trawler. Only two white lights burned on the deck, one fore and one aft. Below deck, it was dark. If Andrik or one of his brothers had been up and awake, she would have signalled to them with the small torch she had taken from Brigid's porch. She would make them turn back, tell them what Brigid had said, convince them to heed the warnings. But, in the darkness, there was no-one to listen.

Chapter 56

Deirdre

The next morning, Deirdre sat at the window watching as the shadows receded across the valley and the sun rose over the hills behind the McIntyre farm. She had forgotten about her father, until now. He would be getting his porridge, thinking about what needed to be done on his land, and waiting for Cathel to arrive. He would know she had returned. He, too, would be waiting, like all the others, to see what would happen. Was he hoping for a reconciliation? Or was he expecting a different outcome? Sebastian's absence must have surprised them all.

The wind had picked up overnight, small clouds accumulating on the horizon. The sea was choppy, with white cresting waves rolling in on the tide.

Just before seven, Deirdre decided to walk down to the store for milk and Marge's freshly-baked bread which always sold out quickly. She was early, and the shop was still shuttered; but Fergus was already unloading crates of beer from the back of his van and carrying them into the pub. She walked on towards him.

'Good morning, Fergus.'

'Good morning to ye. But I'm thinking the morning is not so good to go out looking for fish with untried equipment. It'd be better another day, in calmer seas.'

'You mean the sonar?'

'Aye, that's it,' he paused. 'And perhaps when Carlyle

himself is returned.'

'When will that be, do you suppose?'

'The man's a law unto himself. He doesna advise me of his movements.'

'Have you spoken to them, Andrik and the brothers, about the weather and waiting for Sebastian?'

'Folks must decide for themselves. It's not for me to interfere.'

Deirdre ate breakfast with Brigid and walked back down to the cliffside where she had looked out at the trawler the previous night. The boat had not moved. It was still at anchor; as far as she could see, no-one was moving about on deck. She had no way to reach Andrik, and she had not thought to ask Fergus about the ship-to-shore radio. She considered climbing the hill behind the farm to look for Iolaire, but decided she needed to be nearby. The ship might set sail at any time.

As the day wore on, she became increasingly anxious. She trekked back and forth between the cliff and Brigid's house. The trawler rose and fell with the tides, but each time she looked, it remained at anchor. Once she saw Arron on deck, checking the winches, and waved. But he did not see her and turned back quickly into the cabin, out of the wind.

It was late afternoon when the wind died down and the sea calmed. In the now cloudless sky she watched the sun as it began to sink a little lower and move a little further towards the distant hills. The tide was now running high, and Deirdre knew that Andrik would give the order to weigh anchor and go fishing. With luck and the new sonar, they would make a good catch.

She held her breath and prayed to whatever god the brothers worshipped to keep them safe. She closed her eyes and silently called on all the spirits of the dead, those to whom she and Brigid had chanted at *Samhain* round the bonfire on the hill behind the Auld Village, to save Andrik from whatever danger her dream had predicted. Surely, the spirits and the elements were united tonight. And if prayers were answered and beliefs justified, gods and spirits must surely be moved by her pleas.

She believed all this, until she saw Sebastian walk down the road towards her.

Chapter 57

Deirdre

'Hello, Deirdre.'

'Sebastian.'

'They're about to set out, I believe.'

'Why, Sebastian?'

'The weather has changed, and it's the perfect time of day for herring fishing.'

She turned and faced him. Even in the bright light of the setting sun, his eyes looked sallow, dull.

'No. Why did you follow me? Why did you invest in the fleet? Why are you here now?'

'You know why, Deirdre. Don't be naïve. It's always been about you.'

'You could stop it now, Sebastian.'

'You could too.'

'By agreeing to give up Andrik and marry you? Why is it so hard to understand my decision? You once said you loved me. Surely you know how I feel.'

'I still love you, Deirdre; I can't let you go. I knew that the first time I saw you on the beach in the moonlight. You sensed it too. I know you did.'

'If you love someone, Sebastian, you give them the right to be themselves, the freedom to make their own choices,' she paused. 'What are you afraid of? Losing face? People around here admire honesty, truth …'

'And vengeance. Don't forget vengeance. A trait of the

highland psyche, I believe.'

'You live in the past, Mr Carlyle. Today, most of us just want to live peacefully. You may be the nominal laird …'

'Nominal laird?'

'Yes, only in name. Your fiefdom does not give you *le droit de seigneur* – the right to take a lady against her wishes.'

'Fancy words for a young girl who promised so much and ran away with her new lover.'

'I never promised to marry you, Sebastian, never. I never said the words.'

'Semantics, my dear. Your every action spoke to me of a future together. And you can still change your mind. Call it off, save your exotic Eastern European lover. He'll find someone else; and I'll look after you. You'll never want for anything, never have to run away again. I'll always be here for you.'

'You still don't understand, do you? I can't … I won't abandon Andrik. What you've planned, Sebastian – and I know you've planned something – won't change the way I feel,' she paused. 'I *saw* it all before we left the city. I told Andrik not to come. And Brigid knows it too. Your vengeance will destroy everyone, including you.'

Sebastian turned away and looked out across the bay.

'Ah, at last, they're leaving.'

Deirdre saw the anchor slowly rise above the surface of the water, seaweed falling from its curved blades as it settled in place against the hull of the trawler. The boat turned, water frothing in its wake as the engine kicked into gear. She waited, hoping to see Andrik or one of the others on deck, wanting to wave and let them know she was there, onshore, watching. But no-one appeared. Perhaps, even now, Sebastian might forgive her, change his plans. Perhaps, she could persuade him. But, as the boat pulled out into the open sea, she knew that it was already too late.

She imagined herself on deck again with Andrik, facing

the dying sun in all its glory, holding tightly onto each other as they sailed towards the horizon. Was he thinking of her now as they slipped farther and farther away from each other? But she knew his only thoughts, at that moment, would be of the boat, how it sailed under the guidance of the new equipment, and how good a catch they could expect when they found the shoals of herring. He did not know what she did. It was better this way.

Deirdre's eyes fixed on the receding trawler, willing it to cross the horizon unharmed. For a few minutes, the boat was framed perfectly, seemingly motionless at the centre of the dazzling red orb of the sun. And then, as the sun continued on its path across the horizon, a warm glow seemed to bathe the deck of the *Purvi*, growing in intensity. A minute or two later, the horizon erupted. Burning timbers shot into the air and scattered across the surface of the water until the sea itself seemed to be on fire. And the air continued to rebound with the sounds of a volley of miniature explosions. But, when the flames cleared, and only a pall of black smoke hovered over the water, the boat had vanished, the ripples of its passing coursing across the surface of the water for a short distance until they, too, were swallowed up by the breadth of the surrounding ocean.

She let out a death wail, calling out for Andrik. Her keening echoed across the valley and up into the hills beyond, as if she wanted to fill the space where Andrik and Arron and Jan had once existed. The noise of the explosion and Deirdre's cries of anguish brought people outside. They left the shelter of their houses and the warm conviviality of the pub, knowing that, once again, there had been a disaster out at sea. Some were already running to the cliffside where Deirdre stood. Others were calling for the coastguard to be alerted.

By the time Brigid reached her side, no-one remembered seeing Sebastian leave.

Chapter 58

Meghan

'She's there, where she always was.'

Fergus pointed to the flat ground where the grass and heather had taken hold. An unspoilt space next to the gaping hole.

I stepped nearer and looked down into the darkness of the open grave. If this was really not where Deirdre had been buried, if her skeleton wasn't lying there, exposed and degraded, then I was not so afraid. But I hesitated when I saw white bones laid out carefully, the skull at one end and the semblance of a framework for the rest. Most of the larger bones were in place, but many bone fragments were placed haphazardly, an unidentifiable miscellany. A collector's display, like an archaeological exhibit in the British Museum. This had to be …

'Is this Sebastian Carlyle?'

'Nae. That bastard is long gone. He didna wait to see what happened with the lass. This here's the lad our Deirdre loved, the one she killed hersel' for.'

'There was someone else? Not Sebastian?'

'Aye, a trawlerman, a foreigner from Eastern Europe somewhere.'

'So, why didn't you bury her inside the cemetery, beside her mother, near Brigid?'

'Because of Carlyle.'

'I don't understand.'

'Aye, I know that fine. You're awfu' quick with the accusations when you know nought about it. I've to do this, for the both of them.'

'Will you help me understand?' I hesitated. 'This'll sound foolish. But ever since I moved into the cottage up at the McIntyre farm, I've felt her spirit following me, as if she has unfinished business and wants me to help. If you tell me what happened, explain why you're collecting bones and laying them next to her …'

'Aye, the lass will not rest until I'm done. It was all my fault. Ma knew, and told me it was my penance to pay. But, after so many years, I'm tired.'

'Then let me help, Fergus. Perhaps we can sit up there on the hill and you can rest while we talk?'

We sat for a few minutes in silence, in a place where we could no longer see the graves, only the canopy of the yew trees which sheltered them.

'I shouldna have persuaded her to come back. But I ne'er believed he'd go so far.'

He no longer seemed defiant and defensive, but an old man whose sad eyes betrayed half a lifetime of regret as they scanned the horizon. I waited, allowing him time and space to remember. This was not a story to be hurried nor easily told after his years of silence and secrecy.

'Carlyle – the grand laird,' Fergus spat out the words, 'wanted to marry the lass. She was an outstanding beauty, and he knew it. He tried everything to persuade her. But she fell in love with this other man and she ran away with him to the city.'

'And he's the one in the other grave?'

He nodded, 'His name was Andrik.'

'So, Sebastian Carlyle killed him?'

'Aye, Andrik and both his brothers.'

'He killed three people? So, why wasn't he arrested?'

'He ran away, disappeared. Even if he'd stayed and they'd

265

questioned him, it would've probably been impossible to prove it were his fault,' he paused. 'It was a good plan. The three brothers worked for their uncle, who owned the trawler fleet. He needed an investor, and Carlyle stepped in. He equipped their boat with all that fancy equipment, and asked them to start the trials out in the bay beyond the village. And he asked me to persuade Deirdre to come home with them. No hard feelings, he said.'

'The accident at sea, after Deirdre had been seen arguing with Sebastian on the cliffside!'

'Aye. But it was no accident. He had the boat rigged. He wasna one to get his own hands dirty! There would be a fault in the wiring for the new sonar, a short circuit which would cause the fuel tank to explode. We knew – my ma, and the lass, and me. If he couldna have her, he would kill the lad, and his two brothers with him.'

'And you didn't try to stop him?'

'Deirdre and Ma sensed there was something wrong. I … I just hoped he'd see Deirdre, understand how she felt, and be able to forgive her.'

'But I still don't understand about the graves. You said there were three brothers.'

'The bodies of the two younger brothers floated ashore, along the coast a wee bit. The coastguard said they must've been on deck, but that Andrik was probably in the wheelhouse and took the worst of it. The uncle took the bodies of the two younger brothers to be buried in the city. But Andrik's body was never found,' he cleared his throat. 'The coastguard said there'd be little left of him to bury anyway, possibly only fragments of bones. Then, after a few months, after a storm, they started to wash ashore, on the tide, often wi' the seaweed.'

'And these are what you collect in your basket?'

'I promised Ma. I shouldha known the man wasna telling the truth. He was infatuated with the lass, and he was a proud

266

and jealous man.'

'So, you laid Deirdre next to …'

'To Andrik, aye. I can add the bones to the open grave out here, where nobody will notice; but not inside the cemetery. We chose two wooden coffins to rot and crumble into the hillside. Soon he and Deirdre will lie together, beside each other, for eternity.'

I looked down at the yew trees, bright green umbrellas spreading over the graves below. And, in the darkness, away from prying eyes, I imagined their roots already wrapping the lovers in an embrace. It was a sad but beautiful picture. But first, Fergus had to finish his task and agree to close Andrik's grave.

'How will you know when you've collected all of Andrik's bones, Fergus? How will you know when you can let them rest in peace?'

'I dinna know that for sure. But you can help by returning the one you took.'

'I haven't touched the grave.'

'No. But your wee beastie here claimed one that first day I saw you on the beach.'

'That was Andrik's?'

'I canna say for sure, lass. But what you've felt must make it so.'

'I don't even know where it is. I haven't seen it since that day.'

I remembered how Cassie had growled at Ellen that first day. It had been too big for her to carry, but she wouldn't let it go once we were back at the cottage. Shortly afterwards, it had disappeared. Then I remembered that I'd had a feeling there'd been an intruder in the cottage, searching.

'Fergus, did you try to look for it in the cottage? I thought maybe I'd imagined it, the intruder. I was even afraid it might've been Richard, my ex.'

'Aye, I'm sorry for that. I thought, if I could find it, you wouldna be any the wiser. And I'd not have to explain.'

'But you didn't find it?'

'Nae, I didna. It might still be there, hidden by the wee beastie.'

'I'll look for it, I promise. And I'll make the wee beastie help me,' I smiled. 'And then I'll let you know. But there's something else too. I spoke to Ellen about the grave, Andrik's grave, I know now. She told Cathel to ask you if it was where Deirdre had been buried,' I hesitated. 'I'm sorry if that was wrong, but I didn't know who else to ask. She said they'd keep it to themselves.'

'I'll speak to the lad. It's been a hard thing to keep the secret so long.'

Chapter 59

Deirdre

The sky was already a muted grey and purple when the coastguard helicopter circled over the area where the *Purvi* had last been seen. There was no floating debris, no sign of bodies or survivors, only a pale slick of oil mimicking the colours of the fading light. A small cutter was on its way and would stay in the area overnight. A thorough search was planned for the following day. Officially, there was still hope, but Deirdre knew otherwise. She had seen it, she had known it, she had spoken to Sebastian. Andrik had been taken. She had lost her place. There was nowhere for her to run now without him.

In the morning, when the sea once again raged in the bay below the village and the wind groaned in the timbers of Brigid's cottage, Deirdre dried her tears and walked out to the cliffside. But the path she took did not lead to the place where she had stood yesterday. Instead, she took a side turn before the headland, where the sea crashed relentlessly against the piles of jagged rocks below, eating away at the shoreline and forcing its way through the cracks and crevices it had sculpted every day for millennia.

She stepped out onto a mossy outcrop and looked down onto the churning sea below. Stretching out her arms, she swayed with the gusting wind. She wanted to fly like Iolaire, soar up into the hills, and find a resting place near the Auld Village. As she leant into the wind, she felt it carry her with it. She relaxed into the thermal as it swept her up and over the side of the cliff. And, once again, she called Andrik's name, so he would know where she had gone.

Chapter 60

Meghan

The bone – Andrik's bone – lay on a towel on the kitchen counter covered in dust. Ellen and I sat at the kitchen table in silence and stared at it.

I'd told Fergus I would get the wee beastie to help me. So, as soon as I returned to the cottage, I'd played Cassie's favourite game of fetch. There were only two main rooms in the cottage apart from the small kitchenette and the bathroom. And only two rooms where little Cassie could take a bone and hide it. I thought she'd be happy to hunt for her ball if I rolled it under all the furniture and that she'd return with it, but only until she reached her hiding place for the bone. The bone had been her special treasure when she'd first found it. She wouldn't have forgotten the smell or feel of it, and it would distract her from retrieving and returning the ball.

I'd finished looking under the sofa and chair in the sitting room when Ellen had appeared. In my eagerness to start my search, I'd not closed the front door properly. She'd worried it might be another intruder; and Cassie was barking, and I was crawling around on the floor.

'Is everything okay? Can I help?'

'I'm looking for Cassie's bone … well, Andrik's really.'

'And who's Andrik?'

'Deirdre's lover. He's dead, but Fergus needs the bone to add to the grave.'

271

'Deirdre's grave?'

'No. Deirdre's is okay. It's Andrik's that's still open,' I paused, realising that I was confusing her with my truncated answers. 'Perhaps, if you could help us find the bone …?'

'Then you'll make me a cup of tea, and we can start from the beginning?'

'Exactly.'

We moved into the bedroom, and I rolled the ball under the bed. I heard it hit the headboard. Cassie scooted after it and I waited; she didn't come out again. Ellen and I both got down on our hands and knees and peered underneath. The ball had rolled across the floor and was now resting against one of the legs at the bottom of the bed. Cassie, however, was sitting, paws crossed, against the base of the headboard.

'It's there, isn't it?'

'Yes. I think it's behind the headboard, Ellen. It's been there all this time.'

I had to drag Cassie out by the collar, growling and scuffling her claws along the flagstones as she lost traction. I carried her into the bathroom, where she continued to howl in protest behind the closed door.

Together, Ellen and I manhandled the heavy bed frame away from the wall. The bone had wedged itself on top of the skirting board, and it rolled off almost immediately. I was hesitant to touch it, as if doing so was yet another step beyond decency. This was not some ancient relic, anonymous and impersonal, but the not-long-deceased remains of a man beloved by a girl I'd grown to know. At least, that's how it felt. Ellen instinctively understood, and had already been to the kitchen to fetch a clean tea towel.

As we sat, hot tea cooling in our mugs, I relayed everything Fergus had told me just an hour or so earlier.

'Will he close up Andrik's grave, do ye think, when you give him the bone?'

'I'd like to think so. Perhaps then Deirdre's spirit will be at peace, and I'll not feel so haunted.'

'Aye, well, you must convince him, if he's as exhausted as you say. And for your own sake too. I'll tell Cathel, so Fergus won't have to go through it all again,' she paused. 'Yew trees! Brigid's idea, of course, before she passed.'

*

It was nearly two days later when Fergus and I met up again at the cemetery. I'd rung the main number at the pub several times, but it was Liane who kept answering. In the end, Fergus stopped me on our morning walk.

I watched as he placed the bone where Andrik's left arm would have been. The grave no longer seemed threatening or something to be afraid of. I could look at the skeleton and imagine the man. The skull was cracked, parts broken away. Most of the other larger bones were almost intact.

'It's time, don't you think Fergus, to lay him to rest? You can't spend the rest of your life ...'

'Aye, well that's easy for you to say, lass. You see,' he hesitated, 'I didna tell you all of it.'

I waited in silence, not wanting to interrupt or, worse still, for him to turn away again from the ending of Deirdre's story.

'Sebastian was on the phone in his study. I'd returned from the city, let myself in as usual. I wanted to tell him I thought Deirdre might come with Andrik and his brothers for the sea trials. I was waiting in the hall for him to finish his call, when I heard him mention the sonar – "Is it wired to short circuit as soon as it's switched on, so it'll look like an accident?" he asked, then, "you paid him enough and kept my name out of it?" – I don't know who was at the other end of the line, but Sebastian seemed to be satisfied with the answers he got. As he put down the receiver, and turned, he saw me in the hall. He knew I'd heard.'

'And what did you say?'

273

'I was horrified. I couldn't believe he'd go that far. I told him I'd stop him, speak to Deirdre and tell her everything I'd heard, warn them not to come. And he laughed.'

'He laughed?'

'Aye. He said he'd ruin me if I told what I'd heard.'

'How was he proposing to do that?'

'I've a problem, always have, with gambling – the horses and the dogs. Liane knew I owed some and was always nagging me about it. In fact, I owed tens of thousands, more than I could borrow and pay back in a lifetime. I'd mortgaged the pub twice over. When Carlyle arrived, he was free with his money, wanting to be the generous laird, everyone's friend. He offered freeholds on most of the cottages in the village for pennies on the pound as interest repayments. He paid off my debts on the pub on the same basis. Without his help …'

'So, he blackmailed you?'

'Aye. If he'd told Liane and called in the loan, our marriage would've been over. We'd have been out in the street,' he paused. 'I shoulda called the police and not been so afeart. But he told me he'd no intention of going through with it as long as Deirdre returned with Andrik. And, when she did, and I saw them talking, I thought it'd be over. But I know now – he didn't just want to see her again, he wanted her to give up Andrik and go back to him. It was me that killed her and those young men, me with my greed and my fear.'

Fergus collapsed on the ground beside the graves.

'I'll close the graves now, for the young folks' sake. But I canna live with myself knowing what I've done. And, when I go, the devil will have his way with me.'

'Oh no, Fergus. What you've told me, yes, it's terrible. But living is exactly what you must do. Your mother said collecting the bones was your penance. I'm not a church-goer. I don't believe in all that heaven and hell stuff. Surely, accepting what happened and your part in it, however damning, is enough penance for any man to bear in this world or the next. And,' I paused, 'it seems to me that Sebastian knew Deirdre well enough to realise that she'd never turn her back on Andrik.'

Fergus looked up at me, his eyes brimming with tears.

'What you've told me here today, Fergus, will go no further. I'll be leaving soon. Ellen and Cathel don't need to know more than they do already,' I hesitated. 'But I do have one more question.'

'Aye?'

'Was it you who daubed the image of the Horned God on the front door of my cottage, in black paint, on New Year's Eve?'

'*Cernunnos*?'

'You know who he is then?'

'Of course, my ma knew all the Celtic gods, told me when I was just a bairn. But I didna paint his image on your door. Why would I?'

'To scare me into returning the bone.'

'No, it wasna me, nor any that I know of. You don't go messing with the likes of him around here, unless you're seriously wanting trouble. Even the wee kids ken that well enough. You may not believe in him, but there are some folks who do. It'd be best to hold your peace on that account.'

Chapter 61

Meghan

It was Midsummer's Eve, the longest day of the year when the sky would barely darken before the sun rose again. The sea was soaking up the colours of a seemingly endless sunset, yellows and oranges phasing slowly into reds and purples as the sun moved another day nearer to its winter arc behind the distant hills.

In less than two months, my time here in the village would be over. I'd planned a year's retreat, twelve months to get my life back on track. But my preconceptions of village life, a time for solitude and reflection, had been dashed from the moment I'd become involved with Deirdre. Her presence in my life had taken me to a strange, unearthly place. I'd garnered friends. I'd begun to feel comfortable and accepted. And yet, there were forces here which belied reason. My rational, legal mind wanted to deny what I'd felt, what I'd seen with my own eyes. And, in the end, in my last conversation with Fergus at Andrik's graveside, I'd provided comfort in the face of betrayal, and offered solace to someone whose guilt made him complicit in the deaths of four young people. A year ago, I don't believe I would've been capable of such compassion or forgiveness.

From where I stood with Cassie on the cliffside, I could look down over the pebbled beach below. When we'd arrived, oh-so-many months ago now, I'd convinced myself we wouldn't make it down the steep, slippery track. But today, I could see a couple making the climb without effort. It was definitely something we, too, should do before the weather turned and the track became treacherous again.

I turned away from the cliffside and crossed onto the common grazing land where Cassie was already sniffing out her familiar trails. The couple, now hand-in-hand, were following the path which led to the road through the village. Silhouetted against the glowing seascape, it was difficult to see their features; but I could see that the girl was nearly as tall as her companion. For a moment, she seemed to say something to him. Then, together, they turned to face me. I smiled and waved, and the girl gave a slight nod in my direction. Caught in the umber light of the changing sky, her hair gleamed as if it had been touched by fire.

And then, as I watched, they walked on up the road, growing fainter and fainter as they crossed into the lengthening shadows of the hills and faded into the distance.

Acknowledgements

My gratitude and love goes to family and friends who listened to my ideas, read my drafts, encouraged me, and initiated me into the world of social media and influencer marketing.

And a special hug for my lifelong partner, Don – always at my side, always there to hold my hand along the way. Together we found our haven in the Highlands, a perfect place to imagine new ideas and envision the future.

A huge 'thank you' to everyone at Ringwood Publishing who supported me on my first journey as a published author.

Specific thanks to Editor, Olivia Jackson; Assistant Editor Hayley Bannon; Support/ Marketing Sarah Georges and Ashleigh Tucker; and Cover Designer, Skye Galloway.

The final presentation of *The Bone on the Beach* is due in large part to this talented team who, with their knowledge and expertise, worked long and hard to ensure that it was as good as it could be.

Also thanks to Sandy Jamieson, Chief Executive, and Isobel Freeman, Chief Editor, who were enthusiastic supporters from the outset.

About the Author

Born to Scottish parents, Fiona Gillan Kerr was educated in Ceylon (now Sri Lanka), at Berkhamsted School in Hertfordshire, and at Durham University. She has been a teacher and an investment analyst; sold magazine advertising and package holidays; worked in a large international airline in reservations, PR and commercial training and as a fund-raiser for several schools and a modern classical music foundation.

She divides her time between the United States, where her four sons live, and her Scottish home in the Highlands – a restored crofter's cottage in a small village by the sea.

Other Titles from Ringwood

All titles are available from the Ringwood website in both
print and ebook format, as well as from usual outlets.

www.ringwoodpublishing.com
mail@ringwoodpublishing.com

Bodysnatcher
Carol Margaret Davison

'Theirs, not mine, are the stories that should have been told, but all we hear in their wake is silence. Dead silence.'

In the late 1820s, two Irish immigrants, William Burke and William Hare, murdered 16 individuals and sold their corpses to Dr Robert Knox, who used them for anatomical dissections at the University of Edinburgh However, the question of whether their female accomplices, Nelly McDougal and Margaret Hare, were involved, has never been conclusively determined.

In *Bodysnatcher*, Carol Margaret Davison, a professor in English Literature and Women's Studies, places Nelly centre stage in this sordid story, granting a voice to a woman whose perspective has never been heard. Told by way of alternating confessions, *Bodysnatcher* is both a graphic depiction of one of Edinburgh's most notorious crimes, and a domestic story of a relationship unravelled by secrecy and violence. The novel dives deep into the twisted psychology of William Burke, giving the reader an inside look at a mind descending into madness.

ISBN: 9778-1-901514-83-4

£12.99

What You Call Free
Flora Johnston

Scotland, 1687. An unforgiving place for women who won't conform.

Pregnant and betrayed, eighteen-year-old Jonet believes nothing could be worse than her weekly public humiliation in sackcloth. But soon she discovers that a far darker fate awaits her. Desperate to escape, she takes refuge among an outlawed group of religious dissidents. This extraordinary tale of love and loss, struggle and sacrifice, autonomy and entrapment, urges us to consider what it means to be free and who *can* be free – if freedom exists at all.

ISBN: 978-1-901514-96-4
£9.99

ISBN: 978-1-901514-76-6
£9.99

Raise Dragon
L.A. Kristiansen

In the year of 1306, Scotland is in turmoil. Robert the Bruce and the fighting Bishop Wishart's plans for rebellion put the Scottish kingdom at risk, whilst the hostile kingdom of England seems more invincible than ever. But Bishop Wishart has got a final card left to play: four brave Scottish knights set off in search of a mysterious ancient treasure that will bring Scotland to the centre of an international plot, changing both the kingdoms of Europe and the course of history once and for all.

Inference
Stephanie McDonald

Natalie Byron had a happy life in Glasgow. She had a steady job, supportive friends and a loving family. Or at least, she thought she did. The morning after a date, Natalie wakes up inside a strange house, in a strange bed, sleeping next to a man named Jamie who claims he is her boyfriend. Outside the window are rugged cliffs surrounded by an endless sea. Fearing she's been kidnapped, Natalie flees, but when everyone around her insists that her life back in Glasgow is nothing but a delusion, Natalie begins to doubt her own sanity. There is one thing Natalie is sure of. She needs to get off this island.

ISBN: 978-1-901514-68-1

£9.99

ISBN: 9781901514995

£9.99

Embers
Stephanie McDonald

When the shy and mild-mannered Graham meets Angie at university, he is instantly besotted. The two soon embark on an all-encompassing love affair, later marrying and settling down together. But Angie has a past unknown to Graham – one which threatens to shatter the loving family they have created. An intimate and heart-breaking story, told from the perspective of both partners, the novel confronts the question – does the love that burns the brightest, eventually risk destroying those whom it consumes?

Two Closes and a Referendum
Mary McCabe

Two Closes and a Referendum is an engaging tale of ordinary people in an extraordinary time. This novel brilliantly captures the growing excitement and fervour of the 2014 Independence Referendum that changed Scotland for ever, as ordinary citizens explored their identity and wrestled with the hopes and fears that surrounded the choice they were asked to make.

Elspeth King, Director of the Stirling Smith Art Gallery and Museum praised the book, commenting that it 'summons up the magic and pace of the political contest in 2014.'

ISBN: 9781901514483

£9.99

ISBN: 9781901514902

£9.99

Murder at the Mela
Leela Soma

Newly appointed as Glasgow's first Asian DI, Alok Patel's first assignment is the investigation of the brutal murder of Nadia, an Asian woman. Her body was discovered in the aftermath of the Mela festival in Kelvingrove Park. During the Mela, a small fight erupted between a BNP group and an Asian gang. Then Nadia is accused of having an affair with a local man. Was her murder a crime of passion, or was it racially motivated? The deep-rooted tensions within Glasgow's Asian communities bubble to the surface in this gripping Tartan Noir novel.